Praise for The Dark Tower Series

"King is today's master storyteller,
and here he has latched onto a story
worthy of his talents."
—*Los Angeles Daily News*

"Gripping . . . compelling . . .
King mesmerizes the reader."
—*Chicago Sun-Times*

"An impressive work of mythic magnitude.
May turn out to be Stephen King's
greatest literary achievement."
— *The Atlanta Journal-Constitution*

"A compelling whirlpool of a story that draws one
irretrievably to its center."
—*Milwaukee Journal Sentinel*

"King is a master at creating living,
breathing, believable characters."
—*Baltimore Sun*

"Superb . . . through King's vivid imagery
the reader thirsts, cries and nearly dies with Roland."
—*Chicago Herald-Wheaton*

"Enjoyable . . . whets the appetite for more."
—*Bangor Daily News*

"Prime King . . . suspenseful . . .
reams of virtuoso horror writing . . .
an epic in the making."
—*Kirkus Reviews*

Also by Stephen King

FICTION

Carrie
'Salem's Lot
The Shining
Night Shift
The Stand
The Dead Zone
Firestarter
Cujo
Creepshow
Different Seasons
Cycle of the Werewolf
Christine
Pet Sematary
IT
Skeleton Crew
The Eyes of the Dragon
Misery
The Tommyknockers
The Dark Half
Four Past Midnight
Needful Things
Gerald's Game
Dolores Claiborne
Nightmares & Dreamscapes
Insomnia
Rose Madder
The Green Mile
Desperation
Bag of Bones
The Girl Who Loved Tom Gordon
Hearts in Atlantis
Dreamcatcher
Everything's Eventual
From a Buick 8
The Colorado Kid
Cell
Lisey's Story
Duma Key
Just After Sunset

Under the Dome
Stephen King Goes to the Movies
Full Dark, No Stars
11/22/63
Doctor Sleep
Mr. Mercedes
Revival
Finders Keepers
The Bazaar of Bad Dreams
End of Watch

**NOVELS IN THE DARK
TOWER SERIES**

The Dark Tower II:
The Drawing of the Three
The Dark Tower III: The Waste Lands
The Dark Tower IV: Wizard and Glass
The Dark Tower V: Wolves of the Calla
The Dark Tower VI: Song of Susannah
The Dark Tower VII:
The Dark Tower
The Wind Through the Keyhole:
A Dark Tower Novel

**BY STEPHEN KING
AS RICHARD BACHMAN**

Thinner
The Running Man
The Long Walk
Roadwork
The Regulators
Blaze

WITH PETER STRAUB

The Talisman
Black House

NONFICTION

Danse Macabre
On Writing (A Memoir of the Craft)

THE DARK TOWER I

STEPHEN KING

THE GUNSLINGER

SCRIBNER

NEW YORK LONDON TORONTO SYDNEY NEW DELHI

Scribner
An Imprint of Simon & Schuster, Inc.
1230 Avenue of the Americas
New York, NY 10020

First Scribner trade paperback edition April 2016

SCRIBNER and design are registered trademarks of The Gale Group, Inc., used under license by Simon & Schuster, Inc., the publisher of this work.

For information about special discounts for bulk purchases, please contact Simon & Schuster Special Sales at 1-866-506-1949 or business@simonandschuster.com.

The Simon & Schuster Speakers Bureau can bring authors to your live event. For more information or to book an event, contact the Simon & Schuster Speakers Bureau at 1-866-248-3049 or visit our website at www.simonspeakers.com.

Manufactured in the United States of America

13 15 17 19 20 18 16 14

Library of Congress Cataloging-in-Publication Data is available.

ISBN 978-1-5011-4351-9
ISBN 978-1-5011-4138-6 (ebook)

Permissions acknowledgments appear on page 253.

To
ED FERMAN
who took a chance on these stories,
one by one

CONTENTS

INTRODUCTION

On Being Nineteen
(and a Few Other Things)

I

Hobbits were big when I was nineteen (a number of some import in the stories you are about to read).

There were probably half a dozen Merrys and Pippins slogging through the mud at Max Yasgur's farm during the Great Woodstock Music Festival, twice as many Frodos, and hippie Gandalfs without number. J. R. R. Tolkien's *The Lord of the Rings* was madly popular in those days, and while I never made it to Woodstock (say sorry), I suppose I was at least a halfling-hippie. Enough of one, at any rate, to have read the books and fallen in love with them. The *Dark Tower* books, like most long fantasy tales written by men and women of my generation (*The Chronicles of Thomas Covenant*, by Stephen Donaldson, and *The Sword of Shannara*, by Terry Brooks, are just two of many), were born out of Tolkien's.

But although I read the books in 1966 and 1967, I held off writing. I responded (and with rather touching wholeheartedness) to the sweep of Tolkien's imagination—to the ambition of his story—but I wanted to write my own kind of story, and had I started then, I would have written his. That, as the late Tricky Dick Nixon was fond of saying, would have been wrong. Thanks to Mr. Tolkien, the twentieth century had all the elves and wizards it needed.

In 1967, I didn't have any idea what my kind of story might be, but that didn't matter; I felt positive I'd know it when it passed me on the street. I was nineteen and arrogant. Certainly arrogant enough to feel I could wait a little while on my muse and my masterpiece (as I was sure it would be). At nineteen, it seems to me, one has a right to be arrogant; time has usually not begun its stealthy and rotten subtractions. It takes away your hair and your jump-shot, according to a popular country song, but in truth it takes away a lot more than that. I didn't know it in 1966 and '67, and if I had, I wouldn't have cared. I could imagine—barely—being forty, but fifty? No. *Sixty?* Never! Sixty was out of the question. And at nineteen, that's just the way to be. Nineteen is the age where you say *Look out, world, I'm smokin' TNT and I'm drinkin' dynamite, so if you know what's good for ya, get out of my way—here comes Stevie.*

Nineteen's a selfish age and finds one's cares tightly circumscribed. I had a lot of reach, and I cared about that. I had a lot of ambition, and I cared about that. I had a typewriter that I carried from one shithole apartment to the next, always with a deck of smokes in my pocket and a smile on my face. The compromises of middle age were distant, the insults of old age over the horizon. Like the protagonist in that Bob Seger song they now use to sell the trucks, I felt endlessly powerful and endlessly optimistic; my pockets were empty, but my head was full of things I wanted to say and my heart was full of stories I wanted to tell. Sounds corny now; felt wonderful then. Felt very cool. More than anything else I wanted to get inside my readers' defenses, wanted to rip them and ravish them and change them forever with nothing but story. And I felt I could do those things. I felt I had been *made* to do those things.

How conceited does that sound? A lot or a little? Either way, I don't apologize. I was nineteen. There was not so much as a strand of gray in my beard. I had three pairs of jeans, one pair of boots, the idea that the world was my oyster, and nothing that happened in the next twenty years proved me wrong. Then, around the age of thirty-nine, my troubles set in: drink, drugs, a road accident that changed the way I walked (among other things). I've written about them at length and need not write about them here. Besides, it's the same for you, right? The world eventually sends out a mean-ass Patrol Boy to slow your progress and show you who's boss. You reading this have undoubtedly met yours (or will); I met mine, and I'm sure he'll be back. He's got my address. He's a mean guy, a Bad Lieutenant, the sworn enemy of goofery, fuckery, pride, ambition, loud music, and all things nineteen.

But I still think that's a pretty fine age. Maybe the best age. You can rock and roll all night, but when the music dies out and the beer wears off, you're able to think. And dream big dreams. The mean Patrol Boy cuts you down to size eventually, and if you start out small, why, there's almost nothing left but the cuffs of your pants when he's done with you. "Got another one!" he shouts, and strides on with his citation book in his hand. So a little arrogance (or even a lot) isn't such a bad thing, although your mother undoubtedly told you different. Mine did. *Pride goeth before a fall, Stephen,* she said . . . and then I found out—right around the age that is 19 x 2— that eventually you fall down, anyway. Or get pushed into the ditch. At nineteen they can card you in the bars and tell you to get the fuck out, put your sorry act (and sorrier ass) back on the street, but they can't card you when you sit down to paint a picture, write a poem, or tell a story, by God, and if you reading this happen to be very young, don't let your elders and supposed betters tell you any different. Sure, you've never been to Paris. No, you never ran with the bulls at Pamplona. Yes, you're a pissant who had no hair in your armpits until three years ago—but so what? If you don't start out too big for your britches, how are you gonna fill 'em when you grow up? Let it rip regardless of what anybody tells you, that's my idea; sit down and *smoke* that baby.

II

I think novelists come in two types, and that includes the sort of fledgling novelist I was by 1970. Those who are bound for the more literary or "serious" side of the job examine every possible subject in the light of this question: *What would writing this sort of story mean to me?* Those whose destiny (or ka, if you like) is to include the writing of popular novels are apt to ask a very different one: *What would writing this sort of story mean to others?* The "serious" novelist is looking for answers and keys to the self; the "popular" novelist is looking for an audience. Both kinds of writer are equally selfish. I've known a good many, and will set my watch and warrant upon it.

Anyway, I believe that even at the age of nineteen, I recognized the story of Frodo and his efforts to rid himself of the One Great Ring as one belonging to the second group. They were the adventures of an essentially British band of pilgrims set against a backdrop of vaguely Norse mythology. I liked the idea of the quest—*loved* it, in fact—but I had no interest in either Tolkien's sturdy peasant characters (that's not to say I didn't like them, because I did) or his bosky Scandinavian settings. If I tried going in that direction, I'd get it all wrong.

So I waited. By 1970 I was twenty-two, the first strands of gray had showed up in my beard (I think smoking two and a half packs of Pall Malls a day probably had something to do with that), but even at twenty-two, one can afford to wait. At twenty-two, time is still on one's side, although even then that bad old Patrol Boy's in the neighborhood and asking questions.

Then, in an almost completely empty movie theater (the Bijou, in Bangor, Maine, if it matters), I saw a film directed by Sergio Leone. It was called *The Good, the Bad, and the Ugly,* and before the film was even half over, I realized that what I wanted to write was a novel that contained Tolkien's sense of quest and magic but set against Leone's almost absurdly majestic Western backdrop. If you've only seen this gonzo Western on your television screen, you don't understand what I'm talking about— cry your pardon, but it's true. On a movie screen, projected through the correct Panavision lenses, *TG, TB, & TU* is an epic to rival *Ben-Hur.* Clint Eastwood appears roughly eighteen feet tall, with each wiry jut of stubble on his cheeks looking roughly the size of a young redwood tree. The grooves bracketing Lee Van Cleef's mouth are as deep as canyons, and there could be a thinny (see *Wizard and Glass*) at the bottom of each one. The desert settings appear to stretch at least out as far as the orbit of the planet Neptune. And the barrel of each gun looks to be roughly as large as the Holland Tunnel.

What I wanted even more than the setting was that feeling of epic, apocalyptic *size*. The fact that Leone knew jack shit about American geography (according to one of the characters, Chicago is somewhere in the vicinity of Phoenix, Arizona) added to the film's sense of magnificent dislocation. And in my enthusiasm—the sort only a young person can muster, I think—I wanted to write not just a *long* book, but *the longest popular novel in history*. I did not succeed in doing that, but I feel I had a decent rip; *The Dark Tower*, volumes one through seven, really comprise a single tale, and the first four volumes run to just over two thousand pages in paperback. The final three volumes run another twenty-five hundred in manuscript. I'm not trying to imply here that length has anything whatsoever to do with quality; I'm just saying that I wanted to write an epic, and in some ways, I succeeded. If you were to ask me *why* I wanted to do that, I couldn't tell you. Maybe it's a part of growing up American: build the tallest, dig the deepest, write the longest. And that head-scratching puzzlement when the question of motivation comes up? Seems to me that that is also part of being an American. In the end we are reduced to saying *It seemed like a good idea at the time.*

III

Another thing about being nineteen, do it please ya: it is the age, I think, where a lot of us somehow get stuck (mentally and emotionally, if not physically). The years slide by and one day you find yourself looking into the mirror with real puzzlement. *Why are those lines on my face?* you wonder. *Where did that stupid potbelly come from? Hell, I'm only nineteen!* This is hardly an original concept, but that in no way subtracts from one's amazement.

Time puts gray in your beard, time takes away your jump-shot, and all the while you're thinking—silly you—that it's still on your side. The logical side of you knows better, but your heart refuses to believe it. If you're lucky, the Patrol Boy who cited you for going too fast and having too much fun also gives you a dose of smelling salts. That was more or less what happened to me near the end of the twentieth century. It came in the form of a Plymouth van that knocked me into the ditch beside a road in my hometown.

About three years after that accident I did a book signing for *From a Buick 8* at a Borders store in Dearborn, Michigan. When one guy got to the head of the line, he said he was really, really glad that I was still alive. (I get this a lot, and it beats the *shit* out of "Why the hell didn't you die?")

"I was with this good friend of mine when we heard you got popped," he said. "Man, we just started shaking our heads and saying 'There goes the Tower, it's tilting, it's falling, ahhh, shit, he'll *never* finish it now.' "

A version of the same idea had occurred to me—the

troubling idea that, having built the Dark Tower in the collective imagination of a million readers, I might have a responsibility to make it safe for as long as people wanted to read about it. That might be for only five years; for all I know, it might be five hundred. Fantasy stories, the bad as well as the good (even now, someone out there is probably reading *Varney the Vampire* or *The Monk*), seem to have long shelf lives. Roland's way of protecting the Tower is to try to remove the threat to the Beams that hold the Tower up. I would have to do it, I realized after my accident, by finishing the gunslinger's story.

During the long pauses between the writing and publication of the first four *Dark Tower* tales, I received hundreds of "pack your bags, we're going on a guilt trip" letters. In 1998 (when I was laboring under the mistaken impression that I was still basically nineteen, in other words), I got one from an "82-yr-old Gramma, don't mean to Bother You w/ My Troubles BUT!! very Sick These Days." The Gramma told me she probably had only a year to live ("14 Mo's at Outside, Cancer all thru Me"), and while she didn't expect me to finish Roland's tale in that time just for her, she wanted to know if I couldn't please (*please*) just tell her how it came out. The line that wrenched my heart (although not quite enough to start writing again) was her promise to "not tell a Single Soul." A year later—probably after the accident that landed me in the hospital—one of my assistants, Marsha DiFilippo, got a letter from a fellow on death row in either Texas or Florida, wanting to know essentially the same thing: how does it come out? (He promised to take the secret to the grave with him, which gave me the creeps.)

I would have given both of these folks what they wanted—a summary of Roland's further adventures—if I could have done, but alas, I couldn't. I had no idea of how things were going to turn out with the gunslinger and his friends. To know, I have to write. I once had an outline, but I lost it along the way. (It probably wasn't worth a tin shit, anyway.) All I had was a few notes (*"Chussit, chissit, chassit,* something-something-*basket"* reads one lying on the desk as I write this). Eventually, starting in July of 2001, I began to write again. I knew by then I was no longer nineteen, nor exempt from any of the ills to which the flesh is heir. I knew I was going to be sixty, maybe even seventy. And I wanted to finish my story before the bad Patrol Boy came for the last time. I had no urge to be filed away with *The Canterbury Tales* and *The Mystery of Edwin Drood.*

The result—for better or worse—lies before you, Constant Reader, whether you reading this are starting with Volume One or are preparing for Volume Five. Like it or hate it, the story of Roland is now done. I hope you enjoy it.

As for me, I had the time of my life.

Stephen King
January 25, 2003

F O R E W O R D

Most of what writers write about their work is ill-informed bullshit.* That is why you have never seen a book entitled *One Hundred Great Introductions of Western Civilization* or *Best-Loved Forewords of the American People.* This is a judgment call on my part, of course, but after writing at least fifty introductions and forewords—not to mention an entire book about the craft of fiction—I think it's one I have a right to make. And I think you can take me seriously when I tell you this might be one of those rare occasions upon which I actually have something worth saying.

A few years ago, I created some furor among my readers by offering a revised and expanded version of my novel *The Stand.* I was justifiably nervous about that book, because *The Stand* has always been the novel my readers have loved the best (as far as the most passionate of the "*Stand*-fans" are concerned, I could have died in 1980 without making the world a noticeably poorer place).

If there is a story that rivals *The Stand* in the imagination of King readers, it's probably the tale of Roland

---

* For a fuller discussion of the Bullshit Factor, see *On Writing*, published by Scribner in 2000.

Deschain and his search for the Dark Tower. And now—goddamn!—I've gone and done the same thing again.

Except I haven't, not really, and I want you to know it. I also want you to know what I *have* done, and why. It may not be important to you, but it's *very* important to me, and thus this foreword is exempt (I hope) from King's Bullshit Rule.

First, please be reminded that *The Stand* sustained deep cuts in manuscript not for editorial reasons but for financial ones. (There were binding limitations, too, but I don't even want to go there.) What I re-instated in the late eighties were revised sections of pre-existing manuscript. I also revised the work as a whole, mostly to acknowledge the AIDS epidemic, which blossomed (if that is the word) between the first issue of *The Stand* and the publication of the revised version eight or nine years later. The result was a volume about 100,000 words longer than the original.

In the case of *The Gunslinger*, the original volume was slim, and the added material in this version amounts to a mere thirty-five pages, or about nine thousand words. If you have read *The Gunslinger* before, you'll only find two or three totally new scenes here. Dark Tower purists (of which there are a surprising number—just check the Web) will want to read the book again, of course, and most of them are apt to do so with a mixture of curiosity and irritation. I sympathize, but must say I'm less concerned with them than with readers who have never encountered Roland and his ka-tet.[*]

In spite of its fervent followers, the tale of the Tower

---

[*] Those bound by destiny.

is far less known by my readers than is *The Stand.* Sometimes, when I do readings, I'll ask those present to raise
their hands if they've read one or more of my novels. Since they've bothered to come at all—sometimes
going to the added inconvenience of hiring a baby-sitter
and incurring the added expense of gassing up the old
sedan—it comes as no surprise that most of them raise
their hands. Then I'll ask them to keep their hands
up if they've read one or more of the Dark Tower stories. When I do that, at least half the hands in the hall
invariably go down. The conclusion is clear enough:
although I've spent an inordinate amount of time writing these books in the thirty-three years between 1970
and 2003, comparatively few people have read them.
Yet those who have are passionate about them, and I'm
fairly passionate myself—enough so, in any case, that I
was never able to let Roland creep away into that exile
which is the unhappy home of unfulfilled characters
(think of Chaucer's pilgrims on the way to Canterbury,
or the people who populate Charles Dickens's unfinished final novel, *The Mystery of Edwin Drood*).

I think that I'd always assumed (somewhere in the
back of my mind, for I cannot ever remember thinking about this consciously) that there would be time to
finish, that perhaps God would even send me a singing telegram at the appointed hour: "Deedle-dum,
deedle-dower/Get back to work, Stephen,/Finish the
Tower." And in a way, something like that really did happen, although it wasn't a singing telegram but a close
encounter with a Plymouth minivan that got me going
again. If the vehicle that struck me that day had been a
little bigger, or if the hit had been just a little squarer, it

would have been a case of mourners please omit flowers, the King family thanks you for your sympathy. And Roland's quest would have remained forever unfinished, at least by me.

In any case, in 2001—by which time I'd begun to feel more myself again—I decided the time had come to finish Roland's story. I pushed everything else aside and set to work on the final three books. As always, I did this not so much for the readers who demanded it as for myself.

Although the revisions of the last two volumes still remain to be done as I write this in the winter of 2003, the books themselves were finished last summer. And, in the hiatus between the editorial work on Volume Five (*Wolves of the Calla*) and Volume Six (*Song of Susannah*), I decided the time had come to go back to the beginning and start the final overall revisions. Why? Because these seven volumes were never really separate stories at all, but sections of a single long novel called *The Dark Tower*, and the beginning was out of sync with the ending.

My approach to revision hasn't changed much over the years. I know there are writers who do it as they go along, but my method of attack has always been to plunge in and go as fast as I can, keeping the edge of my narrative blade as sharp as possible by constant use, and trying to outrun the novelist's most insidious enemy, which is doubt. Looking back prompts too many questions: How believable are my characters? How interesting is my story? How good is this, really? Will anyone care? Do I care myself?

When my first draft of a novel is done, I put it away, warts and all, to mellow. Some period of time later—six months, a year, two years, it doesn't really matter—I can come back to it with a cooler (but still loving) eye, and begin the task of revising. And although each book of the Tower series was revised as a separate entity, I never really looked at the work as a whole until I'd finished Volume Seven, *The Dark Tower.*

When I looked back at the first volume, which you now hold in your hands, three obvious truths presented themselves. The first was that *The Gunslinger* had been written by a very young man, and had all the problems of a very young man's book. The second was that it contained a great many errors and false starts, particularly in light of the volumes that followed.* The third was that *The Gunslinger* did not even *sound* like the later books—it was, frankly, rather difficult to read. All too often I heard myself apologizing for it, and telling people that if they persevered, they would find the story really found its voice in *The Drawing of the Three.*

At one point in *The Gunslinger,* Roland is described as the sort of man who would straighten pictures in strange hotel rooms. I'm that sort of guy myself, and to some extent, that is all that rewriting amounts to: straightening the pictures, vacuuming the floors, scrubbing the toilets. I did a great deal of housework in the course of this revision, and have had a chance to do what any writer wants to do with a work that is finished but still needs a final polish and tune-up: *just make it right.* Once you know how things come out, you owe it

---

* One example of this will probably serve for all. In the previously issued text of *The Gunslinger,* Farson is the name of a town. In later volumes, it somehow became the name of a *man:* the rebel John Farson, who engineers the fall of Gilead, the city-state where Roland spends his childhood.

to the potential reader—and to yourself—to go back and put things in order. That is what I have tried to do here, always being careful that no addition or change should give away the secrets hidden in the last three books of the cycle, secrets I have been patiently keeping for as long as thirty years in some cases.

Before I close, I should say a word about the younger man who dared to write this book. That young man had been exposed to far too many writing seminars, and had grown far too used to the ideas those seminars promulgate: that one is writing for other people rather than one's self; that language is more important than story; that ambiguity is to be preferred over clarity and simplicity, which are usually signs of a thick and literal mind. As a result, I was not surprised to find a high degree of pretension in Roland's debut appearance (not to mention what seemed like thousands of unnecessary adverbs). I removed as much of this hollow blather as I could, and do not regret a single cut made in that regard. In other places—invariably those where I'd been seduced into forgetting the writing seminar ideas by some particularly entrancing piece of story—I was able to let the writing almost entirely alone, save for the usual bits of revision any writer needs to do. As I have pointed out in another context, only God gets it right the first time.

In any case, I didn't want to muzzle or even really change the way this story is told; for all its faults, it has its own special charms, it seems to me. To change it too completely would have been to repudiate the person who first wrote of the gunslinger in the late spring and early summer of 1970, and that I did not want to do.

What I *did* want to do—and before the final volumes
of the series came out, if possible—was to give newcom-
ers to the tale of the Tower (and old readers who want
to refresh their memories) a clearer start and a slightly
easier entry into Roland's world. I also wanted them
to have a volume that more effectively foreshadowed
coming events. I hope I have done that. And if you are
one of those who have never visited the strange world
through which Roland and his friends move, I hope you
will enjoy the marvels you find there. More than anything else, I wanted to tell a tale of wonder. If you find
yourself falling under the spell of the Dark Tower, even
a little bit, I reckon I will have done my job, which was
begun in 1970 and largely finished in 2003. Yet Roland
would be the first to point out that such a span of time
means very little. In fact, when one quests for the Dark
Tower, time is a matter of no concern at all.

—February 6, 2003

. . . a stone, a leaf, an unfound door; of a leaf, a stone, a door. And of all the forgotten faces.

Naked and alone we came into exile. In her dark womb, we did not know our mother's face; from the prison of her flesh have we come into the unspeakable and incommunicable prison of this earth.

Which of us has known his brother? Which of us has looked into his father's heart? Which of us has not remained forever prison-pent? Which of us is not forever a stranger and alone?

. . . O lost, and by the wind grieved, ghost, come back again.

Thomas Wolfe
Look Homeward, Angel

19

RESUMPTION

THE GUNSLINGER

CHAPTER 1

The Gunslinger

I

The man in black fled across the desert, and the gunslinger followed.

The desert was the apotheosis of all deserts, huge, standing to the sky for what looked like eternity in all directions. It was white and blinding and waterless and without feature save for the faint, cloudy haze of the mountains which sketched themselves on the horizon and the devil-grass which brought sweet dreams, nightmares, death. An occasional tombstone sign pointed the way, for once the drifted track that cut its way through the thick crust of alkali had been a highway. Coaches and buckas had followed it. The world had moved on since then. The world had emptied.

The gunslinger had been struck by a momentary dizziness, a kind of yawing sensation that made the entire world seem ephemeral, almost a thing that could be looked through. It passed and, like the world upon whose hide he walked, he moved on. He passed the miles stolidly, not hurrying, not loafing. A hide waterbag was slung around his middle like a bloated sausage. It was almost full. He had progressed through the *khef* over many years, and had reached perhaps the fifth level. Had he been a Manni holy man, he might not have even been thirsty; he could have watched his own body dehydrate with clinical, detached attention, watering its crevices and dark inner hollows only when his logic told him it must be done. He was not a Manni, however, nor a follower of the Man Jesus, and considered himself in no way holy. He was just an ordinary pilgrim, in other words, and all he could say with real certainty was that he was thirsty. And even so, he had no particular urge to drink. In a vague way, all this pleased him. It was what the country required, it was a thirsty country, and he had in his long life been nothing if not adaptable.

Below the waterbag were his guns, carefully weighted to his hands; a plate had been added to each when they had come to him from his father, who had been lighter and not so tall. The two belts crisscrossed above his crotch. The holsters were oiled too deeply for even this Philistine sun to crack. The stocks of the guns were sandalwood, yellow and finely grained. Rawhide tiedowns held the holsters loosely to his thighs, and they swung a bit with his step; they had rubbed away the bluing of his jeans (and thinned the cloth) in a pair of arcs that looked almost like smiles. The brass casings of the cartridges looped into the gun-belts heliographed in the sun. There were fewer now. The leather made subtle creaking noises.

His shirt, the no-color of rain or dust, was open at the throat, with a rawhide thong dangling loosely in hand-punched eyelets. His hat was gone. So was the horn he had once carried; gone for years, that horn, spilled from the hand of a dying friend, and he missed them both.

He breasted a gently rising dune (although there was no sand here; the desert was hardpan, and even the harsh winds that blew when dark came raised only an aggravating harsh dust like scouring powder) and saw the kicked remains of a tiny campfire on the lee side, the side the sun would quit earliest. Small signs like this, once more affirming the man in black's possible humanity, never failed to please him. His lips stretched in the pitted, flaked remains of his face. The grin was gruesome, painful. He squatted.

His quarry had burned the devil-grass, of course. It was the only thing out here that *would* burn. It burned with a greasy, flat light, and it burned slow. Border dwellers had told him that devils lived even in the flames. They burned it but would not look into the light. They said the devils hypnotized, beckoned, would eventually draw the one who looked into the fires. And the next man foolish enough to look into the fire might see you.

The burned grass was crisscrossed in the now familiar ideographic pattern, and crumbled to gray senselessness before the gunslinger's prodding hand. There was nothing in the remains but a charred scrap of bacon, which he ate thoughtfully. It had always been this way. The gunslinger had followed the man in black across the desert for two months now, across the endless, screamingly monotonous purgatorial wastes, and had yet to find spoor other than the hygienic sterile ideographs of the man in black's campfires. He had not found a can, a bottle, or a waterbag (the gunslinger had left four of those behind, like dead snakeskins). He hadn't found any dung. He assumed the man in black buried it.

Perhaps the campfires were a message, spelled out one Great Letter at a time. *Keep your distance, partner,* it might say. Or, *The end draweth nigh.* Or maybe even, *Come and get me.* It didn't matter what they said or didn't say. He had no interest in messages, if messages they were. What mattered was that these remains were as cold as all the others. Yet he had gained. He knew he was closer, but did not know how he knew. A kind of smell, perhaps. That didn't matter, either. He would keep going until something changed, and if nothing changed, he would keep going, anyway. There would be water if God willed it, the old-timers said. Water if God willed it, even in the desert. The gunslinger stood up, brushing his hands.

No other trace; the wind, razor-sharp, had of course filed away even what scant tracks the hardpan might once have held. No man-scat, no cast-off trash, never a sign of where those things might have been buried. Nothing. Only these cold campfires along the ancient highway moving southeast and the relentless range-finder in his own head. Although of course it was more than that; the pull southeast was more than just a sense of direction, was even more than magnetism.

He sat down and allowed himself a short pull from the waterbag. He thought of that momentary dizziness earlier in the day, that sense of being almost untethered from the world, and wondered what it might have meant. Why should that dizziness make him think of his horn and the last of his old friends, both lost so long ago at Jericho Hill? He still had the guns—his father's guns—and surely they were more important than horns . . . or even friends.

Weren't they?

The question was oddly troubling, but since there seemed to be no answer but the obvious one, he put it aside, possibly for later consideration. He scanned the desert and then looked up at the sun, which was now sliding into a far quadrant of the sky that was, disturbingly, not quite true west. He got up, removed his threadbare gloves from his belt, and began to pull devilgrass for his own fire, which he laid over the ashes the man in black had left. He found the irony, like his thirst, bitterly appealing.

He did not take the flint and steel from his purse until the remains of the day were only fugitive heat in the ground beneath him and a sardonic orange line on the monochrome horizon. He sat with his gunna drawn across his lap and watched the southeast patiently, looking toward the mountains, not hoping to see the thin straight line of smoke from a new campfire, not expecting to see an orange spark of flame, but watching anyway because watching was a part of it, and had its own bitter satisfaction. *You will not see what you do not look for, maggot,* Cort would have said. *Open the gobs the gods gave ya, will ya not?*

But there was nothing. He was close, but only relatively so. Not close enough to see smoke at dusk, or the orange wink of a campfire.

He laid the flint down the steel rod and struck his spark to the dry, shredded grass, muttering the old and powerful nonsense words as he did: "Spark-a-dark, where's my sire? Will I lay me? Will I stay me? Bless this camp with fire." It was strange how some of childhood's words and ways fell at the wayside and were left behind, while others clamped tight and rode for life, growing the heavier to carry as time passed.

He lay down upwind of his little blazon, letting the dreamsmoke blow out toward the waste. The wind, except for occasional gyrating dust-devils, was constant.

Above, the stars were unwinking, also constant. Suns and worlds by the million. Dizzying constellations, cold fire in every primary hue. As he watched, the sky washed from violet to ebony. A meteor etched a brief, spectacular arc below Old Mother and winked out. The fire threw strange shadows as the devil-grass burned its slow way down into new patterns—not ideograms but a straightforward crisscross vaguely frightening in its own no-nonsense surety. He had laid his fuel in a pattern that was not artful but only workable. It spoke of blacks and whites. It spoke of a man who might straighten bad pictures in strange hotel rooms. The fire burned its steady, slow flame, and phantoms danced in its incandescent core. The gunslinger did not see. The two patterns, art and craft, were welded together as he slept. The wind moaned, a witch with cancer in her belly. Every now and then a perverse downdraft would make the smoke whirl and puff toward him and he breathed some of it in. It built dreams in the same way that a small irritant may build a pearl in an oyster. The gunslinger occasionally moaned with the wind. The stars were as indifferent to this as they were to wars, crucifixions, resurrections. This also would have pleased him.

II

He had come down off the last of the foothills leading
the mule, whose eyes were already dead and bulging
with the heat. He had passed the last town three weeks
before, and since then there had only been the deserted
coach track and an occasional huddle of border dwellers' sod dwellings. The huddles had degenerated into
single dwellings, most inhabited by lepers or madmen.
He found the madmen better company. One had given
him a stainless steel Silva compass and bade him give it
to the Man Jesus. The gunslinger took it gravely. If he saw
Him, he would turn over the compass. He did not expect
that he would, but anything was possible. Once he saw
a taheen—this one a man with a raven's head—but the
misbegotten thing fled at his hail, cawing what might
have been words. What might even have been curses.

Five days had passed since the last hut, and he had
begun to suspect there would be no more when he
topped the last eroded hill and saw the familiar low-
backed sod roof.

The dweller, a surprisingly young man with a wild
shock of strawberry hair that reached almost to his
waist, was weeding a scrawny stand of corn with zealous
abandon. The mule let out a wheezing grunt and the
dweller looked up, glaring blue eyes coming target-
center on the gunslinger in a moment. The dweller was
unarmed, with no bolt nor bah the gunslinger could
see. He raised both hands in curt salute to the stranger
and then bent to the corn again, humping up the row
next to his hut with back bent, tossing devil-grass and

an occasional stunted corn plant over his shoulder. His hair flopped and flew in the wind that now came directly from the desert, with nothing to break it.

The gunslinger came down the hill slowly, leading the donkey on which his waterskins sloshed. He paused by the edge of the lifeless-looking cornpatch, drew a drink from one of his skins to start the saliva, and spat into the arid soil.

"Life for your crop."

"Life for your own," the dweller answered and stood up. His back popped audibly. He surveyed the gunslinger without fear. The little of his face visible between beard and hair seemed unmarked by the rot, and his eyes, while a bit wild, seemed sane. "Long days and pleasant nights, stranger."

"And may you have twice the number."

"Unlikely," the dweller replied, and voiced a curt laugh. "I don't have nobbut corn and beans," he said. "Corn's free, but you'll have to kick something in for the beans. A man brings them out once in a while. He don't stay long." The dweller laughed shortly. "Afraid of spirits. Afraid of the bird-man, too."

"I saw him. The bird-man, I mean. He fled me."

"Yar, he's lost his way. Claims to be looking for a place called Algul Siento, only sometimes he calls it Blue Haven or Heaven, I can't make out which. Has thee heard of it?"

The gunslinger shook his head.

"Well . . . he don't bite and he don't bide, so fuck him. Is thee alive or dead?"

"Alive," the gunslinger said. "You speak as the Manni do."

"I was with 'em awhile, but that was no life for me; too chummy, they are, and always looking for holes in the world."

This was true, the gunslinger reflected. The Manni-folk were great travelers.

The two of them looked at each other in silence for a moment, and then the dweller put out his hand. "Brown is my name."

The gunslinger shook and gave his own name. As he did so, a scrawny raven croaked from the low peak of the sod roof. The dweller gestured at it briefly: "That's Zoltan."

At the sound of its name the raven croaked again and flew across to Brown. It landed on the dweller's head and roosted, talons firmly twined in the wild thatch of hair.

"Screw you," Zoltan croaked brightly. "Screw you and the horse you rode in on."

The gunslinger nodded amiably.

"Beans, beans, the musical fruit," the raven recited, inspired. "The more you eat, the more you toot."

"You teach him that?"

"That's all he wants to learn, I guess," Brown said. "Tried to teach him The Lord's Prayer once." His eyes traveled out beyond the hut for a moment, toward the gritty, featureless hardpan. "Guess this ain't Lord's Prayer country. You're a gunslinger. That right?"

"Yes." He hunkered down and brought out his mak-ings. Zoltan launched himself from Brown's head and landed, flittering, on the gunslinger's shoulder.

"Thought your kind was gone."

"Then you see different, don't you?"

"Did'ee come from In-World?"

"Long ago," the gunslinger agreed.

"Anything left there?"

To this the gunslinger made no reply, but his face suggested this was a topic better not pursued.

"After the other one, I guess."

"Yes." The inevitable question followed: "How long since he passed by?"

Brown shrugged. "I don't know. Time's funny out here. Distance and direction, too. More than two weeks. Less than two months. The bean man's been twice since he passed. I'd guess six weeks. That's probably wrong."

"The more you eat, the more you toot," Zoltan said.

"Did he lay by?" the gunslinger asked.

Brown nodded. "He stayed supper, same as you will, I guess. We passed the time."

The gunslinger stood up and the bird flew back to the roof, squawking. He felt an odd, trembling eagerness. "What did he talk about?"

Brown cocked an eyebrow at him. "Not much. Did it ever rain and when did I come here and had I buried my wife. He asked was she of the Manni-folk and I said yar, because it seemed like he already knew. I did most of the talking, which ain't usual." He paused, and the only sound was the stark wind. "He's a sorcerer, ain't he?"

"Among other things."

Brown nodded slowly. "I knew. He dropped a rabbit out of his sleeve, all gutted and ready for the pot. Are you?"

"A sorcerer?" He laughed. "I'm just a man."

"You'll never catch him."

"I'll catch him."

They looked at each other, a sudden depth of feeling between them, the dweller upon his dust-puff-dry ground, the gunslinger on the hardpan that shelved down to the desert. He reached for his flint.

"Here." Brown produced a sulfur-headed match and struck it with a grimed nail. The gunslinger pushed the tip of his smoke into the flame and drew.

"Thanks."

"You'll want to fill your skins," the dweller said, turning away. "Spring's under the eaves in back. I'll start dinner."

The gunslinger stepped gingerly over the rows of corn and went around back. The spring was at the bottom of a hand-dug well, lined with stones to keep the powdery earth from caving. As he descended the rickety ladder, the gunslinger reflected that the stones must represent two years' work easily—hauling, dragging, laying. The water was clear but slow-moving, and filling the skins was a long chore. While he was topping the second, Zoltan perched on the lip of the well.

"Screw you and the horse you rode in on," he advised.

The gunslinger looked up, startled. The shaft was about fifteen feet deep: easy enough for Brown to drop a rock on him, break his head, and steal everything on him. A crazy or a rotter wouldn't do it; Brown was neither. Yet he liked Brown, and so he pushed the thought out of his mind and got the rest of the water God had willed. Whatever else God willed was ka's business, not his.

When he came through the hut's door and walked down the steps (the hovel proper was set below ground level, designed to catch and hold the coolness of the nights), Brown was poking ears of corn into the embers of a tiny fire with a crude hardwood spatula. Two ragged plates had been set at opposite ends of a dun blanket. Water for the beans was just beginning to bubble in a pot hung over the fire.

"I'll pay for the water, too."

Brown did not look up. "The water's a gift from God, as I think thee knows. Pappa Doc brings the beans."

The gunslinger grunted a laugh and sat down with his back against one rude wall, folded his arms, and closed his eyes. After a little, the smell of roasting corn came to his nose. There was a pebbly rattle as Brown dumped a paper of dry beans into the pot. An occasional *tak-tak-tak* as Zoltan walked restlessly on the roof. He was tired; he had been going sixteen and sometimes eighteen hours a day between here and the horror that had occurred in Tull, the last village. And he had been afoot for the last twelve days; the mule was at the end of its endurance, only living because it was a habit. Once he had known a boy named Sheemie who'd had a mule. Sheemie was gone now; they were all gone now and there was only the two of them: him, and the man in black. He had heard rumor of other lands beyond this, green lands in a place called Mid-World, but it was hard to believe. Out here, green lands seemed like a child's fantasy.

Tak-tak-tak.

Two weeks, Brown had said, or as many as six. Didn't matter. There had been calendars in Tull, and they had remembered the man in black because of the old man he had healed on his way through. Just an old man dying of the weed. An old man of thirty-five. And if Brown was right, he had closed a good deal of distance on the man in black since then. But the desert was next. And the desert would be hell.

Tak-tak-tak . . .

Lend me your wings, bird. I'll spread them and fly on the thermals.

He slept.

III

Brown woke him up an hour later. It was dark. The only light was the dull cherry glare of the banked embers.

"Your mule has passed on," Brown said. "Tell ya sorry. Dinner's ready."

"How?"

Brown shrugged. "Roasted and boiled, how else? You picky?"

"No, the mule."

"It just laid over, that's all. It looked like an old mule." And with a touch of apology: "Zoltan et the eyes."

"Oh." He might have expected it. "All right."

Brown surprised him again when they sat down to the blanket that served as a table by asking a brief blessing: Rain, health, expansion to the spirit.

"Do you believe in an afterlife?" the gunslinger asked him as Brown dropped three ears of hot corn onto his plate.

Brown nodded. "I think this is it."

IV

The beans were like bullets, the corn tough. Outside, the prevailing wind snuffled and whined around the

ground-level eaves. The gunslinger ate quickly, raven-
ously, drinking four cups of water with the meal. Halfway
through, there was a machine-gun rapping at the door.
Brown got up and let Zoltan in. The bird flew across the
room and hunched moodily in the corner.

"Musical fruit," he muttered.

"You ever think about eating him?" the gunslinger
asked.

The dweller laughed. "Animals that talk be tough,"
he said. "Birds, billy-bumblers, human beans. They be
tough eatin'."

After dinner, the gunslinger offered his tobacco. The
dweller, Brown, accepted eagerly.

Now, the gunslinger thought. *Now the questions will
come.*

But Brown asked no questions. He smoked tobacco
that had been grown in Garlan years before and looked
at the dying embers of the fire. It was already noticeably
cooler in the hovel.

"Lead us not into temptation," Zoltan said suddenly,
apocalyptically.

The gunslinger started as if he had been shot at. He
was suddenly sure all this was an illusion, that the man
in black had spun a spell and was trying to tell him
something in a maddeningly obtuse, symbolic way.

"Do you know Tull?" he asked suddenly.

Brown nodded. "Came through it to get here, went
back once to sell corn and drink a glass of whiskey. It
rained that year. Lasted maybe fifteen minutes. The
ground just seemed to open and suck it up. An hour
later it was just as white and dry as ever. But the corn—
God, the corn. You could see it grow. That wasn't so

bad. But you could *hear* it, as if the rain had given it a mouth. It wasn't a happy sound. It seemed to be sighing and groaning its way out of the earth." He paused. "I had extra, so I took it and sold it. Pappa Doc said he'd do it, but he would have cheated me. So I went."

"You don't like town?"

"No."

"I almost got killed there," the gunslinger said.

"Do you say so?"

"Set my watch and warrant on it. And I killed a man that was touched by God," the gunslinger said. "Only it wasn't God. It was the man with the rabbit up his sleeve. The man in black."

"He laid you a trap."

"You say true, I say thank ya."

They looked at each other across the shadows, the moment taking on overtones of finality.

Now *the questions will come.*

But Brown still had no questions to ask. His cigarette was down to a smoldering roach, but when the gunslinger tapped his poke, Brown shook his head.

Zoltan shifted restlessly, seemed about to speak, subsided.

"Will I tell you about it?" the gunslinger asked. "Ordinarily I'm not much of a talker, but . . ."

"Sometimes talking helps. I'll listen."

The gunslinger searched for words to begin and found none. "I have to pass water," he said.

Brown nodded. "Pass it in the corn, please."

"Sure."

He went up the stairs and out into the dark. The stars glittered overhead. The wind pulsed. His urine arched out over the powdery cornfield in a wavering stream. The man in black had drawn him here. It wasn't beyond possibility that Brown *was* the man in black. He might be . . .

The gunslinger shut these useless and upsetting thoughts away. The only contingency he had not learned how to bear was the possibility of his own madness. He went back inside.

"Have you decided if I'm an enchantment yet?" Brown asked, amused.

The gunslinger paused on the tiny landing, startled. Then he came down slowly and sat. "The thought crossed my mind. Are you?"

"If I am, I don't know it."

This wasn't a terribly helpful answer, but the gunslinger decided to let it pass. "I started to tell you about Tull."

"Is it growing?"

"It's dead," the gunslinger said. "I killed it." He thought of adding: *And now I'm going to kill you, if for no other reason than I don't want to have to sleep with one eye open.* But had he come to such behavior? If so, why bother to go on at all? Why, if he had become what he pursued?

Brown said, "I don't want nothing from you, gunslinger, except to still be here when you move on. I won't beg for my life, but that don't mean I don't want it yet awhile longer."

The gunslinger closed his eyes. His mind whirled.

"Tell me what you are," he said thickly.

"Just a man. One who means you no harm. And I'm still willing to listen if you're willing to talk."

To this the gunslinger made no reply.

"I guess you won't feel right about it unless I invite you," Brown said, "and so I do. Will you tell me about Tull?"

The gunslinger was surprised to find that this time the words were there. He began to speak in flat bursts that slowly spread into an even, slightly toneless narrative. He found himself oddly excited. He talked deep into the night. Brown did not interrupt at all. Neither did the bird.

V

He'd bought the mule in Pricetown, and when he reached Tull, it was still fresh. The sun had set an hour earlier, but the gunslinger had continued traveling, guided by the town glow in the sky, then by the uncannily clear notes of a honky-tonk piano playing "Hey Jude." The road widened as it took on tributaries. Here and there were overhead sparklights, all of them long dead.

The forests were long gone now, replaced by the monotonous flat prairie country: endless, desolate fields gone to timothy and low shrubs; eerie, deserted estates guarded by brooding, shadowed mansions where demons undeniably walked; leering, empty shanties where the people had either moved on or had been moved along; an occasional dweller's hovel, given away by a single flickering point of light in the dark, or by sullen, inbred clan-fams toiling silently in the fields by day. Corn was the main crop, but there were beans and also some pokeberries. An occasional scrawny cow stared at him lumpishly from between peeled alder poles. Coaches had passed him four times, twice coming and twice going, nearly empty as they came up on him from behind and bypassed him and his mule, fuller as they headed back toward the forests of the north. Now and then a farmer passed with his feet up on the splashboard of his bucka, careful not to look at the man with the guns.

It was ugly country. It had showered twice since he had left Pricetown, grudgingly both times. Even the timothy looked yellow and dispirited. Pass-on-by country. He had seen no sign of the man in black. Perhaps he had taken a coach.

The road made a bend, and beyond it the gunslinger clucked the mule to a stop and looked down at Tull. It was at the floor of a circular, bowl-shaped hollow, a shoddy jewel in a cheap setting. There were a number of lights, most of them clustered around the area of the music. There looked to be four streets, three running at right angles to the coach road, which was the main avenue of the town. Perhaps there would be a cafe. He doubted it, but perhaps. He clucked at the mule.

More houses sporadically lined the road now, most of them still deserted. He passed a tiny graveyard with moldy, leaning wooden slabs overgrown and choked by the rank devil-grass. Perhaps five hundred feet further on he passed a chewed sign which said: TULL.

The paint was flaked almost to the point of illegibility. There was another further on, but the gunslinger was not able to read that one at all.

A fool's chorus of half-stoned voices was rising in the

final protracted lyric of "Hey Jude"—"Naa-naa-naa naa-na-na-na . . . hey, Jude . . ."—as he entered the town proper. It was a dead sound, like the wind in the hollow of a rotted tree. Only the prosaic thump and pound of the honky-tonk piano saved him from seriously wondering if the man in black might not have raised ghosts to inhabit a deserted town. He smiled a little at the thought.

There were people on the streets, but not many. Three ladies wearing black slacks and identical high-collared blouses passed by on the opposite boardwalk, not looking at him with pointed curiosity. Their faces seemed to swim above their all-but-invisible bodies like pallid balls with eyes. A solemn old man with a straw hat perched firmly on top of his head watched him from the steps of a boarded-up mercantile store. A scrawny tailor with a late customer paused to watch him go by; he held up the lamp in his window for a better look. The gunslinger nodded. Neither the tailor nor his customer nodded back. He could feel their eyes resting heavily upon the low-slung holsters that lay against his hips. A young boy, perhaps thirteen, and a girl who might have been his sissa or his jilly-child crossed the street a block up, pausing imperceptibly. Their footfalls raised little hanging clouds of dust. Here in town most of the streetside lamps worked, but they weren't electric; their isinglass sides were cloudy with congealed oil. Some had been crashed out. There was a livery with a just-hanging-on look to it, probably depending on the coach line for its survival. Three boys were crouched silently around a marble ring drawn in the dust to one side of the barn's gaping maw, smoking cornshuck cigarettes. They made long shadows in the yard. One had a scorpion's tail poked in the band of his hat. Another had a bloated left eye bulging sightlessly from its socket.

The gunslinger led his mule past them and looked into the dim depths of the barn. One lamp glowed sunkenly. A shadow jumped and flickered as a gangling old man in bib overalls forked loose timothy hay into the hayloft with big, grunting swipes of his fork.

"Hey!" the gunslinger called.

The fork faltered and the hostler looked around with yellow-tinged eyes. "Hey yourself!"

"I got a mule here."

"Good for you."

The gunslinger flicked a heavy, unevenly milled gold piece into the semidark. It rang on the old, chaff-drifted boards and glittered.

The hostler came forward, bent, picked it up, squinted at the gunslinger. His eyes dropped to the gunbelts and he nodded sourly. "How long you want him put up?"

"A night or two. Maybe longer."

"I ain't got no change for gold."

"Didn't ask for any."

"Shoot-up money," the hostler muttered.

"What did you say?"

"Nothing." The hostler caught the mule's bridle and led him inside.

"Rub him down!" the gunslinger called. "I expect to smell it on him when I come back, hear me well!"

The old man did not turn. The gunslinger walked out to the boys crouched around the marble ring. They had watched the entire exchange with contemptuous interest.

"Long days and pleasant nights," the gunslinger offered conversationally.

No answer.

"You fellas live in town?"

No answer, unless the scorpion's tail gave one: it seemed to nod.

One of the boys removed a crazily tilted twist of corn-shuck from his mouth, grasped a green cat's-eye marble, and squirted it into the dirt circle. It struck a croaker and knocked it outside. He picked up the cat's-eye and prepared to shoot again.

"There a cafe in this town?" the gunslinger asked.

One of them looked up, the youngest. There was a huge cold-sore at the corner of his mouth, but his eyes were both the same size, and full of an innocence that wouldn't last long in this shithole. He looked at the gunslinger with hooded brimming wonder that was touching and frightening.

"Might get a burger at Sheb's."

"That the honky-tonk?"

The boy nodded. "Yar." The eyes of his mates had turned ugly and hostile. He would probably pay for having spoken up in kindness.

The gunslinger touched the brim of his hat. "I'm grateful. It's good to know someone in this town is bright enough to talk."

He walked past, mounted the boardwalk, and started down toward Sheb's, hearing the clear, contemptuous voice of one of the others, hardly more than a childish treble: "Weed-eater! How long you been screwin' your sister, Charlie? Weed-eater!" Then the sound of a blow and a cry.

There were three flaring kerosene lamps in front of Sheb's, one to each side and one nailed above the drunk-hung batwing doors. The chorus of "Hey Jude" had petered out, and the piano was plinking some other old ballad. Voices murmured like broken threads. The gun-slinger paused outside for a moment, looking in. Saw-dust floor, spittoons by the tipsy-legged tables. A plank bar on sawhorses. A gummy mirror behind it, reflect-ing the piano player, who wore an inevitable piano-stool slouch. The front of the piano had been removed so you could watch the wooden keys whonk up and down as the contraption was played. The bartender was a straw-haired woman wearing a dirty blue dress. One strap was held with a safety pin. There were perhaps six townies in the back of the room, juicing and playing Watch Me apathetically. Another half-dozen were grouped loosely about the piano. Four or five at the bar. And an old man with wild gray hair collapsed at a table by the doors. The gunslinger went in.

Heads swiveled to look at him and his guns. There was a moment of near silence, except for the oblivious piano player, who continued to tinkle. Then the woman mopped at the bar, and things shifted back.

"Watch me," one of the players in the corner said and matched three hearts with four spades, emptying his hand. The one with the hearts swore, pushed over his stake, and the next hand was dealt.

The gunslinger approached the woman at the bar. "You got meat?" he asked.

"Sure." She looked him in the eye, and she might have been pretty when she started out, but the world had moved on since then. Now her face was lumpy and there a livid scar went corkscrewing across her forehead. She had powdered it heavily, and the powder called attention to what it had been meant to camouflage. "Clean beef. Threaded stock. It's dear, though."

Threaded stock, my ass, the gunslinger thought. *What you got in your cooler came from something with three eyes, six legs, or both—that's my guess, lady-sai.*

"I want three burgers and a beer, would it please ya."

Again that subtle shift in tone. Three hamburgers. Mouths watered and tongues licked at saliva with slow lust. Three hamburgers. Had anyone here ever seen anyone eat three hamburgers at a go?

"That would go you five bocks. Do you ken bocks?"

"Dollars?"

She nodded, so she was probably saying *bucks.* That was his guess, anyway.

"That with the beer?" he asked, smiling a little. "Or is the beer extra?"

She didn't return the smile. "I'll throw in the suds. Once I see the color of your money, that is."

The gunslinger put a gold piece on the bar, and every eye followed it.

There was a smoldering charcoal cooker behind the bar and to the left of the mirror. The woman disappeared into a small room behind it and returned with meat on a paper. She scrimped out three patties and put them on the grill. The smell that arose was maddening. The gunslinger stood with stolid indifference, only peripherally aware of the faltering piano, the slowing of the card game, the sidelong glances of the barflies.

The man was halfway up behind him when the gunslinger saw him in the mirror. The man was almost completely bald, and his hand was wrapped around the haft of a gigantic hunting knife that was looped onto his belt like a holster.

"Go sit down," the gunslinger said. "Do yourself a favor, cully."

The man stopped. His upper lip lifted unconsciously, like a dog's, and there was a moment of silence. Then he went back to his table, and the atmosphere shifted back again.

Beer came in a cracked glass schooner. "I ain't got change for gold," the woman said truculently.

"Don't expect any."

She nodded angrily, as if this show of wealth, even at her benefit, incensed her. But she took his gold, and a moment later the hamburgers came on a cloudy plate, still red around the edges.

"Do you have salt?"

She gave it to him in a little crock she took from underneath the bar, white lumps he'd have to crumble with his fingers. "Bread?"

"No bread." He knew she was lying, but he also knew why and didn't push it. The bald man was staring at him with cyanosed eyes, his hands clenching and unclenching on the splintered and gouged surface of his table. His nostrils flared with pulsating regularity, scooping up the smell of the meat. That, at least, was free.

The gunslinger began to eat steadily, not seeming to taste, merely chopping the meat apart and forking it into his mouth, trying not to think of what the cow this had come from must have looked like. Threaded stock, she had said. Yes, quite likely! And pigs would dance the commala in the light of the Peddler's Moon.

He was almost through, ready to call for another beer and roll a smoke, when the hand fell on his shoulder.

He suddenly became aware that the room had once more gone silent, and he tasted tension in the air. He turned around and stared into the face of the man who had been asleep by the door when he entered. It was a terrible face. The odor of the devil-grass was a rank miasma. The eyes were damned, the staring, glaring eyes of one who sees but does not see, eyes ever turned inward to the sterile hell of dreams beyond control, dreams unleashed, risen out of the stinking swamps of the unconscious.

The woman behind the bar made a small moaning sound.

The cracked lips writhed, lifted, revealing the green, mossy teeth, and the gunslinger thought: *He's not even smoking it anymore. He's chewing it. He's really chewing it.*

And on the heels of that: *He's a dead man. He should have been dead a year ago.*

And on the heels of that: *The man in black did this.*

They stared at each other, the gunslinger and the man who had gone around the rim of madness.

He spoke, and the gunslinger, dumbfounded, heard himself addressed in the High Speech of Gilead.

"The gold for a favor, gunslinger-sai. Just one? For a pretty."

The High Speech. For a moment his mind refused to track it. It had been years—God!—centuries, millenniums; there was no more High Speech; he was the last, the last gunslinger. The others were all . . .

Numbed, he reached into his breast pocket and produced a gold piece. The split, scabbed, gangrenous hand reached for it, fondled it, held it up to reflect the greasy glare of the kerosene lamps. It threw off its proud civilized glow; golden, reddish, bloody.

"Ahhhhhh . . ." An inarticulate sound of pleasure. The old man did a weaving turn and began moving back to his table, holding the coin at eye level, turning it, flashing it.

The room was emptying rapidly, the batwings shuttling madly back and forth. The piano player closed the lid of his instrument with a bang and exited after the others in long, comic-opera strides.

"Sheb!" the woman screamed after him, her voice an odd mixture of fear and shrewishness, "Sheb, you come back here! Goddammit!" Was that a name the gunslinger had heard before? He thought yes, but there was no time to reflect upon it now, or to cast his mind back.

The old man, meanwhile, had gone back to his table. He spun the gold piece on the gouged wood, and the dead-alive eyes followed it with empty fascination. He spun it a second time, a third, and his eyelids drooped. The fourth time, and his head settled to the wood before the coin stopped.

"There," she said softly, furiously. "You've driven out my trade. Are you satisfied?"

"They'll be back," the gunslinger said.

"Not tonight they won't."

"Who is he?" He gestured at the weed-eater.

"Go fuck yourself. *Sai.*"

"I have to know," the gunslinger said patiently. "He—"

"He talked to you funny," she said. "Nort never talked like that in his life."

"I'm looking for a man. You would know him."

She stared at him, the anger dying. It was replaced
with speculation, then with a high, wet gleam he had
seen before. The rickety building ticked thoughtfully
to itself. A dog barked brayingly, far away. The gunslinger waited. She saw his knowledge and the gleam
was replaced by hopelessness, by a dumb need that had
no mouth.

"I guess maybe you know my price," she said. "I got
an itch I used to be able to take care of, but now I can't."

He looked at her steadily. The scar would not show in
the dark. Her body was lean enough so the desert and
grit and grind hadn't been able to sag everything. And
she'd once been pretty, maybe even beautiful. Not that
it mattered. It would not have mattered if the grave-
beetles had nested in the arid blackness of her womb. It
had all been written. Somewhere some hand had put it
all down in ka's book.

Her hands came up to her face and there was still
some juice left in her—enough to weep.

"Don't *look!* You don't have to look at me so mean!"

"I'm sorry," the gunslinger said. "I didn't mean to be
mean."

"None of you mean it!" she cried at him.

"Close the place up and put out the lights."

She wept, hands at her face. He was glad she had her
hands at her face. Not because of the scar but because it
gave her back her maidenhood, if not her maidenhead.
The pin that held the strap of her dress glittered in the
greasy light.

"Will he steal anything? I'll put him out if he will."

"No," she whispered. "Nort don't steal."

"Then put out the lights."

She would not remove her hands until she was behind him and she doused the lamps one by one, turning down the wicks and breathing the flames into extinction. Then she took his hand in the dark and it was warm. She led him upstairs. There was no light to hide their act.

VI

He made cigarettes in the dark, then lit them and passed one to her. The room held her scent, fresh lilac, pathetic. The smell of the desert had overlaid it. He realized he was afraid of the desert ahead.

"His name is Nort," she said. No harshness had been worn out of her voice. "Just Nort. He died."

The gunslinger waited.

"He was touched by God."

The gunslinger said, "I have never seen Him."

"He was here ever since I can remember—Nort, I mean, not God." She laughed jaggedly into the dark. "He had a honeywagon for a while. Started to drink. Started to smell the grass. Then to smoke it. The kids started to follow him around and sic their dogs onto him. He wore old green pants that stank. Do you understand?"

"Yes."

"He started to chew it. At the last he just sat in there and didn't eat anything. He might have been a king, in his mind. The children might have been his jesters, and the dogs his princes."

"Yes."

"He died right in front of this place," she said. "Came clumping down the boardwalk—his boots wouldn't wear out, they were engineer boots he found in the old train-yard—with the children and dogs behind him. He looked like wire clothes hangers all wrapped and twirled together. You could see all the lights of hell in his eyes, but he was grinning, just like the grins the children carve into their sharproots and pumpkins, come Reap. You could smell the dirt and the rot and the weed. It was running down from the corners of his mouth like green blood. I think he meant to come in and listen to Sheb play the piano. And right in front, he stopped and cocked his head. I could see him, and I thought he heard a coach, although there was none due. Then he puked, and it was black and full of blood. It went right through that grin like sewer water through a grate. The stink was enough to make you want to run mad. He raised up his arms and just threw over. That was all. He died in his own vomit with that grin on his face."

"A nice story."

"Oh yes, thankee-sai. This be a nice place."

She was trembling beside him. Outside, the wind kept up its steady whine, and somewhere far away a door was banging, like a sound heard in a dream. Mice ran in the walls. The gunslinger thought in the back of his mind that it was probably the only place in town prosperous enough to support mice. He put a hand on her belly and she started violently, then relaxed.

"The man in black," he said.

"You have to have it, don't you? You couldn't just throw me a fuck and go to sleep."

"I have to have it."

"All right. I'll tell you." She grasped his hand in both of hers and told him.

VII

He came in the late afternoon of the day Nort died, and the wind was whooping it up, pulling away the loose topsoil, sending sheets of grit and uprooted stalks of corn windmilling past. Jubal Kennerly had padlocked the livery, and the few other merchants had shuttered their windows and laid boards across the shutters. The sky was the yellow color of old cheese and the clouds flew across it, as if they had seen something horrifying in the desert wastes where they had so lately been.

The gunslinger's quarry came in a rickety rig with a rippling tarp tied across its bed. There was a big howdy-do of a grin on his face. They watched him come, and old man Kennerly, lying by the window with a bottle in one hand and the loose, hot flesh of his second-eldest daughter's left breast in the other, resolved not to be there if he should knock.

But the man in black went by without slowing the bay that pulled his rig, and the spinning wheels spumed up dust that the wind clutched eagerly. He might have been a priest or a monk; he wore a black robe that had been floured with dust, and a loose hood covered his head and obscured his features, but not that horrid happy grin. The robe rippled and flapped. From beneath the garment's hem there peeped heavy buckled boots with square toes.

He pulled up in front of Sheb's and tethered the

horse, which lowered its head and grunted at the ground. Around the back of the rig he untied one flap, found a weathered saddlebag, threw it over his shoulder, and went in through the batwings.

Alice watched him curiously, but no one else noticed his arrival. The regulars were drunk as lords. Sheb was playing Methodist hymns ragtime, and the grizzled layabouts who had come in early to avoid the storm and to attend Nort's wake had sung themselves hoarse. Sheb, drunk nearly to the point of senselessness, intoxicated and horny with his own continued existence, played with hectic, shuttlecock speed, fingers flying like looms.

Voices screeched and hollered, never overcoming the wind but sometimes seeming to challenge it. In the corner, Zachary had thrown Amy Feldon's skirts over her head and was painting Reap-charms on her knees. A few other women circulated. A fever seemed to be on all of them. The dull stormglow that filtered through the batwings seemed to mock them, however.

Nort had been laid out on two tables in the center of the room. His engineer boots made a mystical V. His mouth hung open in a slack grin, although someone had closed his eyes and put slugs on them. His hands had been folded on his chest with a sprig of devil-grass in them. He smelled like poison.

The man in black pushed back his hood and came to the bar. Alice watched him, feeling trepidation mixed with the familiar want that hid within her. There was no religious symbol on him, although that meant nothing by itself.

"Whiskey," he said. His voice was soft and pleasant. "I want the good stuff, honey."

She reached under the counter and brought out a bottle of Star. She could have palmed off the local pop-skull on him as her best, but did not. She poured, and the man in black watched her. His eyes were large, luminous. The shadows were too thick to determine their color exactly. Her need intensified. The hollering and whooping went on behind, unabated. Sheb, the worthless gelding, was playing about the Christian Soldiers and somebody had persuaded Aunt Mill to sing. Her voice, warped and distorted, cut through the babble like a dull ax through a calf's brain.

"Hey, Allie!"

She went to serve, resentful of the stranger's silence, resentful of his no-color eyes and her own restless groin. She was afraid of her needs. They were capricious and beyond her control. They might be the signal of change, which would in turn signal the beginning of her old age—a condition which in Tull was usually as short and bitter as a winter sunset.

She drew beer until the keg was empty, then broached another. She knew better than to ask Sheb; he would come willingly enough, like the dog he was, and would either chop off his own fingers or spume beer all over everything. The stranger's eyes were on her as she went about it; she could feel them.

"It's busy," he said when she returned. He had not touched his drink, merely rolled it between his palms to warm it.

"Wake," she said.

"I noticed the departed."

"They're bums," she said with sudden hatred. "All bums."

"It excites them. He's dead. They're not."

"He was their butt when he was alive. It's not right that he should be their butt now. It's . . ." She trailed off, not able to express what it was, or how it was obscene.

"Weed-eater?"

"Yes! What else did he have?"

Her tone was accusing, but he did not drop his eyes, and she felt the blood rush to her face. "I'm sorry. Are you a priest? This must revolt you."

"I'm not and it doesn't." He knocked the whiskey back neatly and did not grimace. "Once more, please. Once more with feeling, as they say in the world next door."

She had no idea what that might mean, and was afraid to ask. "I'll have to see the color of your coin first. I'm sorry."

"No need to be."

He put a rough silver coin on the counter, thick on one edge, thin on the other, and she said as she would say later: "I don't have change for this."

He shook his head, dismissing it, and watched absently as she poured again.

"Are you only passing through?" she asked.

He did not reply for a long time, and she was about to repeat when he shook his head impatiently. "Don't talk trivialities. You're here with death."

She recoiled, hurt and amazed, her first thought being that he had lied about his holiness to test her.

"You cared for him," he said flatly. "Isn't that true?"

"Who? Nort?" She laughed, affecting annoyance to cover her confusion. "I think you better—"

"You're soft-hearted and a little afraid," he went on,

"and he was on the weed, looking out hell's back door. And there he is, they've even slammed the door now, and you don't think they'll open it until it's time for you to walk through, isn't it so?"

"What are you, drunk?"

"Mistuh Norton, he *daid*," the man in black intoned, giving the words a sardonic little twist. "Dead as anybody. Dead as you or anybody."

"Get out of my place." She felt a trembling loathing spring up in her, but the warmth still radiated from her belly.

"It's all right," he said softly. "It's all right. Wait. Just wait."

The eyes were blue. She felt suddenly easy in her mind, as if she had taken a drug.

"Dead as anybody," he said. "Do you see?"

She nodded dumbly and he laughed aloud—a fine, strong, untainted laugh that swung heads around. He whirled and faced them, suddenly the center of attention. Aunt Mill faltered and subsided, leaving a cracked high note bleeding on the air. Sheb struck a discord and halted. They looked at the stranger uneasily. Sand rattled against the sides of the building.

The silence held, spun itself out. Her breath had clogged in her throat and she looked down and saw both hands pressed to her belly beneath the bar. They all looked at him and he looked at them. Then the laugh burst forth again, strong, rich, beyond denial. But there was no urge to laugh along with him.

"I'll show you a wonder!" he cried at them. But they only watched him, like obedient children taken to see a magician in whom they have grown too old to believe.

The man in black sprang forward, and Aunt Mill drew away from him. He grinned fiercely and slapped her broad belly. A short, unwitting cackle was forced out of her, and the man in black threw back his head.

"It's better, isn't it?"

Aunt Mill cackled again, suddenly broke into sobs, and fled blindly through the doors. The others watched her go silently. The storm was beginning; shadows followed each other, rising and falling on the white cyclorama of the sky. A man near the piano with a forgotten beer in one hand made a groaning, slobbering sound.

The man in black stood over Nort, grinning down at him. The wind howled and shrieked and thrummed. Something large struck the side of the building hard enough to make it shake and then bounced away. One of the men at the bar tore himself free and headed for some quieter locale, moving in great grotesque strides. Thunder racketed the sky with a sound like some god coughing.

"All *right!*" the man in black grinned. "All right, let's get down *to* it!"

He began to spit into Nort's face, aiming carefully. The spittle gleamed on the corpse's forehead, pearled down the shaven beak of his nose.

Under the bar, her hands worked faster.

Sheb laughed, loon-like, and hunched over. He began to cough up phlegm, huge and sticky gobs of it, and let fly. The man in black roared approval and pounded him on the back. Sheb grinned, one gold tooth twinkling.

Some fled. Others gathered in a loose ring around Nort. His face and the dewlapped rooster-wrinkles of his neck and upper chest gleamed with liquid—liquid so precious in this dry country. And suddenly the rain of spit stopped, as if on signal. There was ragged, heavy breathing.

The man in black suddenly lunged across the body, jackknifing over it in a smooth arc. It was pretty, like a flash of water. He caught himself on his hands, sprang to his feet in a twist, grinning, and went over again. One of the watchers forgot himself, began to applaud, and suddenly backed away, eyes cloudy with terror. He slobbered a hand across his mouth and made for the door.

Nort twitched the third time the man in black went across.

A sound went through the watchers—a grunt—and then they were silent. The man in black threw his head back and howled. His chest moved in a quick, shallow rhythm as he sucked air. He began to go back and forth at a faster clip, pouring over Nort's body like water poured from one glass to another and then back again. The only sound in the room was the tearing rasp of his respiration and the rising pulse of the storm.

There came the moment when Nort drew a deep, dry breath. His hands rattled and pounded aimlessly on the table. Sheb screeched and exited. One of the women followed him, her eyes wide and her wimple billowing.

The man in black went across once more, twice, thrice. The body on the table was vibrating now, trembling and rapping and twitching like a large yet essentially lifeless doll with some monstrous clockwork hidden inside. The smell of rot and excrement and decay billowed up in choking waves. There came a moment when his eyes opened.

Allie felt her numb and feelingless feet propelling

her backward. She struck the mirror, making it shiver, and blind panic took over. She bolted like a steer.

"So here's your wonder," the man in black called after her, panting. "I've given it to you. Now you can sleep easy. Even *that* isn't irreversible. Although it's . . . so . . . god-damned . . . *funny!*" And he began to laugh again. The sound faded as she raced up the stairs, not stopping until the door to the three rooms above the bar was bolted.

She began to giggle then, rocking back and forth on her haunches by the door. The sound rose to a keening wail that mixed with the wind. She kept hearing the sound Nort had made when he came back to life—the sound of fists knocking blindly on the lid of a coffin. What thoughts, she wondered, could be left in his reanimated brain? What had he seen while dead? How much did he remember? Would he tell? Were the secrets of the grave waiting downstairs? The most terrible thing about such questions, she reckoned, was that part of you really wanted to ask.

Below her, Nort wandered absently out into the storm to pull some weed. The man in black, now the only patron in the bar, perhaps watched him go, perhaps still grinning.

When she forced herself to go back down that evening, carrying a lamp in one hand and a heavy stick of stovewood in the other, the man in black was gone, rig and all. But Nort was there, sitting at the table by the door as if he had never been away. The smell of the weed was on him, but not as heavily as she might have expected.

He looked up at her and smiled tentatively. "Hello, Allie."

"Hello, Nort." She put the stovewood down and began lighting the lamps, not turning her back to him.

"I been touched by God," he said presently. "I ain't going to die no more. He said so. It was a promise."

"How nice for you, Nort." The spill she was holding dropped through her trembling fingers and she picked it up.

"I'd like to stop chewing the grass," he said. "I don't enjoy it no more. It don't seem right for a man touched by God to be chewing the weed."

"Then why don't you stop?"

Her exasperation had startled her into looking at him as a man again, rather than an infernal miracle. What she saw was a rather sad-looking specimen only half-stoned, looking hangdog and ashamed. She could not be frightened by him anymore.

"I shake," he said. "And I want it. I can't stop. Allie, you was always good to me . . ." He began to weep. "I can't even stop peeing myself. What am I? *What am I?*"

She walked to the table and hesitated there, uncertain.

"He could have made me not want it," he said through the tears. "He could have done that if he could have made me be alive. I ain't complaining . . . I don't want to complain . . ." He stared around hauntedly and whispered, "He might strike me dead if I did."

"Maybe it's a joke. He seemed to have quite a sense of humor."

Nort took his poke from where it dangled inside his shirt and brought out a handful of grass. Unthinkingly she knocked it away and then drew her hand back, horrified.

"I can't help it, Allie, I can't," and he made a crippled dive for the poke. She could have stopped him, but she made no effort. She went back to lighting the lamps, tired although the evening had barely begun. But nobody came in that night except old man Kennerly, who had missed everything. He did not seem particularly surprised to see Nort. Perhaps someone had told him what had happened. He ordered beer, asked where Sheb was, and pawed her.

Later, Nort came to her and held out a folded piece of paper in one shaky no-right-to-be-alive hand. "He left you this," he said. "I near forgot. If I'd forgot, he woulda come back and killed me, sure."

Paper was valuable, a commodity much to be treasured, but she didn't like to handle this. It felt heavy, nasty. Written on it was a single word:

Allie

"How'd he know my name?" she asked Nort, and Nort only shook his head.

She opened it and read this:

You want to know about Death. I left him a word. That word is NINETEEN. If you say it to him his mind will be opened. He will tell you what lies beyond. He will tell you what he saw.

The word is NINETEEN.

Knowing will drive you mad.

But sooner or later you will ask.

You won't be able to help yourself.

Have a nice day! ☺

Walter o' Dim

P.S. The word is NINETEEN.
You will try to forget but sooner or later it will come out of your mouth like vomit.
NINETEEN.

And oh dear God, she knew that she would. Already it trembled on her lips. *Nineteen,* she would say—*Nort, listen: Nineteen.* And the secrets of Death and the land beyond would be opened to her.

Sooner or later you will ask.

The next day things were almost normal, although none of the children followed Nort. The day after that, the catcalls resumed. Life had gotten back on its own sweet keel. The uprooted corn was gathered together by the children, and a week after Nort's resurrection, they burned it in the middle of the street. The fire was momentarily bright and most of the barflies stepped or staggered out to watch. They looked primitive. Their faces seemed to float between the flames and the ice-chip brilliance of the sky. Allie watched them and felt a pang of fleeting despair for the sad times of this world. The loss. Things had stretched apart. There was no glue at the center anymore. Somewhere something was tottering, and when it fell, all would end. She had never seen the ocean, never would.

"If I had *guts,*" she murmured. "If I had guts, guts, *guts . . .*"

Nort raised his head at the sound of her voice and smiled emptily at her from hell. She had no guts. Only a bar and a scar. And a word. It struggled behind her closed lips. Suppose she were to call him over now and draw him close despite his stink? Suppose she said the word into the waxy buggerlug he called an ear? His eyes would change. They would turn into *his* eyes—those of the man in the robe. And then Nort would tell what he'd seen in the Land of Death, what lay beyond the earth and the worms.

I'll never say that word to him.

But the man who had brought Nort back to life and left her a note—left her a word like a cocked pistol she would someday put to her temple—had known better.

Nineteen would open the secret.

Nineteen *was* the secret.

She caught herself writing it in a puddle on the bar— NꓱNE ꓔEEN—and skidded it to nothingness when she saw Nort watching her.

The fire burned down rapidly and her customers came back in. She began to dose herself with the Star Whiskey, and by midnight she was blackly drunk.

VIII

She ceased her narrative, and when he made no immediate comment, she thought at first that the story had put him to sleep. She began to drowse herself when he asked: "That's all?"

"Yes. That's all. It's very late."

"Um." He was rolling another cigarette.

"Don't go getting your tobacco dandruff in my bed," she told him, more sharply than she had intended.

"No."

Silence again. The tip of his cigarette winked off and on.

"You'll be leaving in the morning," she said dully.

"I should. I think he's left a trap for me here. Just like he left one for you."

"Do you really think that number would—"

"If you like your sanity, you don't ever want to say that word to Nort," the gunslinger said. "Put it out of your head. If you can, teach yourself that the number after eighteen is twenty. That half of thirty-eight is seventeen. The man who signed himself Walter o' Dim is a lot of things, but a liar isn't one of them."

"But—"

"When the urge comes and it's strong, come up here and hide under your quilts and say it over and over again—scream it, if you have to—until the urge passes."

"A time will come when it won't pass."

The gunslinger made no reply, for he knew this was true. The trap had a ghastly perfection. If someone told you you'd go to hell if you thought about seeing your mother naked (once when the gunslinger was very young he had been told this very thing), you'd eventually do it. And why? Because you did *not* want to imagine your mother naked. Because you did *not* want to go to hell. Because, if given a knife and a hand in which to hold it, the mind would eventually eat itself. Not because it wanted to; because it did *not* want to.

Sooner or later Allie would call Nort over and say the word.

"Don't go," she said.

"We'll see."

He turned on his side away from her, but she was comforted. He would stay, at least for a little while. She drowsed.

On the edge of sleep she thought again about the way Nort had addressed him, in that strange talk. It was the only time she had seen her strange new lover express emotion. Even his lovemaking had been a silent thing, and only at the last had his breathing roughened and then stopped for a second or two. He was like something out of a fairytale or a myth, a fabulous, dangerous creature. Could he grant wishes? She thought the answer was yes, and that she would have hers. He would stay awhile. That was wish enough for a luckless scarred bitch such as she. Tomorrow was time enough to think of another, or a third. She slept.

IX

In the morning she cooked him grits, which he ate without comment. He shoveled them in without thinking about her, hardly seeing her. He knew he should go. Every minute he sat here the man in black was further away—probably out of the hardpan and arroyos and into the desert by now. His path had been undeviatingly southeast, and the gunslinger knew why.

"Do you have a map?" he asked, looking up.

"Of the town?" she laughed. "There isn't enough of it to need a map."

"No. Of what's southeast of here."

Her smile faded. "The desert. Just the desert. I thought you'd stay for a little."

"What's on the other side of the desert?"

"How would I know? Nobody crosses it. Nobody's tried since I was here." She wiped her hands on her apron, got potholders, and dumped the tub of water she had been heating into the sink, where it splashed and steamed. "The clouds all go that way. It's like something sucks them—"

He got up.

"Where are you going?" She heard the shrill fear in her voice and hated it.

"To the stable. If anyone knows, the hostler will." He put his hands on her shoulders. The hands were hard, but they were also warm. "And to arrange for my mule. If I'm going to be here, he should be taken care of. For when I leave."

But not yet. She looked up at him. "But you watch that Kennerly. If he doesn't know a thing, he'll make it up."

"Thank you, Allie."

When he left she turned to the sink, feeling the hot, warm drift of her grateful tears. How long since anyone had thanked her? Someone who mattered?

X

Kennerly was a toothless and unpleasant old satyr who had buried two wives and was plagued with daughters. Two half-grown ones peeked at the gunslinger from the dusty shadows of the barn. A baby drooled happily in the dirt. A full-grown one, blond, dirty, and sensual, watched with a speculative curiosity as she drew water from the groaning pump beside the building. She caught the gunslinger's eye, pinched her nipples between her fingers, dropped him a wink, and then went back to pumping.

The hostler met him halfway between the door to

his establishment and the street. His manner vacillated between a kind of hateful hostility and craven fawning.

"Hit's bein' cared for, never fear 'at," he said, and before the gunslinger could reply, Kennerly turned on his daughter with his fists up, a desperate scrawny rooster of a man. "You get in, Soobie! You get right the hell in!"

Soobie began to drag her bucket sullenly toward the shack appended to the barn.

"You meant my mule," the gunslinger said.

"Yes, sai. Ain't seen no mule in quite a time, specially one that looks as threaded as your'n—two eyes, four legs . . ." His face squinched together alarmingly in an expression meant to convey either extreme pain or the notion that a joke had been made. The gunslinger assumed it was the latter, although he had little or no sense of humor himself.

"Time was they used to grow up wild for want of 'em," Kennerly continued, "but the world has moved on. Ain't seen nothin' but a few mutie oxen and the coach horses and—Soobie, I'll whale you, 'fore God!"

"I don't bite," the gunslinger said pleasantly.

Kennerly cringed and grinned. The gunslinger saw the murder in his eyes quite clearly, and although he did not fear it, he marked it as a man might mark a page in a book, one that contained potentially valuable instructions. "It ain't *you*. Gods, no, it ain't *you*." He grinned loosely. "She just naturally gawky. She got a devil. She wild." His eyes darkened. "It's coming to Last Times, mister. You know how it says in the Book. Children won't obey their parents, and a plague'll be visited on the multitudes. You only have to listen to the preacher-woman to know it."

The gunslinger nodded, then pointed southeast. "What's out there?"

Kennerly grinned again, showing gums and a few sociable yellow teeth. "Dwellers. Weed. Desert. What else?" He cackled, and his eyes measured the gunslinger coldly.

"How big is the desert?"

"Big." Kennerly endeavored to look serious, as if answering a serious question. "Maybe a thousand wheels. Maybe two thousand. I can't tell you, mister. There's nothin' out there but devil-grass and maybe demons. Heard there was a speakin'-ring sommers on the far side, but that 'us prolly a lie. That's the way the other fella went. The one who fixed up Norty when he was sick."

"Sick? I heard he was dead."

Kennerly kept grinning. "Well, well. Maybe. But we're growed-up men, ain't we?"

"But you believe in demons."

Kennerly looked affronted. "That's a lot different. Preacher-woman says . . ."

He blathered and palavered ever onward. The gunslinger took off his hat and wiped his forehead. The sun was hot, beating steadily. Kennerly seemed not to notice. Kennerly had a lot to say, none of it sensible. In the thin shadow by the livery, the baby girl was gravely smearing dirt on her face.

The gunslinger finally grew impatient and cut the man off in mid-spate. "You don't know what's after the desert?"

Kennerly shrugged. "Some might. The coach ran through part of it fifty years ago. My pap said so. He used to say 'twas mountains. Others say an ocean . . . a green ocean with monsters. And some say that's where the world ends. That there ain't nothing but lights that'll drive a man blind and the face of God with his mouth open to eat them up."

"Drivel," the gunslinger said shortly.

"Sure it is," Kennerly cried happily. He cringed again, hating, fearing, wanting to please.

"You see my mule is looked after." He flicked Kennerly another coin, which Kennerly caught on the fly. The gunslinger thought of the way a dog will catch a ball.

"Surely. You stayin' a little?"

"I guess I might. There'll be water—"

"—if God wills it! Sure, sure!" Kennerly laughed unhappily, and his eyes went on wanting the gunslinger stretched out dead at his feet. "That Allie's pretty nice when she wants to be, ain't she?" The hostler made a loose circle with his left fist and began poking his right finger rapidly in and out of it.

"Did you say something?" the gunslinger asked remotely.

Sudden terror dawned in Kennerly's eyes, like twin moons coming over the horizon. He put his hands behind his back like a naughty child caught with the jamjar. "No, sai, not a word. And I'm right sorry if I did." He caught sight of Soobie leaning out a window and whirled on her. "I'll whale you now, you little slut-whore! 'Fore God! I'll—"

The gunslinger walked away, aware that Kennerly had turned to watch him, aware of the fact that he could whirl and catch the hostler with some true and untinc-tured emotion distilled on his face. Why bother? It was hot, and he knew what the emotion would be: just hate.

Hate of the outsider. He'd gotten all the man had to offer. The only sure thing about the desert was its size. The only sure thing about the town was that it wasn't all played out here. Not yet.

XI

He and Allie were in bed when Sheb kicked the door open and came in with the knife.

It had been four days, and they had gone by in a blinking haze. He ate. He slept. He had sex with Allie. He found that she played the fiddle and he made her play it for him. She sat by the window in the milky light of daybreak, only a profile, and played something haltingly that might have been good if she'd had some training. He felt a growing (but strangely absentminded) affection for her and thought this might be the trap the man in black had left behind. He walked out sometimes. He thought very little about everything.

He didn't hear the little piano player come up—his reflexes had sunk. That didn't seem to matter, either, although it would have frightened him badly in another time and place.

Allie was naked, the sheet below her breasts, and they were preparing to make love.

"Please," she was saying. "Like before, I want that, I want—"

The door crashed open and the piano player made his ridiculous, knock-kneed run for the sun. Allie did not scream, although Sheb held an eight-inch carving knife in his hand. He was making a noise, an inarticulate

blabbering. He sounded like a man being drowned in a
bucket of mud. Spittle flew. He brought the knife down
with both hands, and the gunslinger caught his wrists
and turned them. The knife went flying. Sheb made
a high screeching noise, like a rusty screen door. His
hands fluttered in marionette movements, both wrists
broken. The wind gritted against the window. Allie's
looking glass on the wall, faintly clouded and distorted,
reflected the room.

"She was mine!" He wept. "She was mine first! Mine!"

Allie looked at him and got out of bed. She put on
a wrapper, and the gunslinger felt a moment of empa-
thy for a man who must be seeing himself coming out
on the far end of what he once had. He was just a little
man. And the gunslinger suddenly knew where he had
seen him before. Known him before.

"It was for you," Sheb sobbed. "It was only for you,
Allie. It was you first and it was all for you. I—ah, oh
God, dear God . . ." The words dissolved into a par-
oxysm of unintelligibilities, finally to tears. He rocked
back and forth holding his broken wrists to his belly.

"Shhh. Shhh. Let me see." She knelt beside him. "Broken. Sheb, you ass. How will you make your living now?
Didn't you know you were never strong?" She helped
him to his feet. He tried to hold his hands to his face,
but they would not obey, and he wept nakedly. "Come
on over to the table and let me see what I can do."

She led him to the table and set his wrists with slats
of kindling from the fire box. He wept weakly and without volition.

"Mejis," the gunslinger said, and the little piano
player looked around, eyes wide. The gunslinger nod-

ded, amiably enough now that Sheb was no longer trying to stick a knife in his lights. *"Mejis,"* he said again.
"On the Clean Sea."

"What about it?"

"You were there, weren't you? Many and many-a, as
they did say."

"What if I was? I don't remember you."

"But you remember the girl, don't you? The girl
named Susan? And Reap night?" His voice took on an
edge. "Were you there for the bonfire?"

The little man's lips trembled. They were covered
with spit. His eyes said he knew the truth: He was closer
to dead now than when he'd come bursting in with a
knife in his hand.

"Get out of here," the gunslinger said.

Understanding dawned in Sheb's eyes. "But you was just
a *boy!* One of them three *boys!* You come to count stock,
and Eldred Jonas was there, the Coffin Hunter, and—"

"Get out while you still can," the gunslinger said, and
Sheb went, holding his broken wrists before him.

She came back to the bed. "What was that about?"

"Never mind," he said.

"All right—then where were we?"

"Nowhere." He rolled on his side, away from her.

She said patiently, "You knew about him and me. He
did what he could, which wasn't much, and I took what
I could, because I had to. There's nothing to be done.
What else is there?" She touched his shoulder. "Except
I'm glad that you are so strong."

"Not now," he said.

"Who was she?" And then, answering her own question: "A girl you loved."

"Leave it, Allie."

"I can make you strong—"

"No," he said. "You can't do that."

XII

The next night the bar was closed. It was whatever passed for the Sabbath in Tull. The gunslinger went to the tiny, leaning church by the graveyard while Allie washed tables with strong disinfectant and rinsed kerosene lamp chimneys in soapy water.

An odd purple dusk had fallen, and the church, lit from the inside, looked almost like a blast furnace from the road.

"I don't go," Allie had said shortly. "The woman who preaches has poison religion. Let the respectable ones go."

He stood in the vestibule, hidden in a shadow, looking in. The pews were gone and the congregation stood (he saw Kennerly and his brood; Castner, owner of the town's scrawny dry-goods emporium and his slat-sided wife; a few barflies; a few "town" women he had never seen before; and, surprisingly, Sheb). They were singing a hymn raggedly, *a cappella*. He looked curiously at the mountainous woman at the pulpit. Allie had said: "She lives alone, hardly ever sees anybody. Only comes out on Sunday to serve up the hellfire. Her name is Sylvia Pittston. She's crazy, but she's got the hoodoo on them. They like it that way. It suits them."

No description could take the measure of the woman. Breasts like earthworks. A huge pillar of a neck overtopped by a pasty white moon of a face, in which blinked eyes so large and so dark that they seemed to be bottomless tarns. Her hair was a beautiful rich brown and it was piled atop her head in a haphazard sprawl, held by a hairpin almost big enough to be a meat skewer. She wore a dress that seemed to be made of burlap. The arms that held the hymnal were slabs. Her skin was creamy, unmarked, lovely. He thought that she must top three hundred pounds. He felt a sudden red lust for her that made him feel shaky, and he turned his head and looked away.

"Shall we gather at the river,
The beautiful, the beautiful,
The riiiiver,
Shall we gather at the river,
That flows by the kingdom of God."

The last note of the last chorus faded off, and there was a moment of shuffling and coughing.

She waited. When they were settled, she spread her hands over them, as if in benediction. It was an evocative gesture.

"My dear little brothers and sisters in Christ."

It was a haunting line. For a moment the gunslinger felt mixed feelings of nostalgia and fear, stitched in with an eerie feeling of *déjà vu,* and he thought: *I dreamed this. Or I was here before. If so, when? Not Mejis.* No, not there. He shook the feeling off. The audience—perhaps twenty-five all told—had become dead silent. Every eye touched the preacher-woman.

"The subject of our meditation tonight is The Interloper." Her voice was sweet, melodious, the speaking voice of a well-trained contralto.

A little rustle ran through the audience.

"I feel," Sylvia Pittston said reflectively, "that I know almost everyone in the Good Book personally. In the last five years I have worn out three of 'em, precious though any book be in this ill world, and uncountable numbers before that. I love the story, and I love the players in that story. I have walked arm in arm in the lion's den with Daniel. I stood with David when he was tempted by Bathsheba as she bathed at the pool. I have been in the fiery furnace with Shadrach, Meschach, and Abednego. I slew two thousand with Samson when he swung the jawbone, and was blinded with St. Paul on the road to Damascus. I wept with Mary at Golgotha."

A soft, shurring sigh in the audience.

"I have known and loved them. There is only one"— she held up a finger—"only one player in the greatest of all dramas that I do not know.

"Only one who stands outside with his face in the shadow.

"Only one who makes my body tremble and my spirit quail.

"I fear him.

"I don't know his mind and I fear him.

"I fear The Interloper."

Another sigh. One of the women had put a hand over her mouth as if to stop a sound and was rocking, rocking.

"The Interloper who came to Eve as a snake on its belly in the dust, grinning and writhing. The Interloper who walked among the Children of Israel while Moses was up on the Mount, who whispered to them to make a golden idol, a golden calf, and to worship it with foulness and fornication."

Moans, nods.

"The Interloper!

"He stood on the balcony with Jezebel and watched as King Ahaz fell screaming to his death, and he and she grinned as the dogs gathered and lapped up his blood. Oh, my little brothers and sisters, watch thou for The Interloper."

"Yes, O Jesus—" This was the man the gunslinger had first noticed coming into town, the one with the straw hat.

"He's always been there, my brothers and sisters. But I don't know his mind. And *you* don't know his mind. Who could understand the awful darkness that swirls there, the pride and the titanic blasphemy, the unholy glee? And the madness! The gibbering madness that walks and crawls and wriggles through men's most awful wants and desires?"

"O Jesus Savior—"

"It was *him* who took our Lord up on the mountain—"

"Yes—"

"It was *him* that tempted him and shewed him all the world and the world's pleasures—"

"*Yesss*—"

"It's *him* that will return when Last Times come on the world . . . and they are coming, my brothers and sisters, can't you feel they are?"

"*Yesss*—"

Rocking and sobbing, the congregation became a sea; the woman seemed to point at all of them and none of them.

"It's *him* that will come as the Antichrist, a crimson king with bloody eyes, to lead men into the flaming bowels of perdition, to the bloody end of wickedness, as Star Wormword hangs blazing in the sky, as gall gnaws at the vitals of the children, as women's wombs give forth monstrosities, as the works of men's hands turn to blood—"

"Ahhh—"

"Ah, God—"

"Gawwwwwwwww—"

A woman fell on the floor, her legs crashing up and down against the wood. One of her shoes flew off.

"It's *him* that stands behind every fleshly pleasure . . . him who made the machines with LaMerk stamped on them, *him!* The Interloper!"

LaMerk, the gunslinger thought. *Or maybe she said LeMark.* The word had some vague resonance for him, but nothing he could put his finger on. Nonetheless, he filed it away in his memory, which was capacious.

"Yes, Lord!" they were screaming.

A man fell on his knees, holding his head and braying.

"When you take a drink, who holds the bottle?"

"The Interloper!"

"When you sit down to a faro or a Watch Me table, who turns the cards?"

"The Interloper!"

"When you riot in the flesh of another's body, when you pollute yourself with your solitary hand, to whom do you sell your soul?"

"In—"

"ter—"

"Oh, Jesus . . . Oh—"

"—loper—"

"Aw . . . Aw . . . Aw . . ."

"And who is he?" she cried. But calm within, he could sense the calmness, the mastery, the control and domination. He thought suddenly, with terror and absolute surety, that the man who called himself Walter had left a demon in her. She was haunted. He felt the hot ripple of sexual desire again through his fear, and thought this was somehow like the word the man in black had left in Allie's mind like a loaded trap.

The man who was holding his head crashed and blundered forward.

"I'm in hell!" he screamed up at her. His face twisted and writhed as if snakes crawled beneath his skin. "I done fornications! I done gambling! I done weed! I done *sins!* I—" But his voice rose skyward in a dreadful, hysterical wail that drowned articulation. He held his head as if it would burst like an overripe cantaloupe at any moment.

The audience stilled as if a cue had been given, frozen in their half-erotic poses of ecstasy.

Sylvia Pittston reached down and grasped his head. The man's cry ceased as her fingers, strong and white, unblemished and gentle, worked through his hair. He looked up at her dumbly.

"Who was with you in sin?" she asked. Her eyes looked into his, deep enough, gentle enough, cold enough to drown in.

"The . . . The Interloper."

"Called who?"

"Called Lord High Satan." Raw, oozing whisper.

"Will you renounce?"

Eagerly: "Yes! Yes! Oh, my Jesus Savior!"

She rocked his head; he stared at her with the blank, shiny eyes of the zealot. "If he walked through that door"—she hammered a finger at the vestibule shadows where the gunslinger stood—"would you renounce him to his face?"

"On my mother's name!"

"Do you believe in the eternal love of Jesus?"

He began to weep. "You're fucking-A I do—"

"He forgives you that, Jonson."

"Praise God," Jonson said, still weeping.

"I know he forgives you just as I know he will cast out the unrepentant from his palaces and into the place of burning darkness beyond the end of End-World."

"Praise God." The congregation, drained, spoke it solemnly.

"Just as I know this Interloper, this Satan, this Lord of Flies and Serpents, will be cast down and crushed . . . will you crush him if you see him, Jonson?"

"Yes and praise God!" Jonson wept. "Wit' bote feet!"

"Will you crush him if you see him, brothers and sisters?"

"*Yess* . . ." Sated.

"If you see him sashaying down Main Street tomorrow?"

"Praise God . . ."

The gunslinger faded back out the door and headed

for town. The smell of the desert was clear in the air.
Almost time to move on.

Almost.

XIII

In bed again.

"She won't see you," Allie said. She sounded frightened. "She doesn't see anybody. She only comes out on
Sunday evenings to scare the hell out of everybody."

"How long has she been here?"

"Twelve years. Or maybe only two. Time's funny, as
thou knows. Let's not talk about her."

"Where did she come from? Which direction?"

"I don't know." Lying.

"Allie?"

"I don't know!"

"Allie?"

"All right! All right! She came from the dwellers! From
the desert!"

"I thought so." He relaxed a little. Southeast, in other
words. Along the path he followed. The one he could
even see in the sky, sometimes. And he guessed the
preacher-woman had come a lot further than from the
dwellers or even the desert. How had she traveled so
far? By way of some old machine that still worked? A
train, mayhap? "Where does she live?"

Her voice dropped a notch. "If I tell you, will you
make love to me?"

"I'll make love to you, anyway. But I want to know."

Allie sighed. It was an old, yellow sound, like turning

pages. "She has a house over the knoll in back of the church. A little shack. It's where the . . . the real minister used to live until he moved out. Is that enough? Are you satisfied?"

"No. Not yet." And he rolled on top of her.

XIV

It was the last day, and he knew it.

The sky was an ugly, bruised purple, weirdly lit from above with the first fingers of dawn. Allie moved about like a wraith, lighting lamps, tending corn fritters that sputtered in the skillet. He had loved her hard after she had told him what he had to know, and she had sensed the coming end and had given more than she had ever given, and she had given it with desperation against the coming of dawn, given it with the tireless energy of sixteen. But she was pale this morning, on the brink of menopause again.

She served him without a word. He ate rapidly, chewing, swallowing, chasing each bite with hot coffee. Allie went to the batwings and stood staring out at the morning, at the silent battalions of slow-moving clouds.

"It's going to dust up today."

"I'm not surprised."

"Are you ever?" she asked ironically, and turned to watch him get his hat. He clapped it on his head and brushed past her.

"Sometimes," he told her. He only saw her once more alive.

XV

By the time he reached Sylvia Pittston's shack, the wind
had died utterly and the whole world seemed to wait.
He had been in desert country long enough to know
that the longer the lull, the harder the blow when it
finally came. A queer, flat light hung over everything.

There was a large wooden cross nailed to the door of
the place, which was leaning and tired. He rapped and
waited. No answer. He rapped again. No answer. He
drew back and kicked in the door with one hard shot
of his right boot. A small bolt on the inside ripped free.
The door banged against a haphazardly planked wall
and scared rats into skittering flight. Sylvia Pittston sat
in the hall, in a mammoth ironwood rocker, and looked
at him calmly with those great and dark eyes. The storm-
light fell on her cheeks in crazy half-tones. She wore a
shawl. The rocker made tiny squeaking noises.

They looked at each other for a long, clockless
moment.

"You will never catch him," she said. "You walk in the
way of evil."

"He came to you," the gunslinger said.

"And to my bed. He spoke to me in the Tongue. The
High Speech. He—"

"He screwed you. In every sense of the word."

She did not flinch. "You walk an evil way, gunslinger.
You stand in shadows. You stood in the shadows of the
holy place last night. Did you think I couldn't see you?"

"Why did he heal the weed-eater?"

"He's an angel of God. He said so."

"I hope he smiled when he said it."

She drew her lip back from her teeth in an unconsciously feral gesture. "He told me you would follow. He told me what to do. He said you are the Antichrist."

The gunslinger shook his head. "He didn't say that."

She smiled up at him lazily. "He said you would want to bed me. Is it true?"

"Did you ever meet a man who didn't want to bed you?"

"The price of my flesh would be your life, gunslinger. He has got me with child. Not his, but the child of a great king. If you invade me . . ." She let the lazy smile complete her thought. At the same time she gestured with her huge, mountainous thighs. They stretched beneath her garment like pure marble slabs. The effect was dizzying.

The gunslinger dropped his hands to the butts of his pistols. "You have a demon, woman, not a king. Yet fear not. I can remove it."

The effect was instantaneous. She recoiled against the chair, and a weasel look flashed on her face. "Don't touch me! Don't come near me! You dare not touch the Bride of God!"

"Want to bet?" the gunslinger said. He stepped toward her. "As the gambler said when he laid down a handful of cups and wands, just watch me."

The flesh on the huge frame quaked. Her face had become a caricature of terror, and she stabbed the sign of the Eye at him with pronged fingers.

"The desert," the gunslinger said. "What after the desert?"

"You'll never catch him! Never! Never! You'll burn! He told me so!"

"I'll catch him," the gunslinger said. "We both know it. What is beyond the desert?"

"No!"

"Answer me!"

"No!"

He slid forward, dropped to his knees, and grabbed her thighs. Her legs locked like a vise. She made strange, lustful keening noises.

"The demon, then," he said. "Out it comes."

"No—"

He pried the legs apart and unholstered one of his guns.

"No! No! No!" Her breath came in short, savage grunts.

"Answer me."

She rocked in the chair and the floor trembled. Prayers and garbled bits of scripture flew from her lips.

He rammed the barrel of the gun forward. He could feel the terrified wind sucked into her lungs more than he could hear it. Her hands beat at his head; her legs drummed against the floor. And at the same time the huge body tried to suck the invader in. Outside nothing watched them but the bruised and dusty sky.

She screamed something, high and inarticulate.

"What?"

"Mountains!"

"What about them?"

"He stops . . . on the other side . . . s-s-sweet *Jesus!* . . . to m-make his strength. Med-m-meditation, do you understand? Oh . . . I'm . . . I'm . . ."

The whole huge mountain of flesh suddenly strained forward and upward, yet he was careful not to let her secret flesh touch him.

Then she seemed to wilt and grow smaller, and she wept with her hands in her lap.

"So," he said, getting up. "The demon is served, eh?"

"Get out. You've killed the child of the Crimson King. But you will be repaid. I set my watch and warrant on it. Now get out. Get out."

He stopped at the door and looked back. "No child," he said briefly. "No angel, prince, no demon."

"Leave me alone."

He did.

XVI

By the time he arrived at Kennerly's, a queer obscurity had come over the northern horizon and he knew it was dust. Over Tull the air was still dead quiet.

Kennerly was waiting for him on the chaff-strewn stage that was the floor of his barn. "Leaving?" He grinned abjectly at the gunslinger.

"Yar."

"Not before the storm?"

"Ahead of it."

"The wind goes faster than any man on a mule. In the open it can kill you."

"I'll want the mule now," the gunslinger said simply.

"Sure." But Kennerly did not turn away, merely stood as if searching for something further to say, grinning his groveling, hate-filled grin, and his eyes flicked up and over the gunslinger's shoulder.

The gunslinger sidestepped and turned at the same time, and the heavy stick of stovewood that the girl

Soobie held swished through the air, grazing his elbow only. She lost hold of it with the force of her swing and it clattered over the floor. In the explosive height of the loft, barnswallows took shadowed wing.

The girl looked at him bovinely. Her breasts thrust with overripe grandeur at the wash-faded shirt she wore. One thumb sought the haven of her mouth with dream-like slowness.

The gunslinger turned back to Kennerly. Kennerly's grin was huge. His skin was waxy yellow. His eyes rolled in their sockets. "I . . ." he began in a phlegm-filled whisper and could not continue.

"The mule," the gunslinger prodded gently.

"Sure, sure, sure," Kennerly whispered, the grin now touched with incredulity that he should still be alive. He shuffled to get it.

The gunslinger moved to where he could watch the man go. The hostler brought the mule back and handed him the bridle. "You get in an' tend your sister," he said to Soobie.

Soobie tossed her head and didn't move.

The gunslinger left them there, staring at each other across the dusty, droppings-strewn floor, he with his sick grin, she with dumb, inanimate defiance. Outside the heat was still like a hammer.

XVII

He walked the mule up the center of the street, his boots sending up squirts of dust. His waterbags, swollen with water, were strapped across the mule's back.

He stopped at the tonk, but Allie was not there. The place was deserted, battened down for the storm, but still dirty from the night before. It stank of sour beer.

He filled his tote sack with corn meal, dried and roasted corn, and half of the raw hamburg in the cooler. He left four gold pieces stacked on the planked counter. Allie did not come down. Sheb's piano bid him a silent, yellow-toothed toodle-oo. He stepped back out and cinched the tote sack across the mule's back. There was a tight feeling in his throat. He might still avoid the trap, but the chances were small. He was, after all, The Interloper.

He walked past the shuttered, waiting buildings, feeling the eyes that peered through cracks and chinks. The man in black had played God in Tull. He had spoken of a King's child, a red prince. Was it only a sense of the cosmic comic, or a matter of desperation? It was a question of some importance.

There was a shrill, harried scream from behind him, and doors suddenly threw themselves open. Forms lunged. The trap was sprung. Men in longhandles and men in dirty dungarees. Women in slacks and in faded dresses. Even children, tagging after their parents. And in every hand there was a chunk of wood or a knife.

His reaction was automatic, instantaneous, inbred. He whirled on his heels while his hands pulled the guns from their holsters, the butts heavy and sure in his hands. It was Allie, and of course it had to be Allie, coming at him with her face distorted, the scar a hellish purple in the lowering light. He saw that she was held hostage; the distorted, grimacing face of Sheb peered over her shoulder like a witch's familiar. She was his shield and sacrifice. He saw it all, clear and shadowless in the frozen, deathless light of the sterile calm, and heard her:

"Kill me, Roland, kill me! I said the word, *nineteen,* I said, and he told me . . . *I can't bear it—*"

The hands were trained to give her what she wanted. He was the last of his breed and it was not only his mouth that knew the High Speech. The guns beat their heavy, atonal music into the air. Her mouth flapped and she sagged and the guns fired again. The last expression on her face might have been gratitude. Sheb's head snapped back. They both fell into the dust.

They've gone to the land of Nineteen, he thought. *Whatever is there.*

Sticks flew through the air, rained on him. He staggered, fended them off. One with a nail pounded raggedly through it ripped at his arm and drew blood. A man with a beard stubble and sweat-stained armpits lunged, flying at him with a dull kitchen knife held in one paw. The gunslinger shot him dead and the man thumped into the street. His false teeth shot out as his chin struck and grinned, spit-shiny, in the dirt.

"SATAN!" someone was screaming: "THE ACCURSED! BRING HIM DOWN!"

"THE INTERLOPER!" another voice cried. Sticks rained on him. A knife struck his boot and bounced. "THE INTERLOPER! THE ANTICHRIST!"

He blasted his way through the middle of them, running as the bodies fell, his hands picking the targets with ease and dreadful accuracy. Two men and a woman went down, and he ran through the hole they left.

He led them a feverish parade across the street and

toward the rickety general store/barber shop that faced Sheb's. He mounted the boardwalk, turned again, and fired the rest of his loads into the charging crowd. Behind them, Sheb and Allie and the others lay crucified in the dust.

They never hesitated or faltered, although every shot he fired found a vital spot and although they had probably never seen a gun.

He retreated, moving his body like a dancer to avoid the flying missiles. He reloaded as he went, with a rapidity that had also been trained into his fingers. They shuttled busily between gunbelts and cylinders. The mob came up over the boardwalk and he stepped into the general store and rammed the door closed. The large display window to the right shattered inward and three men crowded through. Their faces were zealously blank, their eyes filled with bland fire. He shot them all, and the two that followed them. They fell in the window, hung on the jutting shards of glass, choking the opening.

The door crashed and shuddered with their weight and he could hear *her* voice: "THE KILLER! YOUR SOULS! THE CLOVEN HOOF!"

The door ripped off its hinges and fell straight in, making a flat handclap. Dust puffed up from the floor. Men, women, and children charged him. Spittle and stovewood flew. He shot his guns empty and they fell like ninepins in a game of Points. He retreated into the barber shop, shoving over a flour barrel, rolling it at them, throwing a pan of boiling water that contained two nicked straight-razors. They came on, screaming with frantic incoherency. From somewhere, Sylvia Pittston exhorted them, her voice rising and falling in blind inflections. He pushed shells into hot chambers, smelling the aromas of shave and tonsure, smelling his own flesh as the calluses at the tips of his fingers singed.

He went through the back door and onto the porch. The flat scrubland was at his back now, flatly denying the town that crouched against its dirty haunch. Three men hustled around the corner, with large betrayer grins on their faces. They saw him, saw him seeing them, and the grins curdled in the second before he mowed them down. A woman had followed them, howling. She was large and fat and known to the patrons of Sheb's as Aunt Mill. The gunslinger blew her backwards and she landed in a whorish sprawl, her skirt rucked up between her thighs.

He went down the steps and walked backwards into the desert: ten paces, twenty. The back door of the barber shop flew open and they boiled out. He caught a glimpse of Sylvia Pittston. He opened up. They fell in squats, they fell backwards, they tumbled over the railing into the dust. They cast no shadows in the deathless purple light of the day. He realized he was screaming. He had been screaming all along. His eyes felt like cracked ball bearings. His balls had drawn up against his belly. His legs were wood. His ears were iron.

The guns were empty and they boiled at him, transmogrified into an Eye and a Hand, and he stood, screaming and reloading, his mind far away and absent, letting his hands do their reloading trick. Could he hold up a hand, tell them he had spent a thousand years learning this trick and others, tell them of the guns and the blood that had blessed them? Not with his mouth. But his hands could speak their own tale.

They were in throwing range as he finished reloading, and a stick struck him on the forehead and brought
blood in abraded drops. In two seconds they would be
in gripping distance. In the forefront he saw Kennerly;
Kennerly's younger daughter, perhaps eleven; Soobie;
two male barflies; a whore named Amy Feldon. He let
them all have it, and the ones behind them. Their bodies thumped like scarecrows. Blood and brains flew in
streamers.

They halted for a moment, startled, the mob face
shivering into individual, bewildered faces. A man ran
in a large, screaming circle. A woman with blisters on
her hands turned her head up and cackled feverishly at
the sky. The man whom he had first seen sitting gravely
on the steps of the mercantile store made a sudden and
amazing load in his pants.

He had time to reload one gun.

Then it was Sylvia Pittston, running at him, waving a
wooden cross in each hand. "DEVIL! DEVIL! DEVIL!
CHILDKILLER! MONSTER! DESTROY HIM, BROTH-
ERS AND SISTERS! DESTROY THE CHILDKILLING
INTERLOPER!"

He put a shot into each of the crosspieces, blowing
the roods to splinters, and four more into the woman's
head. She seemed to accordion into herself and waver
like a shimmer of heat.

They all stared at her for a moment in tableau, while
the gunslinger's fingers did their reloading trick. The
tips of his fingers sizzled and burned. Neat circles were
branded into the tips of each one.

There were fewer of them now; he had run through
them like a mower's scythe. He thought they would

break with the woman dead, but someone threw a knife. The hilt struck him squarely between the eyes and knocked him over. They ran at him in a reaching, vicious clot. He fired his guns empty again, lying in his own spent shells. His head hurt and he saw large brown circles in front of his eyes. He missed with one shot, downed eleven with the rest.

But they were on him, the ones that were left. He fired the four shells he had reloaded, and then they were beating him, stabbing him. He threw a pair of them off his left arm and rolled away. His hands began doing their infallible trick. He was stabbed in the shoulder. He was stabbed in the back. He was hit across the ribs. He was stabbed in the ass with what might have been a meat-fork. A small boy squirmed at him and made the only deep cut, across the bulge of his calf. The gunslinger blew his head off.

They were scattering and he let them have it again, back-shooting now. The ones left began to retreat toward the sand-colored, pitted buildings, and still the hands did their business, like overeager dogs that want to do their rolling-over trick for you not once or twice but all night, and the hands were cutting them down as they ran. The last one made it as far as the steps of the barber shop's back porch, and then the gunslinger's bullet took him in the back of the head. *"Yowp!"* the man cried, and fell over. It was Tull's final word on the business.

Silence came back in, filling jagged spaces.

The gunslinger was bleeding from perhaps twenty different wounds, all of them shallow except for the cut across his calf. He bound it with a strip of shirt and then straightened and examined his kill.

They trailed in a twisting, zigzagging path from the back door of the barber shop to where he stood. They lay in all positions. None of them seemed to be sleeping.

He followed the trail of death, counting as he went. In the general store, one man sprawled with his arms wrapped lovingly around the cracked candy jar he had dragged down with him.

He ended up where he had started, in the middle of the deserted main street. He had shot and killed thirty-nine men, fourteen women, and five children. He had shot and killed everyone in Tull.

A sickish-sweet odor came to him on the first of the dry, stirring wind. He followed it, then looked up and nodded. The decaying body of Nort was spread-eagled atop the plank roof of Sheb's, crucified with wooden pegs. Mouth and eyes were open. The mark of a large and purple cloven hoof had been pressed into the skin of his grimy forehead.

The gunslinger walked out of town. His mule was standing in a clump of weed about forty yards further along the remnant of the coach road. The gunslinger led it back to Kennerly's stable. Outside, the wind was playing a jagtime tune. He put the mule up for the time being and went back to the tonk. He found a ladder in the back shed, went up to the roof, and cut Nort loose. The body was lighter than a bag of sticks. He tumbled it down to join the common people, those who would only have to die once. Then he went back inside, ate hamburgers, and drank three beers while the light failed and the sand began to fly. That night he slept in the bed where he and Allie had lain. He had no dreams. The next morning the wind was gone and the sun was its usual bright and forgetful self. The bodies had gone south like tumbleweeds with the wind. At mid-morning, after he had bound all his cuts, he moved on as well.

XVIII

He thought Brown had fallen asleep. The fire was down to no more than a spark and the bird, Zoltan, had put his head under his wing.

Just as he was about to get up and spread a pallet in the corner, Brown said, "There. You've told it. Do you feel better?"

The gunslinger started. "Why would I feel bad?"

"You're human, you said. No demon. Or did you lie?"

"I didn't lie." He felt the grudging admittance in him: he liked Brown. Honestly did. And he hadn't lied to the dweller in any way. "Who are you, Brown? Really, I mean."

"Just me," he said, unperturbed. "Why do you have to think you're in the middle of such a mystery?"

The gunslinger lit a smoke without replying.

"I think you're very close to your man in black," Brown said. "Is he desperate?"

"I don't know."

"Are you?"

"Not yet," the gunslinger said. He looked at Brown with a shade of defiance. "I go where I have to go, do what I have to do."

"That's good then," Brown said and turned over and went to sleep.

XIX

The next morning, Brown fed him and sent him on his way. In the daylight he was an amazing figure with his scrawny, sunburnt chest, pencil-like collarbones, and loony shock of red hair. The bird perched on his shoulder.

"The mule?" the gunslinger asked.

"I'll eat it," Brown said.

"Okay."

Brown offered his hand and the gunslinger shook it. The dweller nodded to the southeast. "Walk easy. Long days and pleasant nights."

"May you have twice the number."

They nodded at each other and then the man Allie had called Roland walked away, his body festooned with guns and water. He looked back once. Brown was rooting furiously at his little cornbed. The crow was perched on the low roof of his dwelling like a gargoyle.

XX

The fire was down, and the stars had begun to pale off. The wind walked restlessly, told its tale to no one. The gunslinger twitched in his sleep and was still again. He dreamed a thirsty dream. In the darkness the shape of the mountains was invisible. Any thoughts of guilt, any feelings of regret, had faded. The desert had baked them out. He found himself thinking more and more about Cort, who had taught him to shoot. Cort had known black from white.

He stirred again and woke. He blinked at the dead fire with its own shape superimposed over the other, more geometrical one. He was a romantic, he knew it, and he guarded the knowledge jealously. It was a secret he had shared with only a few over the years. The girl named Susan, the girl from Mejis, had been one of them.

That, of course, made him think of Cort again. Cort was dead. They were all dead, except for him. The world had moved on.

The gunslinger shouldered his gunna and moved on with it.

THE WAY STATION

CHAPTER 2

The Way Station

I

A nursery rhyme had been playing itself through his mind all day, the maddening kind of thing that will not let go, that mockingly ignores all commands of the conscious mind to cease and desist. The rhyme was:

The rain in Spain falls on the plain.
There is joy and also pain
but the rain in Spain falls on the plain.

Time's a sheet, life's a stain,
All the things we know will change
and all those things remain the same,
but be ye mad or only sane,
the rain in Spain falls on the plain.

We walk in love but fly in chains
And the planes in Spain fall in the rain.

He didn't know what a plane was in the context of the rhyme's last couplet, but knew why the rhyme had occurred to him in the first place. There had been the recurring dream of his room in the castle and of his mother, who had sung it to him as he lay solemnly in the tiny bed by the window of many colors. She did not sing it at bedtimes because all small boys born to the High Speech must face the dark alone, but she sang to him at naptimes and he could remember the heavy gray rainlight that shivered into rainbows on the counterpane; he could feel the coolness of the room and the heavy warmth of blankets, love for his mother and her red lips, the haunting melody of the little nonsense lyric, and her voice.

Now it came back maddeningly, like a dog chasing its own tail in his mind as he walked. All his water was gone, and he knew he was very likely a dead man. He had never expected it to come to this, and he was sorry. Since noon he had been watching his feet rather than the way ahead. Out here even the devil-grass had grown stunted and yellow. The hardpan had disintegrated in places to mere rubble. The mountains were not noticeably clearer, although sixteen days had passed since he had left the hut of the last homesteader, a loony-sane young man on the edge of the desert. He had had a bird, the gunslinger remembered, but he couldn't remember the bird's name.

He watched his feet move up and down like the heddles of a loom, listened to the nonsense rhyme sing itself into a pitiful garble in his mind, and wondered when he would fall down for the first time. He didn't want to fall, even though there was no one to see him. It was a matter of pride. A gunslinger knows pride, that invisible bone that keeps the neck stiff. What hadn't come to him from his father had been kicked into him by Cort, a boy's gentleman if there ever was one. Cort, yar, with his red bulb of a nose and his scarred face.

He stopped and looked up suddenly. It made his head buzz and for a moment his whole body seemed to float. The mountains dreamed against the far horizon. But there was something else up ahead, something much closer. Perhaps only five miles away. He squinted at it, but his eyes were sandblasted and going glareblind. He shook his head and began to walk again. The rhyme circled and buzzed. About an hour later he fell down and skinned his hands. He looked at the tiny beads of blood on his flaked skin with disbelief. The blood looked no thinner; it looked like any blood, now dying in the air. It seemed almost as smug as the desert. He dashed the drops away, hating them blindly. Smug? Why not? The blood was not thirsty. The blood was being served. The blood was being made sacrifice unto. Blood sacrifice. All the blood needed to do was run . . . and run . . . and run.

He looked at the splotches that had landed on the hardpan and watched as they were sucked up with uncanny suddenness. How do you like that, blood? How does that suit you?

O Jesus, I'm far gone.

He got up, holding his hands to his chest, and the thing he'd seen earlier was almost in front of him, so close it made him cry out—a dust-choked crow-croak. It was a building. No, *two* buildings, surrounded by a fallen rail fence. The wood seemed old, fragile to the point of elvishness; it was wood being transmogrified into sand. One of the buildings had been a stable— the shape was clear and unmistakable. The other was a house, or an inn. A way station for the coach line. The tottering sand-house (the wind had crusted the wood with grit until it looked like a sand castle that the sun

had beat upon at low tide and hardened to a tempo-
rary abode) cast a thin line of shadow, and someone sat
in the shadow, leaning against the building. And the
building seemed to lean with the burden of his weight.

Him, then. At last. The man in black.

The gunslinger stood with his hands to his chest,
unaware of his declamatory posture, and gawped. But
instead of the tremendous winging excitement he had
expected (or perhaps fear, or awe), there was nothing
but the dim, atavistic guilt for the sudden, raging hate
of his own blood moments earlier and the endless ring-
a-rosy of the childhood song:

. . . *the rain in Spain* . . .

He moved forward, drawing one gun.

. . . *falls on the plain.*

He came the last quarter mile at a jolting, flat-footed
run, not trying to hide himself; there was nothing to
hide behind. His short shadow raced him. He was not
aware that his face had become a gray and dusty death-
mask of exhaustion; he was aware of nothing but the
figure in the shadow. It did not occur to him until later
that the figure might even have been dead.

He kicked through one of the leaning fence rails (it
broke in two without a sound, almost apologetically)
and lunged across the dazzled and silent stable yard,
bringing the gun up.

"You're covered! You're covered! Hands up, you
whoreson, you're—"

The figure moved restlessly and stood up. The gunslinger thought: *My God, he is worn away to nothing, what's
happened to him?* Because the man in black had shrunk
two full feet and his hair had gone white.

He paused, struck dumb, his head buzzing tunelessly. His heart was racing at a lunatic rate and he thought, *I'm dying right here—*

He sucked the white-hot air into his lungs and hung his head for a moment. When he raised it again, he saw it wasn't the man in black but a boy with sun-bleached hair, regarding him with eyes that did not even seem interested. The gunslinger stared at him blankly and then shook his head in negation. But the boy survived his refusal to believe; he was a strong delusion. One wearing blue jeans with a patch on one knee and a plain brown shirt of rough weave.

The gunslinger shook his head again and started for the stable with his head lowered, gun still in hand. He couldn't think yet. His head was filled with motes and there was a huge, thrumming ache building in it.

The inside of the stable was silent and dark and exploding with heat. The gunslinger stared around himself with huge, floating walleyes. He made a drunken about-face and saw the boy standing in the ruined doorway, staring at him. A blade of pain slipped smoothly into his head, cutting from temple to temple, dividing his brain like an orange. He reholstered his gun, swayed, put out his hands as if to ward off phantoms, and fell over on his face.

II

When he woke up he was on his back, and there was a pile of light, odorless hay beneath his head. The boy had not been able to move him, but he had made him reasonably comfortable. And he was cool. He looked down at himself and saw that his shirt was dark and wet. He licked at his face and tasted water. He blinked at it. His tongue seemed to swell in his mouth.

The boy was hunkered down beside him. When he saw the gunslinger's eyes were open, he reached behind him and gave the gunslinger a dented tin can filled with water. He grasped it with trembling hands and allowed himself to drink a little—just a little. When that was down and sitting in his belly, he drank a little more. Then he spilled the rest over his face and made shocked blowing noises. The boy's pretty lips curved in a solemn little smile.

"Would you want something to eat, sir?"

"Not yet," the gunslinger said. There was still a sick ache in his head from the sunstroke, and the water sat uneasily in his stomach, as if it did not know where to go. "Who are you?"

"My name is John Chambers. You can call me Jake. I have a friend—well, sort of a friend, she works for us— who calls me 'Bama sometimes, but you can call me Jake."

The gunslinger sat up, and the sick ache became hard and immediate. He leaned forward and lost a brief struggle with his stomach.

"There's more," Jake said. He took the can and walked toward the rear of the stable. He paused and smiled back at the gunslinger uncertainly. The gunslinger nodded at him and then put his head down and propped it with his hands. The boy was well-made, handsome, perhaps ten or eleven. There had been a shadow of fear on his face, but that was all right; the gunslinger would have trusted him far less if the boy hadn't shown fear.

A strange, thumping hum began at the rear of the stable. The gunslinger raised his head alertly, hands going to the butts of his guns. The sound lasted for perhaps fifteen seconds and then quit. The boy came back with the can—filled now.

The gunslinger drank sparingly again, and this time it was a little better. The ache in his head was fading.

"I didn't know what to do with you when you fell down," Jake said. "For a couple of seconds there, I thought you were going to shoot me."

"Maybe I was. I thought you were somebody else."

"The priest?"

The gunslinger looked up sharply.

The boy studied him, frowning. "He camped in the yard. I was in the house over there. Or maybe it was a depot. I didn't like him, so I didn't come out. He came in the night and went on the next day. I would have hidden from you, but I was sleeping when you came." He looked darkly over the gunslinger's head. "I don't like people. They fuck me up."

"What did he look like?"

The boy shrugged. "Like a priest. He was wearing black things."

"A hood and a cassock?"

"What's a cassock?"

"A robe. Like a dress."

The boy nodded. "That's about right."

The gunslinger leaned forward, and something in his face made the boy recoil a little. "How long ago? Tell me, for your father's sake."

"I . . . I . . ."

Patiently, the gunslinger said, "I'm not going to hurt you."

"I don't know. I can't remember time. Every day is the same."

For the first time the gunslinger wondered consciously how the boy had come to this place, with dry and man-killing leagues of desert all around it. But he would not make it his concern, not yet, at least. "Make your best guess. Long ago?"

"No. Not long. I haven't been here long."

The fire lit in him again. He snatched up the can and drank from it with hands that trembled the smallest bit. A fragment of the cradle song recurred, but this time, instead of his mother's face, he saw the scarred face of Alice, who had been his jilly in the now-defunct town of Tull. "A week? Two? Three?"

The boy looked at him distractedly. "Yes."

"Which?"

"A week. Or two." He looked aside, blushing a little. "Three poops ago, that's the only way I can measure things now. He didn't even drink. I thought he might be the ghost of a priest, like in this movie I saw once, only Zorro figured out he wasn't a priest at all, or a ghost, either. He was just a banker who wanted some land because there was gold on it. Mrs. Shaw took me to see that movie. It was in Times Square."

None of this made any sense to the gunslinger, so he did not comment on it.

"I was scared," the boy said. "I've been scared almost all the time." His face quivered like crystal on the edge of the ultimate, destructive high note. "He didn't even build a fire. He just sat there. I don't even know if he went to sleep."

Close! Closer than he had ever been, by the gods! In spite of his extreme dehydration, his hands felt faintly moist; greasy.

"There's some dried meat," the boy said.

"All right." The gunslinger nodded. "Good."

The boy got up to fetch it, his knees popping slightly. He made a fine straight figure. The desert had not yet sapped him. His arms were thin, but the skin, although tanned, had not dried and cracked. *He's got juice,* the gunslinger thought. *Mayhap some sand in his craw, as well, or he would have taken one of my guns and shot me right where I lay.*

Or perhaps the boy simply hadn't thought of it.

The gunslinger drank from the can again. *Sand in his craw or not, he didn't come from this place.*

Jake came back with a pile of dried jerky on what looked like a sun-scoured breadboard. The meat was tough, stringy, and salty enough to make the cankered lining of the gunslinger's mouth sing. He ate and drank until he felt logy, and then settled back. The boy ate only a little, picking at the dark strands with an odd delicacy.

The gunslinger regarded him, and the boy looked back at him candidly enough. "Where did you come from, Jake?" he asked finally.

"I don't know." The boy frowned. "I *did* know. I knew when I came here, but it's all fuzzy now, like a bad dream when you wake up. I have lots of bad dreams. Mrs. Shaw used to say it was because I watched too many horror movies on Channel Eleven."

"What's a channel?" A wild idea occurred to him. "Is it like a beam?"

"No—it's TV."

"What's teevee?"

"I—" The boy touched his forehead. "Pictures."

"Did somebody tote you here? This Mrs. Shaw?"

"No," the boy said. "I just *was* here."

"Who is Mrs. Shaw?"

"I don't know."

"Why did she call you 'Bama?"

"I don't remember."

"You're not making any sense," the gunslinger said flatly.

Quite suddenly the boy was on the verge of tears. "I can't help it. I was just here. If you asked me about TV and channels yesterday, I bet I still could have remembered! Tomorrow I probably won't even remember I'm Jake—not unless you tell me, and you won't be here, will you? You're going to go away and I'll starve because you ate up almost all my food. I didn't ask to be here. I don't like it. It's spooky."

"Don't feel so sorry for yourself. Make do."

"I didn't ask to be here," the boy repeated with bewildered defiance.

The gunslinger ate another piece of the meat, chewing the salt out of it before swallowing. The boy had become part of it, and the gunslinger was convinced he told the truth—he had not asked for it. It was too bad. He himself . . . *he* had asked for it. But he had not asked for the game to become this dirty. He had not asked to turn his guns on the townsfolk of Tull; had not asked to shoot Allie, with her sadly pretty face at the end marked by the secret she had finally asked to be let in on, using that word, that nineteen, like a key in a lock; had not asked to be faced with a choice between duty and flat-out murder. It was not fair to ring in innocent bystand-ers and make them speak lines they didn't understand on a strange stage. *Allie,* he thought, *Allie was at least part of this world, in her own self-illusory way. But this boy . . . this God-damned boy . . .*

"Tell me what you can remember," he told Jake.

"It's only a little. It doesn't seem to make any sense anymore."

"Tell me. Maybe I can pick up the sense."

The boy thought about how to begin. He thought about it very hard. "There was a place . . . the one before this one. A high place with lots of rooms and a patio where you could look at tall buildings and water. There was a statue that stood in the water."

"A statue in the water?"

"Yes. A lady with a crown and a torch and . . . I think . . . a book."

"Are you making this up?"

"I guess I must be," the boy said hopelessly. "There were things to ride in on the streets. Big ones and little ones. The big ones were blue and white. The little ones were yellow. A lot of yellow ones. I walked to school. There were cement paths beside the streets. Windows to look in and more statues wearing clothes. The stat-ues sold the clothes. I know it sounds crazy, but the stat-ues sold the clothes."

The gunslinger shook his head and looked for a lie on the boy's face. He saw none.

"I walked to school," the boy repeated doggedly. "And I had a"—his eyes tilted closed and his lips moved gropingly—"a brown . . . book . . . bag. I carried a lunch.

And I wore"—the groping again, agonized groping—"a tie."

"A cravat?"

"I don't know." The boy's fingers made a slow, unconscious clinching motion at his throat, one the gunslinger associated with hanging. "I don't know. It's just all gone." And he looked away.

"May I put you to sleep?" the gunslinger asked.

"I'm not sleepy."

"I can make you sleepy, and I can make you remember."

Doubtfully, Jake asked, "How could you do that?"

"With this."

The gunslinger removed one of the shells from his gunbelt and twirled it in his fingers. The movement was dexterous, as flowing as oil. The shell cartwheeled effortlessly from thumb and index to index and second, to second and ring, to ring and pinky. It popped out of sight and reappeared; seemed to float briefly, then reversed. The shell walked across the gunslinger's fingers. The fingers themselves marched as his feet had marched on his last miles to this place. The boy watched, his initial doubt first replaced with plain delight, then by raptness, then by dawning blankness as he opened. His eyes slipped shut. The shell danced back and forth. Jake's eyes opened again, caught the steady, limpid movement between the gunslinger's fingers a little while longer, and then they closed once more. The gunslinger continued the howken, but Jake's eyes did not open again. The boy breathed with slow and steady calmness. Did this have to be part of it? Yes. It did. There was a certain cold beauty to it, like the lacy frettings that fringe hard blue ice-packs. He once more seemed to hear his mother singing, not the nonsense about the rain in Spain this time, but sweeter nonsense, coming from a great distance as he rocked on the rim of sleep: *Baby-bunting, baby dear, baby bring your basket here.*

Not for the first time the gunslinger tasted the smooth, loden taste of soul-sickness. The shell in his fingers, manipulated with such unknown grace, was suddenly horrific, the spoor of a monster. He dropped it into his palm, made a fist, and squeezed it with painful force. Had it exploded, in that moment he would have rejoiced at the destruction of his talented hand, for its only true talent was murder. There had always been murder in the world, but telling himself so was no comfort. There was murder, there was rape, there were unspeakable practices, and all of them were for the good, the bloody good, the bloody myth, for the grail, for the Tower. Ah, the Tower stood somewhere in the middle of things (so they did say), rearing its black-gray bulk to the sky, and in his desert-scoured ears, the gunslinger heard the faint sweet sound of his mother's voice: *Chussit, chissit, chassit, bring enough to fill your basket.*

He brushed the song, and the sweetness of the song, aside. "Where are you?" he asked.

III

Jake Chambers—sometimes 'Bama—is going downstairs with his bookbag. There is Earth Science, there is Geography, there is a notepad, a pencil, a lunch his mother's cook, Mrs. Greta Shaw, has made for him in the chrome-and-Formica kitchen where a fan whirrs eternally, sucking up alien odors. In his lunch sack he has a peanut butter and jelly sandwich; a bologna, lettuce, and onion sandwich; and four Oreo cookies. His parents do not hate him, but they do seem to have overlooked him. They have abdicated and left him to Mrs. Greta Shaw, to nannies, to a tutor in the summer and The Piper School (which is Private and Nice, and most of all, White) the rest of the time. None of these people have ever pretended to be more than what they are—professional people, the best in their fields. None have folded him to a particularly warm bosom as usually happens in the historical romance novels his mother reads and which Jake has dipped into, looking for the "hot parts." Hysterical novels, his father sometimes calls them, and sometimes "bodice-rippers." You should talk, *his mother says with infinite scorn from behind some closed door where Jake listens. His father works for The Network, and Jake could pick him out of a line-up of skinny men with crewcuts. Probably.*

Jake does not know that he hates all the professional people but Mrs. Shaw. People have always bewildered him. His mother, who is scrawny in a sexy way, often goes to bed with sick friends. His father sometimes talks about people at The Network who are doing "too much Coca-Cola." This statement is always accompanied by a humorless grin and a quick little sniff of the thumbnail.

Now he is on the street, Jake Chambers is on the street, he has "hit the bricks." He is clean and well-mannered, comely, sensitive. He bowls once a week at Mid-Town Lanes. He has no friends, only acquaintances. He has never bothered to think about this, but it hurts him. He does not know or understand that a long association with professional people has caused him to take on many of their traits. Mrs. Greta Shaw (better than the rest of them, but gosh, is that ever a consolation prize) makes very professional sandwiches. She quarters them and cuts off the breadcrusts so that when he eats in the gym period four he looks like he ought to be at a cocktail party with a drink in his other hand instead of a sports novel or a Clay Blaisdell Western from the school library. His father makes a great deal of money because he is a master of "the kill"—that is, placing a stronger show on his Network against a weaker show on a rival Network. His father smokes four packs of cigarettes a day. His father does not cough, but he has a hard grin, and he's not averse to the occasional shot of the old Coca-Cola.

Down the street. His mother leaves cab fare, but he walks every day it doesn't rain, swinging his bookbag (and sometimes his bowling bag, although mostly he leaves it in his locker), a small boy who looks very American with his blond hair and blue eyes. Girls have already begun to notice him (with their mothers' approval), and he does not shy away with skittish little-boy arrogance. He talks to them with unknowing professionalism and puzzles them away. He likes geography and bowling in the afternoon. His father owns stock in a company that makes automatic pin-setting machinery, but Mid-Town Lanes does not use his father's brand. He does not think he has thought about this, but he has.

Walking down the street, he passes Bloomie's, where the models stand dressed in fur coats, in six-button Edwardian suits, some in nothing at all; some are "bare-naked." These models— these mannequins—are perfectly professional, and he hates all professionalism. He is too young to have learned to hate himself yet, but that seed is already there; given time, it will grow, and bear bitter fruit.

He comes to the corner and stands with his bookbag at his side. Traffic roars by—grunting blue-and-white busses, yellow taxis, Volkswagens, a large truck. He is just a boy, but not average, and he sees the man who kills him out of the corner of his eye. It is the man in black, and he doesn't see the face, only the swirling robe, the outstretched hands, and the hard, professional grin. He falls into the street with his arms outstretched, not letting go of the bookbag which contains Mrs. Greta Shaw's extremely professional lunch. There is a brief glance through a polarized windshield at the horrified face of a businessman wearing a dark-blue hat in the band of which is a small, jaunty feather. Somewhere a radio is blasting rock and roll. An old woman on the far curb screams—she is wearing a black hat with a net. Nothing jaunty about that black net; it is like a mourner's veil. Jake feels nothing but surprise and his usual sense of headlong bewilderment—is this how it ends? Before he's bowled better than two-seventy? He lands hard in the street and looks at an asphalt-sealed crack some two inches from his eyes. The bookbag is jolted from his hand. He is wondering if he has skinned his knees when the car belonging to the businessman wearing the blue hat with the jaunty feather passes over him. It is a big blue 1976 Cadillac with whitewall Firestone tires. The car is almost exactly the same color as the businessman's hat. It breaks Jake's back, mushes his guts to gravy, and sends blood from his mouth in a high-pressure jet. He turns his head and sees the Cadillac's flaming taillights and smoke spurting from beneath its locked rear wheels. The car has also run over his bookbag and left a wide black tread on it. He turns his head the other way and sees a large gray Ford screaming to a stop inches from his body. A black fellow who has been selling pretzels and sodas from a pushcart is coming toward him on the run. Blood runs from Jake's nose, ears, eyes, rectum. His genitals have been squashed. He wonders irritably how badly he has skinned his knees. He wonders if he'll be late for school. Now the driver of the Cadillac is running toward him, babbling. Somewhere a terrible, calm voice, the voice of doom, says: "I am a priest. Let me through. An Act of Contrition . . ."

He sees the black robe and knows sudden horror. It is him, the man in black. Jake turns his face away with the last of his strength. Somewhere a radio is playing a song by the rock group Kiss. He sees his own hand trailing on the pavement, small, white, shapely. He has never bitten his nails.

Looking at his hand, Jake dies.

IV

The gunslinger hunkered in frowning thought. He was tired and his body ached and the thoughts came with aggravating slowness. Across from him the amazing boy slept with his hands folded in his lap, still breathing calmly. He had told his tale without much emotion, although his voice had trembled near the end, when he had come to the part about the "priest" and the "Act of Contrition." He had not, of course, told the gunslinger about his family and his own sense of bewildered dichotomy, but that had seeped through anyway—enough for the gunslinger to make out its shape. The fact that there had never been such a city as the boy described (unless it was the mythic city of Lud) was not the most upsetting part of the story, but it was disturbing. It was all disturbing. The gunslinger was afraid of the implications.

"Jake?"

"Uh-huh?"

"Do you want to remember this when you wake up, or forget it?"

"Forget it," the boy said promptly. "When the blood came out of my mouth I could taste my own shit."

"All right. You're going to sleep, understand? Real sleep now. Go ahead and lie over, if it do please ya."

Jake laid over, looking small and peaceful and harmless. The gunslinger did not believe he was harmless. There was a deadly feeling about him, the stink of yet another trap. He didn't like the feeling, but he liked the boy. He liked him a great deal.

"Jake?"

"Shhh. I'm sleeping. I want to sleep."

"Yes. And when you wake up you won't remember any of this."

"Kay. Good."

The gunslinger watched him for a brief time, thinking of his own boyhood, which usually seemed to have happened to another person—to a person who had leaped through some fabulous lens of time to become someone else—but which now seemed poignantly close. It was very hot in the stable of the way station, and he carefully drank some more water. He got up and walked to the back of the building, pausing to look into one of the horse stalls. There was a small pile of white hay in the corner, and a neatly folded blanket, but there was no smell of horse. There was no smell of anything in the stable. The sun had bled away every smell and left nothing. The air was perfectly neutral.

At the back of the stable was a small, dark room with a stainless steel machine in the center. It was untouched by rust or rot. It looked like a butter churn. At the left, a chrome pipe jutted from it, terminating over a drain in the floor. The gunslinger had seen pumps like it in other dry places, but never one so big. He could not contemplate how deep they (some long-gone they) must have drilled before they struck water, secret and forever black under the desert.

Why hadn't they removed the pump when the way station had been abandoned?

Demons, perhaps.

He shuddered abruptly, an abrupt twisting of his back. Heatflesh poked out on his skin, then receded. He went to the control switch and pushed the ON button. The machine began to hum. After perhaps half a minute, a stream of cool, clear water belched from the pipe and went down the drain to be recirculated. Perhaps three gallons flowed out of the pipe before the pump shut itself down with a final click. It was a thing as alien to this place and time as true love, and yet as concrete as a Judgment, a silent reminder of the time when the world had not yet moved on. It probably ran on an atomic slug, as there was no electricity within a thousand miles of here and even dry batteries would have lost their charge long ago. It had been made by a company called North Central Positronics. The gunslinger didn't like it.

He went back and sat down beside the boy, who had put one hand under his cheek. Nice-looking boy. The gunslinger drank some more water and crossed his legs so he was sitting Indian fashion. The boy, like the squatter on the edge of the desert who kept the bird (Zoltan, the gunslinger remembered abruptly, the bird's name was Zoltan), had lost his sense of time, but the fact that the man in black was closer seemed beyond doubt. Not for the first time, the gunslinger wondered if the man in black was letting him catch up for some reason of his own. Perhaps the gunslinger was playing into his hands. He tried to imagine what the confrontation might be like, and could not.

He was very hot, but no longer felt sick. The nursery rhyme occurred to him again, but this time instead of his mother, he thought of Cort—Cort, an ageless engine of a man, his face stitched with the scars of bricks and bullets and blunt instruments. The scars of war and instruction in the arts of war. He wondered if Cort had ever had a love to match those monumental scars. He doubted it. He thought of Susan, and his mother, and of Marten, that incomplete enchanter.

The gunslinger was not a man to dwell on the past; only a shadowy conception of the future and of his own emotional make-up saved him from being a man without imagination, a dangerous dullard. His present run of thought therefore rather amazed him. Each name called up others—Cuthbert, Alain, the old man Jonas with his quavery voice; and again Susan, the lovely girl at the window. Such thoughts always came back to Susan, and the great rolling plain known as the Drop, and fishermen casting their nets in the bays on the edge of the Clean Sea.

The piano player in Tull (also dead, all dead in Tull, and by his hand) had known those places, although he and the gunslinger had only spoken of them that once. Sheb had been fond of the old songs, had once played them in a saloon called the Traveller's Rest, and the gunslinger hummed one tunelessly under his breath:

Love o love o careless love
See what careless love has done.

The gunslinger laughed, bemused. *I am the last of that green and warm-hued world.* And for all his nostalgia, he felt no self-pity. The world had moved on mercilessly, but his legs were still strong, and the man in black was closer. The gunslinger nodded out.

V

When he awoke, it was almost dark and the boy was gone.

The gunslinger got up, hearing his joints pop, and went to the stable door. There was a small flame dancing in darkness on the porch of the inn. He walked toward it, his shadow long and black and trailing in the reddish-ochre light of sunset.

Jake was sitting by a kerosene lamp. "The oil was in a drum," he said, "but I was scared to burn it in the house. Everything's so dry—"

"You did just right." The gunslinger sat down, seeing but not thinking about the dust of years that puffed up around his rump. He thought it something of a wonder that the porch didn't simply collapse beneath their combined weight. The flame from the lamp shadowed the boy's face with delicate tones. The gunslinger produced his poke and rolled a cigarette.

"We have to palaver," he said.

Jake nodded, smiling a little at the word.

"I guess you know I'm on the prod for that man you saw."

"Are you going to kill him?"

"I don't know. I have to make him tell me something. I may have to make him take me someplace."

"Where?"

"To find a tower," the gunslinger said. He held his cigarette over the chimney of the lamp and drew on it; the smoke drifted away on the rising night breeze. Jake watched it. His face showed neither fear nor curiosity, certainly not enthusiasm.

"So I'm going on tomorrow," the gunslinger said. "You'll have to come with me. How much of that meat is left?"

"Only a little."

"Corn?"

"A little more."

The gunslinger nodded. "Is there a cellar?"

"Yes." Jake looked at him. The pupils of his eyes had grown to a huge, fragile size. "You pull up on a ring in the floor, but I didn't go down. I was afraid the ladder would break and I wouldn't be able to get up again. And it smells bad. It's the only thing around here that smells at all."

"We'll get up early and see if there's anything down there worth taking. Then we'll go."

"All right." The boy paused and then said, "I'm glad I didn't kill you when you were sleeping. I had a pitchfork and I thought about doing it. But I didn't, and now I won't have to be afraid to go to sleep."

"What would you be afraid of?"

The boy looked at him ominously. "Spooks. Of *him* coming back."

"The man in black," the gunslinger said. Not a question.

"Yes. Is he a bad man?"

"I guess that depends on where you're standing," the

gunslinger said absently. He got up and pitched his cigarette out onto the hardpan. "I'm going to sleep."

The boy looked at him timidly. "Can I sleep in the stable with you?"

"Of course."

The gunslinger stood on the steps, looking up, and the boy joined him. Old Star was up there, and Old Mother. It seemed to the gunslinger that if he closed his eyes he would be able to hear the croaking of the first spring peepers, smell the green, almost-summer smell of the court lawns after their first cutting (and hear, perhaps, the indolent click of wooden balls as the ladies of the East Wing, attired only in their shifts as dusk glimmered toward dark, played at Points), could almost see Cuthbert and Jamie as they came through the break in the hedges, calling for him to ride out with them . . .

It was not like him to think so much of the past.

He turned back and picked up the lamp. "Let's go to sleep," he said.

They crossed to the stable together.

VI

The next morning he explored the cellar.

Jake was right; it smelled bad. It had a wet, swampy stench that made the gunslinger feel nauseous and a little lightheaded after the antiseptic odorlessness of the desert and the stable. The cellar smelled of cabbages and turnips and potatoes with long, sightless eyes gone to everlasting rot. The ladder, however, seemed quite sturdy, and he climbed down.

The floor was earthen, and his head almost touched the overhead beams. Down here spiders still lived, disturbingly big ones with mottled gray bodies. Many were muties, the true thread long-lost. Some had eyes on stalks, some had what might have been as many as sixteen legs.

The gunslinger peered around and waited for his nighteyes.

"You all right?" Jake called down nervously.

"Yes." He focused on the corner. "There are cans. Wait."

He went carefully to the corner, ducking his head. There was an old box with one side folded down. The cans were vegetables—green beans, yellow beans—and three cans of corned beef.

He scooped up an armload and went back to the ladder. He climbed halfway up and handed them to Jake, who knelt to receive them. He went back for more.

It was on the third trip that he heard the groaning in the foundations.

He turned, looked, and felt a kind of dreamy terror wash over him, a feeling both languid and repellent.

The foundation was composed of huge sandstone blocks that had probably been evenly cornered when the way station was new, but which were now at every zigzag, drunken angle. It made the wall look as if it were inscribed with strange, meandering hieroglyphics. And from the joining of two of these abstruse cracks, a thin spill of sand was running, as if something on the other side was digging itself through with slobbering, agonized intensity.

The groaning rose and fell, becoming louder, until the whole cellar was full of the sound, an abstract noise of ripping pain and dreadful effort.

"Come up!" Jake screamed. "Oh Jesus, mister, come up!"

"Go away," the gunslinger said calmly. "Wait outside. If I don't come up by the time you count to two . . . no, three hundred, get the hell out."

"Come up!" Jake screamed again.

The gunslinger didn't answer. He pulled leather with his right hand.

There was a hole as big as a coin in the wall now. He could hear, through the curtain of his own terror, Jake's pattering feet as the boy ran. Then the spill of sand stopped. The groaning ceased, but there was a sound of steady, labored breathing.

"Who are you?" the gunslinger asked.

No answer.

And in the High Speech, his voice filling with the old thunder of command, Roland demanded: "Who are you, Demon? Speak, if you would speak. My time is short; my patience shorter."

"Go slow," a dragging, clotted voice said from within the wall. And the gunslinger felt the dream-like terror deepen and grow almost solid. It was the voice of Alice, the woman he had stayed with in the town of Tull. But she was dead; he had seen her go down himself, a bullet hole between her eyes. Fathoms seemed to swim by his eyes, descending. "Go slow past the Drawers, gunslinger. Watch for the taheen. While you travel with the boy, the man in black travels with your soul in his pocket."

"What do you mean? Speak on!"

But the breathing was gone.

The gunslinger stood for a moment, frozen, and then one of the huge spiders dropped on his arm and scrambled frantically up to his shoulder. With an involuntary grunt he brushed it away and got his feet moving. He did not want to do the next thing, but custom was strict, inviolable. Take the dead from the dead, the old proverb said; only a corpse may speak true prophecy. He went to the hole and punched at it. The sandstone crumbled easily at the edges, and with a bare stiffening of muscles, he thrust his hand through the wall.

And touched something solid, with raised and fretted knobs. He drew it out. He held a jawbone, rotted at the far hinge. The teeth leaned this way and that.

"All right," he said softly. He thrust it rudely into his back pocket and went back up the ladder, carrying the last cans awkwardly. He left the trapdoor open. The sun would get in and kill the mutie spiders.

Jake was halfway across the stable yard, cowering on the cracked, rubbly hardpan. He screamed when he saw the gunslinger, backed away a step or two, and then ran to him, crying.

"I thought it got you, that it got you. I thought—"

"It didn't. Nothing got me." He held the boy to him, feeling his face, hot against his chest, and his hands, dry against his ribcage. He could feel the rapid beating of the boy's heart. It occurred to him later that this was when he began to love the boy—which was, of course, what the man in black must have planned all along. Was there ever a trap to match the trap of love?

"Was it a demon?" The voice was muffled.

"Yes. A speaking-demon. We don't have to go back there anymore. Come on. Let's shake a mile."

They went to the stable, and the gunslinger made a rough pack from the blanket he'd slept under—it was hot and prickly, but there was nothing else. That done, he filled the waterbags from the pump.

"You carry one of the waterbags," the gunslinger said. "Wear it around your shoulders—see?"

"Yes." The boy looked up at him worshipfully, the look quickly masked. He slung one of the bags over his shoulders.

"Is it too heavy?"

"No. It's fine."

"Tell me the truth, now. I can't carry you if you get a sunstroke."

"I won't have a sunstroke. I'll be okay."

The gunslinger nodded.

"We're going to the mountains, aren't we?"

"Yes."

They walked out into the steady smash of the sun. Jake, his head as high as the swing of the gunslinger's elbows, walked to his right and a little ahead, the rawhide-wrapped ends of the waterbag hanging nearly to his shins. The gunslinger had crisscrossed two more water-bags across his shoulders and carried the sling of food in his armpit, his left arm holding it against his body. In his right hand was his pack, his poke, and the rest of his gunna.

They passed through the far gate of the way station and found the blurred ruts of the stage track again. They had walked perhaps fifteen minutes when Jake turned around and waved at the two buildings. They seemed to huddle in the titanic space of the desert.

"Goodbye!" Jake cried. "Goodbye!" Then he turned back to the gunslinger, looking troubled. "I feel like something's watching us."

"Something or someone," the gunslinger agreed.

"Was someone hiding there? Hiding there all along?"

"I don't know. I don't think so."

"Should we go back? Go back and—"

"No. We're done with that place."

"Good," Jake said fervently.

They walked. The stage track breasted a frozen sand drumlin, and when the gunslinger looked around, the way station was gone. Once again there was the desert, and that only.

VII

They were three days out of the way station; the mountains were deceptively clear now. They could see the smooth, stepped rise of the desert into foothills, the first naked slopes, the bedrock bursting through the skin of the earth in sullen, eroded triumph. Further up, the land gentled off briefly again, and for the first time in months or years the gunslinger could see real, living green. Grass, dwarf spruces, perhaps even willows, all fed by snow runoff from further up. Beyond that the rock took over again, rising in cyclopean, tumbled splendor all the way to the blinding snowcaps. Off to the left, a huge slash showed the way to the smaller, eroded sandstone cliffs and mesas and buttes on the far side. This draw was obscured in the almost continual gray membrane of showers. At night, Jake would sit fascinated for the few minutes before he fell into sleep, watching the brilliant swordplay of the far-off lightning, white and purple, startling in the clarity of the night air.

The boy was fine on the trail. He was tough, but more than that, he seemed to fight exhaustion with a calm reservoir of will which the gunslinger appreciated and admired. He didn't talk much and he didn't ask questions, not even about the jawbone, which the gunslinger turned over and over in his hands during his evening smoke. He caught a sense that the boy felt highly flattered by the gunslinger's companionship—perhaps even exalted by it—and this disturbed him. The boy had been placed in his path—*While you travel with the boy, the man in black travels with your soul in his pocket*—and the fact that Jake was not slowing him down only opened the way to more sinister possibilities.

They passed the symmetrical campfire leavings of the man in black at regular intervals, and it seemed to the gunslinger that these leavings were much fresher now. On the third night, the gunslinger was sure that he could see the distant spark of another campfire, somewhere in the first rising swell of the foothills. This did not please him as much as he once might have believed. One of Cort's sayings occurred to him: *'Ware the man who fakes a limp.*

Near two o'clock on the fourth day out from the way station, Jake reeled and almost fell.

"Here, sit down," the gunslinger said.

"No, I'm okay."

"Sit down."

The boy sat obediently. The gunslinger squatted close by, so Jake would be in his shadow.

"Drink."

"I'm not supposed to until—"

"Drink."

The boy drank, three swallows. The gunslinger wet the tail of the blanket, which held a good deal less now, and applied the damp fabric to the boy's wrists and forehead, which were fever-dry.

"From now on we rest every afternoon at this time. Fifteen minutes. Do you want to sleep?"

"No." The boy looked at him with shame. The gunslinger looked back blandly. In an abstracted way he withdrew one of the bullets from his belt and began to twirl it howken between his fingers. The boy watched, fascinated.

"That's neat," he said.

The gunslinger nodded. "Yar!" He paused. "When I was your age, I lived in a walled city, did I tell you that?"

The boy shook his head sleepily.

"Sure. And there was an evil man—"

"The priest?"

"Well, sometimes I wonder about that, tell you true," the gunslinger said. "If they *were* two, I think now they must have been brothers. Maybe even twins. But did I ever see 'em together? No, I never did. This bad man . . . this Marten . . . he was a wizard. Like Merlin. Do they ken Merlin where you come from?"

"Merlin and Arthur and the knights of the Round Table," Jake said dreamily.

The gunslinger felt a nasty jolt go through him. "Yes," he said. "Arthur Eld, you say true, I say thank ya. I was very young . . ."

But the boy was asleep sitting up, his hands folded neatly in his lap.

"Jake."

"Yar!"

The sound of this word from the boy's mouth startled him badly, but the gunslinger wouldn't let his voice show it. "When I snap my fingers, you'll wake up. You'll be rested and fresh. Do you kennit?"

"Yes."

"Lie over, then."

The gunslinger got makings from his poke and rolled a cigarette. There was something missing. He searched for it in his diligent, careful way and located it. The missing thing was his previous maddening sense of hurry, the feeling that he might be left behind at any time, that the trail would die out and he would be left with only a last fading footprint. All that was gone now, and the gunslinger was slowly becoming sure that the man in black wanted to be caught. *'Ware the man who fakes a limp.*

What would follow?

The question was too vague to catch his interest. Cuthbert would have found interest in it, lively interest (and probably a joke), but Cuthbert was as gone as the Horn o' Deschain, and the gunslinger could only go forward in the way he knew.

He watched the boy as he smoked, and his mind turned back on Cuthbert, who had always laughed (to his death he had gone laughing), and Cort, who never laughed, and on Marten, who sometimes smiled—a thin, silent smile that had its own disquieting gleam . . . like an eye that slips open in the dark and discloses blood. And there had been the falcon, of course. The falcon was named David, after the legend of the boy with the sling. David, he was quite sure, knew nothing but the need for murder, rending, and terror. Like the gunslinger himself. David was no dilettante; he played the center of the court.

Except maybe at the end.

The gunslinger's stomach seemed to rise painfully against his heart, but his face didn't change. He watched the smoke of his cigarette rise into the hot desert air and disappear, and his mind went back.

VIII

The sky was white, perfectly white, the smell of rain strong in the air. The smell of hedges and growing green was sweet. It was deep spring, what some called New Earth.

David sat on Cuthbert's arm, a small engine of destruction with bright golden eyes that glared outward at nothing. The rawhide leash attached to his jesses was looped carelessly about Bert's arm.

Cort stood aside from the two boys, a silent figure in patched leather trousers and a green cotton shirt that had been cinched high with his old, wide infantry belt. The green of his shirt merged with the hedges and the rolling turf of the Back Courts, where the ladies had not yet begun to play at Points.

"Get ready," Roland whispered to Cuthbert.

"We're ready," Cuthbert said confidently. "Aren't we, Davey?"

They spoke the low speech, the language of both scullions and squires; the day when they would be allowed to use their own tongue in the presence of others was still far. "It's a beautiful day for it. Can you smell the rain? It's—"

Cort abruptly raised the trap in his hands and let the side fall open. The dove was out and up, trying for the sky in a quick, fluttering blast of its wings. Cuthbert pulled the leash, but he was slow; the hawk was already up and his takeoff was awkward. The hawk recovered with a brief twitch of its wings. It struck upward, trudging the air, gaining altitude over the dove, moving bullet-swift.

Cort walked over to where the boys stood, casually, and swung his huge and twisted fist at Cuthbert's ear. The boy fell over without a sound, although his lips writhed back from his gums. A trickle of blood flowed slowly from his ear and onto the rich green grass.

"You were slow, maggot," he said.

Cuthbert was struggling to his feet. "I cry your pardon, Cort. It's just that I—"

Cort swung again, and Cuthbert fell over again. The blood flowed more swiftly now.

"Speak the High Speech," he said softly. His voice was flat, with a slight, drunken rasp. "Speak your Act of Contrition in the speech of civilization for which better men than you will ever be have died, maggot."

Cuthbert was getting up again. Tears stood brightly in his eyes, but his lips were pressed together in a tight line of hate which did not quiver.

"I grieve," Cuthbert said in a voice of breathless control. "I have forgotten the face of my father, whose guns I hope someday to bear."

"That's right, brat," Cort said. "You'll consider what you did wrong, and sharpen your reflections with hunger. No supper. No breakfast."

"Look!" Roland cried. He pointed up.

The hawk had climbed above the soaring dove. It

glided for a moment, its stubby wings outstretched and without movement on the still, white spring air. Then it folded its wings and dropped like a stone. The two bodies came together, and for a moment Roland fancied he could see blood in the air. The hawk gave a brief scream of triumph. The dove fluttered, twisting, to the ground, and Roland ran toward the kill, leaving Cort and the chastened Cuthbert behind him.

The hawk had landed beside its prey and was complacently tearing into its plump white breast. A few feathers seesawed slowly downward.

"David!" the boy yelled, and tossed the hawk a piece of rabbit flesh from his poke. The hawk caught it on the fly, ingested it with an upward shaking of its back and throat, and Roland attempted to re-leash the bird.

The hawk whirled, almost absentmindedly, and ripped skin from Roland's arm in a long, dangling gash. Then it went back to its meal.

With a grunt, Roland looped the leash again, this time catching David's diving, slashing beak on the leather gauntlet he wore. He gave the hawk another piece of meat, then hooded it. Docilely, David climbed onto his wrist.

He stood up proudly, the hawk on his arm.

"What's this, can ya tell me?" Cort asked, pointing to the dripping slash on Roland's forearm. The boy stationed himself to receive the blow, locking his throat against any possible cry, but no blow fell.

"He struck me," Roland said.

"You pissed him off," Cort said. "The hawk does not fear you, boy, and the hawk never will. The hawk is God's gunslinger."

Roland merely looked at Cort. He was not an imagi-
native boy, and if Cort had intended to imply a moral, it
was lost on him; he went so far as to believe that it might
have been one of the few foolish statements he had ever
heard Cort make.

Cuthbert came up behind them and stuck his tongue
out at Cort, safely on his blind side. Roland did not
smile, but nodded to him.

"Go in now," Cort said, taking the hawk. He turned
and pointed at Cuthbert. "But remember your reflection, maggot. And your fast. Tonight and tomorrow
morning."

"Yes," Cuthbert said, stiltedly formal now. "Thank you
for this instructive day."

"You learn," Cort said, "but your tongue has a bad
habit of lolling from your stupid mouth when your
instructor's back is turned. Mayhap the day will come
when it and you will learn their respective places." He
struck Cuthbert again, this time solidly between the eyes
and hard enough so that Roland heard a dull thud—the
sound a mallet makes when a scullion taps a keg of beer.
Cuthbert fell backward onto the lawn, his eyes cloudy
and dazed at first. Then they cleared and he stared burn-
ingly up at Cort, his usual easy grin nowhere to be seen,
his hatred unveiled, a pinprick as bright as the dove's
blood in the center of each eye. He nodded and parted
his lips in a scarifying smile that Roland had never seen.

"Then there's hope for you," Cort said. "When you
think you can, you come for me, maggot."

"How did you know?" Cuthbert said between his
teeth.

Cort turned toward Roland so swiftly that Roland

almost fell back a step—and then both of them would have been on the grass, decorating the new green with their blood. "I saw it reflected in this maggot's eyes," he said. "Remember it, Cuthbert Allgood. Last lesson for today."

Cuthbert nodded again, the same frightening smile on his face. "I grieve," he said. "I have forgotten the face—"

"Cut that shit," Cort said, losing interest. He turned to Roland. "Go on, now. The both of you. If I have to look at your stupid maggot faces any longer I'll puke my guts and lose a good dinner."

"Come on," Roland said.

Cuthbert shook his head to clear it and got to his feet. Cort was already walking down the hill in his squat, bowlegged stride, looking powerful and somehow prehistoric. The shaved and grizzled spot at the top of his head glimmered.

"I'll kill the son of a bitch," Cuthbert said, still smiling. A large goose egg, purple and knotted, was rising mystically on his forehead.

"Not you or me," Roland said, suddenly bursting into a grin. "You can have supper in the west kitchen with me. Cook will give us some."

"He'll tell Cort."

"He's no friend of Cort's," Roland said, and then shrugged. "And what if he did?"

Cuthbert grinned back. "Sure. Right. I always wanted to know how the world looked when your head was on backwards and upside down."

They started back together over the green lawns, casting shadows in the fine white springlight.

IX

The cook in the west kitchen was named Hax. He stood huge in foodstained whites, a man with a crude-oil complexion whose ancestry was a quarter black, a quarter yellow, a quarter from the South Islands, now almost forgotten (the world had moved on), and a quarter gods-knew-what. He shuffled about three high-ceilinged steamy rooms like a tractor in low gear, wearing huge, Caliph-like slippers. He was one of those quite rare adults who communicate with small children fairly well and who love them all impartially—not in a sugary way but in a business-like fashion that may sometimes entail a hug, in the same way that closing a big business deal may call for a handshake. He even loved the boys who had begun the way of the gun, although they were different from other children—undemonstrative and always slightly dangerous, not in an adult way, but rather as if they were ordinary children with a slight touch of madness—and Bert was not the first of Cort's students whom he had fed on the sly. At this moment he stood in front of his huge, rambling electric stove—one of six working appliances left on the whole estate. It was his personal domain, and he stood there watching the two boys bolt the gravied meat scraps he had produced. Behind, before, and all around, cookboys, scullions, and various underlings rushed through the steaming, humid air, rattling pans, stirring stew, slaving over potatoes and vegetables in nether regions. In the dimly lit pantry alcove, a washerwoman with a doughy, miserable face and hair caught up in a rag splashed water around on the floor with a mop.

One of the scullery boys rushed up with a man from the Guards in tow. "This man, he wantchoo, Hax."

"All right." Hax nodded to the Guard, and he nodded back. "You boys," he said. "Go over to Maggie, she'll give you some pie. Then scat. Don't get me in trouble."

Later they would both remember he'd said that: *Don't get me in trouble.*

They nodded and went over to Maggie, who gave them huge wedges of pie on dinner plates—but gingerly, as if they were wild dogs that might bite her.

"Let's eat it understairs," Cuthbert said.

"All right."

They sat behind a huge, sweating stone colonnade, out of sight of the kitchen, and gobbled their pie with their fingers. It was only moments later that they saw shadows fall on the far curving wall of the wide staircase. Roland grabbed Cuthbert's arm. "Come on," he said. "Someone's coming." Cuthbert looked up, his face surprised and berry-stained.

But the shadows stopped, still out of sight. It was Hax and the man from the Guards. The boys sat where they were. If they moved now, they might be heard.

". . . the good man," the Guard was saying.

"Farson?"

"In two weeks," the Guard replied. "Maybe three. You have to come with us. There's a shipment from the freight depot . . ." A particularly loud crash of pots and pans and a volley of catcalls directed at the hapless potboy who had dropped them blotted out some of the rest; then the boys heard the Guard finish: ". . . poisoned meat."

"Risky."

"Ask not what the good man can do for you—" the Guard began.

"But what you can do for him." Hax sighed. "Soldier, ask not."

"You know what it could mean," the Guard said quietly.

"Yar. And I know my responsibilities to him; you don't need to lecture me. I love him just as you do. Would foller him into the sea if he asked; so I would."

"All right. The meat will be marked for short-term storage in your coldrooms. But you'll have to be quick. You must understand that."

"There are children in Taunton?" the cook asked. It was not really a question.

"Children everywhere," the Guard said gently. "It's the children we—and he—care about."

"Poisoned meat. Such a strange way to care for children." Hax uttered a heavy, whistling sigh. "Will they curdle and hold their bellies and cry for their mammas? I suppose they will."

"It will be like going to sleep," the Guard said, but his voice was too confidently reasonable.

"Of course," Hax said, and laughed.

"You said it yourself. 'Soldier, ask not.' Do you enjoy seeing children under the rule of the gun, when they could be under his hands, ready to start making a new world?"

Hax did not reply.

"I go on duty in twenty minutes," the Guard said, his voice once more calm. "Give me a joint of mutton and I'll pinch one of your girls and make her giggle. When I leave—"

"My mutton will give no cramps to your belly, Robeson."

"Will you . . ." But the shadows moved away and the voices were lost.

I could have killed them, Roland thought, frozen and fascinated. *I could have killed them both with my knife, slit their throats like hogs.* He looked at his hands, now stained with gravy and berries as well as dirt from the day's lessons.

"Roland."

He looked at Cuthbert. They looked at each other for a long moment in the fragrant semidarkness, and a taste of warm despair rose in Roland's throat. What he felt might have been a sort of death—something as brutal and final as the death of the dove in the white sky over the games field. *Hax?* he thought, bewildered. *Hax who put a poultice on my leg that time? Hax?* And then his mind snapped closed, cutting the subject off.

What he saw, even in Cuthbert's humorous, intelligent face, was nothing—nothing at all. Cuthbert's eyes were flat with Hax's doom. In Cuthbert's eyes, it had already happened. He had fed them and they had gone understairs to eat and then Hax had brought the Guard named Robeson to the wrong corner of the kitchen for their treasonous little *tete-a-tete.* Ka had worked as ka sometimes did, as suddenly as a big stone rolling down a hillside. That was all.

Cuthbert's eyes were gunslinger's eyes.

X

Roland's father was only just back from the uplands, and he looked out of place amid the drapes and the chiffon fripperies of the main receiving hall to which the boy had only lately been granted access, as a sign of his apprenticeship.

Steven Deschain was dressed in black jeans and a blue work shirt. His cloak, dusty and streaked, torn to the lining in one place, was slung carelessly over his shoulder with no regard for the way it and he clashed with the elegance of the room. He was desperately thin and the heavy handlebar mustache below his nose seemed to weight his head as he looked down at his son. The guns crisscrossed over the wings of his hips hung at the perfect angle for his hands, the worn sandalwood grips looking dull and sleepy in this languid indoor light.

"The head cook," his father said softly. "Imagine it! The tracks that were blown upland at the railhead. The dead stock in Hendrickson. And perhaps even . . . imagine! Imagine!"

He looked more closely at his son. "It preys on you."

"Like the hawk," Roland said. "It preys on you." He laughed—at the startling appropriateness of the image rather than at any lightness in the situation.

His father smiled.

"Yes," Roland said. "I guess it . . . it preys on me."

"Cuthbert was with you," his father said. "He will have told his father by now."

"Yes."

"He fed both of you when Cort—"

"Yes."

"And Cuthbert. Does it prey on him, do you think?"

"I don't know." Nor did he care. He was not concerned with how his feelings compared with those of others.

"It preys on you because you feel you've caused a man's death?"

Roland shrugged unwillingly, all at once not content with this probing of his motivations.

"Yet you told. Why?"

The boy's eyes widened. "How could I not? Treason was—"

His father waved a hand curtly. "If you did it for something as cheap as a schoolbook idea, you did it unworthily. I would rather see all of Taunton poisoned."

"I didn't!" The words jerked out of him violently. "I wanted to kill him—both of them! Liars! *Black* liars! Snakes! They—"

"Go ahead."

"They hurt me," he finished, defiant. "They changed something and it hurt. I wanted to kill them for it. I wanted to kill them right there."

His father nodded. "That's crude, Roland, but not unworthy. Not moral, either, but it is not your place to be moral. In fact . . ." He peered at his son. "Morals may always be beyond you. You are not quick, like Cuthbert or Vannay's boy. That's all right, though. It will make you formidable."

The boy felt both pleased and troubled by this. "He'll—"

"Oh, he'll hang."

The boy nodded. "I want to see it."

The elder Deschain threw his head back and roared laughter. "Not as formidable as I thought . . . or perhaps just stupid." He closed his mouth abruptly. An arm shot out and grabbed the boy's upper arm painfully. Roland grimaced but didn't flinch. His father peered at him steadily, and the boy looked back, although it was more difficult than hooding the hawk had been.

"All right," he said, "thee may." And turned abruptly to go.

"Father?"

"What?"

"Do you know who they were talking about? Do you know who the good man is?"

His father turned back and looked at him speculatively. "Yes. I think I do."

"If you caught him," Roland said in his thoughtful, near-plodding way, "no one else like Cook would have to be neck-popped."

His father smiled thinly. "Perhaps not for a while. But in the end, someone always has to have his or her neck popped, as you so quaintly put it. The people demand it. Sooner or later, if there isn't a turncoat, the people make one."

"Yes," Roland said, grasping the concept instantly—it was one he never forgot. "But if you got the good man—"

"No," his father said flatly.

"Why not? Why wouldn't that end it?"

For a moment his father seemed on the verge of saying why, but then shook his head. "We've talked enough for now, I think. Go out from me."

He wanted to tell his father not to forget his promise when the time came for Hax to step through the trap, but he was sensitive to his father's moods. He put his fist to his forehead, crossed one foot in front of the other, and bowed. Then he went out, closing the door quickly. He suspected that what his father wanted now was to fuck. He was aware that his mother and father did that, and he was reasonably well informed as to how it was done, but the mental picture that always condensed with the thought made him feel both uneasy and oddly guilty. Some years later, Susan would tell him the story of Oedipus, and he would absorb it in quiet thoughtfulness, thinking of the odd and bloody triangle formed by his father, his mother, and by Marten—known in some quarters as Farson, the good man. Or perhaps it was a quadrangle, if one wished to add himself.

XI

Gallows Hill was on the Taunton Road, which was nicely poetic; Cuthbert might have appreciated this, but Roland did not. He did appreciate the splendidly ominous scaffold which climbed into the brilliantly blue sky, an angular silhouette which overhung the coach road.

The two boys had been let out of Morning Exercises— Cort had read the notes from their fathers laboriously, lips moving, nodding here and there. When he finished with them, he had carefully put the papers away in his pocket. Even here in Gilead, paper was easily as valuable as gold. When these two sheets of it were safe, he'd looked up at the blue-violet dawn sky and nodded again.

"Wait here," he said, and went toward the leaning stone hut that served him as living quarters. He came back with a slice of rough, unleavened bread, broke it in two, and gave half to each.

"When it's over, each of you will put this beneath his shoes. Mind you do exactly as I say or I'll clout you into next week."

They had not understood until they arrived, riding
double on Cuthbert's gelding. They were the first, fully
two hours ahead of anyone else and four hours before
the hanging, so Gallows Hill stood deserted—except
for the rooks and ravens. The birds were everywhere.
They roosted noisily on the hard, jutting bar that overhung the trap—the armature of death. They sat in a
row along the edge of the platform, they jostled for
position on the stairs.

"They leave the bodies," Cuthbert muttered. "For the
birds."

"Let's go up," Roland said.

Cuthbert looked at him with something like horror.
"Up *there?* Do you think—"

Roland cut him off with a gesture of his hands. "We're
years early. No one will come."

"All right."

They walked slowly toward the gibbet, and the birds
took wing, cawing and circling like a mob of angry dis-
possessed peasants. Their bodies were flat black against
the pure dawnlight of the In-World sky.

For the first time Roland felt the enormity of his
responsibility in the matter; this wood was not noble,
not part of the awesome machine of Civilization, but
merely warped pine from the Forest o' Barony, covered
with splattered white bird droppings. It was splashed
everywhere—stairs, railing, platform—and it stank.

The boy turned to Cuthbert with startled, terrified
eyes and saw Cuthbert looking back at him with the
same expression.

"I can't," Cuthbert whispered. "Ro', I can't watch it."

Roland shook his head slowly. There was a lesson

here, he realized, not a shining thing but something that was old and rusty and misshapen. It was why their fathers had let them come. And with his usual stubborn and inarticulate doggedness, Roland laid mental hands on whatever it was.

"You can, Bert."

"I won't sleep tonight if I do."

"Then you won't," Roland said, not seeing what that had to do with it.

Cuthbert suddenly seized Roland's hand and looked at him with such mute agony that Roland's own doubt came back, and he wished sickly that they had never gone to the west kitchen that night. His father had been right. Better not to know. Better every man, woman, and child in Taunton dead and stinking than this.

But still. Still. Whatever the lesson was, rusty, whatever half-buried thing with sharp edges, he would not let it go or give up his grip on it.

"Let's not go up," Cuthbert said. "We've seen everything."

And Roland nodded reluctantly, feeling his grip on that thing—whatever it was—weaken. Cort, he knew, would have knocked them both sprawling and then forced them up to the platform step by cursing step . . . and sniffing fresh blood back up their noses and down their throats like salty jam as they went. Cort would probably have looped new hemp over the yardarm itself and put the noose around each of their necks in turn, would have made them stand on the trap to feel it; and Cort would have been ready to strike them again if either wept or lost control of his bladder. And Cort, of course, would have been right. For the first time in his life, Roland found himself hating his own childhood. He wished for the long boots of age.

He deliberately pried a splinter from the railing and placed it in his breast pocket before turning away.

"Why did you do that?" Cuthbert asked.

He wished to answer something swaggering: *Oh, the luck of the gallows . . .* , but he only looked at Cuthbert and shook his head. "Just so I'll have it," he said. "Always have it."

They walked away from the gallows, sat down, and waited. In an hour or so the first of the townfolk began to gather, mostly families who had come in broken-down wagons and beat-up buckas, carrying their breakfasts with them—hampers of cold pancakes folded over fillings of wild pokeberry jam. Roland felt his stomach growl hungrily and wondered again, with despair, where the honor and the nobility was. He had been taught of such things, and was now forced to wonder if they had been lies all along, or only treasures buried deep by the wise. He *wanted* to believe that, but it seemed to him that Hax in his dirty whites, walking around and around his steaming, subterranean kitchen and yelling at the potboys, had more honor than this. He fingered the splinter from the gallows tree with sick bewilderment. Cuthbert lay beside him with his face drawn impassive.

XII

In the end it wasn't such of a much, and Roland was glad. Hax was carried in an open cart, but only his huge girth gave him away; he had been blindfolded with a wide black cloth that hung down over his face. A few threw stones, but most merely continued with their breakfasts as they watched.

A gunslinger whom the boy did not know well (he was glad his father had not drawn the black stone) led the fat cook carefully up the steps. Two Guards of the Watch had gone ahead and stood on either side of the trap. When Hax and the gunslinger reached the top, the gunslinger threw the noosed rope over the cross-tree and then put it over the cook's head, dropping the knot until it lay just below the left ear. The birds had all flown, but Roland knew they were waiting.

"Do you wish to make confession?" the gunslinger asked.

"I have nothing to confess," Hax said. His words carried well, and his voice was oddly dignified in spite of the muffle of cloth which hung over his lips. The cloth ruffled slightly in the faint, pleasant breeze that had blown up. "I have not forgotten my father's face; it has been with me through all."

Roland glanced sharply at the crowd and was disturbed by what he saw there—a sense of sympathy? Perhaps admiration? He would ask his father. When traitors are called heroes (or heroes traitors, he supposed in his frowning way), dark times must have fallen. Dark times, indeed. He wished he understood better. His mind flashed to Cort and the bread Cort had given them. He felt contempt; the day was coming when Cort would serve him. Perhaps not Cuthbert; perhaps Bert would buckle under Cort's steady fire and remain a page or a horseboy (or infinitely worse, a perfumed diplomat, dallying in receiving chambers or looking into bogus crystal balls with doddering kings and princes), but he would not. He knew it. He was for the open lands and long rides. That this seemed a *good* fate was something he would marvel over later, in his solitude.

"Roland?"

"I'm here." He took Cuthbert's hand, and their fingers locked together like iron.

"Charge be capital murder and sedition," the gunslinger said. "You have crossed the white, and I, Charles son of Charles, consign you ever to the black."

The crowd murmured, some in protest.

"I never—"

"Tell your tale in the underworld, maggot," said Charles of Charles, and yanked the lever with both yellow-gauntleted hands.

The trap dropped. Hax plummeted through, still trying to talk. Roland never forgot that. The cook went *still trying to talk*. And where did he finish the last sentence he would ever begin on earth? His words were ended by the sound an exploding pineknot makes on the hearth in the cold heart of a winter night.

But on the whole he thought it not so much. The cook's legs kicked out once in a wide Y; the crowd made a satisfied whistling noise; the Guards of the Watch dropped their military pose and began to gather things up negligently. Charles son of Charles walked back down the steps slowly, mounted his horse, and rode off, cutting roughly through one gaggle of picnickers, quirting a few of the slowcoaches, making them scurry.

The crowd dispersed rapidly after that, and in forty minutes the two boys were left alone on the small hill they had chosen. The birds were returning to examine their new prize. One lit on Hax's shoulder and sat there chummily, darting its beak at the bright and shiny hoop Hax had always worn in his right ear.

"It doesn't look like him at all," Cuthbert said.

"Oh yes, it does," Roland said confidently as they walked toward the gallows, the bread in their hands. Bert looked abashed.

They paused beneath the crosstree, looking up at the dangling, twisting body. Cuthbert reached up and touched one hairy ankle, defiantly. The body started on a new, twisting arc.

Then, rapidly, they broke the bread and spread the rough chunks beneath the dangling feet. Roland looked back just once as they rode away. Now there were thousands of birds. The bread—he grasped this only dimly—was symbolic, then.

"It was good," Cuthbert said suddenly. "It . . . I . . . I liked it. I did."

Roland was not shocked by this, although he had not particularly cared for the scene. But he thought he could perhaps understand what Bert was saying. Perhaps he'd not finish as a diplomat after all, jokes and easy line of talk or not.

"I don't know about that," he said, "but it was something. It surely was."

The land did not fall to the good man for another five years, and by that time Roland was a gunslinger, his father was dead, he himself had become a matricide— and the world had moved on.

The long years and long rides had begun.

XIII

"Look," Jake said, pointing upward.

The gunslinger looked up and felt a twinge in his right hip. He winced. They had been in the foothills two days now, and although the waterskins were almost empty again, it didn't matter now. There would soon be all the water they could drink.

He followed the vector of Jake's finger upward, past the rise of the green plain to the naked and flashing cliffs and gorges above it . . . on up toward the snowcap itself.

Faint and far, nothing but a tiny dot (it might have been one of those motes that dance perpetually in front of the eyes, except for its constancy), the gunslinger beheld the man in black, moving up the slopes with deadly progress, a minuscule fly on a huge granite wall.

"Is that him?" Jake asked.

The gunslinger looked at the depersonalized mote doing its faraway acrobatics, feeling nothing but a premonition of sorrow.

"That's him, Jake."

"Do you think we'll catch him?"

"Not on this side. On the other. And not if we stand here talking about it."

"They're so high," Jake said. "What's on the other side?"

"I don't know," the gunslinger said. "I don't think anybody does. Maybe they did once. Come on, boy."

They began to move upward again, sending small runnels of pebbles and sand down toward the desert that washed away behind them in a flat bake-sheet that seemed to never end. Above them, far above, the man in black moved up and up and up. It was impossible to see if he looked back. He seemed to leap across impossible gulfs, to scale sheer faces. Once or twice he disappeared, but always they saw him again, until the violet curtain of dusk shut him from their view. When they made their camp for the evening, the boy spoke little, and the gunslinger wondered if the boy knew what he himself had already intuited. He thought of Cuthbert's face, hot, dismayed, excited. He thought of the bread. He thought of the birds. It ends this way, he thought. Again and again it ends this way. There are quests and roads that lead ever onward, and all of them end in the same place—upon the killing ground.

Except, perhaps, the road to the Tower. There ka might show its true face.

The boy, the sacrifice, his face innocent and very young in the light of their tiny fire, had fallen asleep over his beans. The gunslinger covered him with the horse blanket and then curled up to sleep himself.

THE ORACLE AND THE MOUNTAINS

CHAPTER 3

The Oracle and
the Mountains

I

The boy found the oracle and it almost destroyed him.

Some thin instinct brought the gunslinger up from sleep to the velvet darkness which had fallen on them at dusk. That had been when he and Jake reached the grassy, nearly level oasis above the first rise of tumbled foothills. Even on the hardscrabble below, where they had toiled and fought for every foot in the killer sun, they had been able to hear the sound of crickets rubbing their legs seductively together in the perpetual green of willow groves above them. The gunslinger remained calm in his mind, and the boy had kept up at least the pretense of a façade, and that had made the gunslinger proud. But Jake hadn't been able to hide the wildness in his eyes, which were white and starey, the eyes of a horse scenting water and held back from bolting only by the tenuous chain of its master's mind; like a horse at the point where only understanding, not the spur, could hold it steady. The gunslinger could gauge the need

in Jake by the madness the sounds of the crickets bred
in his own body. His arms seemed to seek out shale to
scrape on, and his knees seemed to beg to be ripped in
tiny, maddening, salty gashes.

The sun trampled them all the way; even when it
turned a swollen, feverish red with sunset, it shone per-
versely through the knife-cut in the hills off to their left,
blinding them and making every teardrop of sweat into
a prism of pain.

Then there was sawgrass: at first only yellow scrub,
clinging with gruesome vitality to the bleak soil where
the last of the runoff reached. Further up there was
witch-grass, first sparse, then green and rank . . . then the
sweet smell of real grass, mixed with timothy and shaded
by the first of the dwarfed firs. There the gunslinger saw
an arc of brown moving in the shadows. He drew, fired,
and felled the rabbit all before Jake could begin to cry
out his surprise. A moment later he had reholstered the
gun.

"Here," the gunslinger said. Up ahead the grass
deepened into a jungle of green willows that was shock-
ing after the parched sterility of the endless hardpan.
There would be a spring, perhaps several of them, and
it would be even cooler, but it was better out here in the
open. The boy had pushed every step he could push,
and there might be suckerbats in the deeper shadows of
the grove. The bats might break the boy's sleep, no matter how deep it was, and if they were vampires, neither
of them might awaken . . . at least, not in this world.

The boy said, "I'll get some wood."

The gunslinger smiled. "No, you won't. Sit yourself,
Jake." Whose phrase had that been? Some woman.

Susan? He couldn't remember. *Time's the thief of memory:* that one he knew. That one had been Vannay's.

The boy sat. When the gunslinger got back, Jake was asleep in the grass. A large praying mantis was performing ablutions on the springy stem of the kid's cowlick. The gunslinger snorted laughter—the first in gods knew how long—and set the fire and went after water.

The willow jungle was deeper than he had suspected, and confusing in the failing light. But he found a spring, richly guarded by frogs and peepers. He filled one of their waterskins . . . and paused. The sounds that filled the night awoke an uneasy sensuality in him, a feeling that not even Allie, the woman he had bedded with in Tull, had been able to bring out—too much of his time with Allie had been business. He chalked it up to the sudden blinding change from the desert. After all those miles of bleak hardpan, the softness of the dark seemed nearly decadent.

He returned to the camp and skinned the rabbit while water boiled over the fire. Mixed with the last of their canned veg, the rabbit made an excellent stew. He woke Jake and watched him as he ate, bleary but ravenous.

"We stay here tomorrow," the gunslinger said.

"But that man you're after . . . that priest . . ."

"He's no priest. And don't worry. He'll keep."

"How do you know that?"

The gunslinger could only shake his head. The intuition was strong in him . . . but it was not a good intuition.

After the meal, he rinsed the cans from which they had eaten (marveling again at his own water extravagance), and when he turned around, Jake was asleep again. The gunslinger felt the now-familiar rising and falling in his chest that he could only identify with Cuthbert. Cuthbert had been Roland's own age, but he had seemed so much younger.

His cigarette drooped toward the grass, and he tossed it into the fire. He looked at it, the clear yellow burn so different, so much cleaner, from the way the devil-grass burned. The air was wonderfully cool, and he lay down with his back to the fire.

Far away, through the gash that led the way into the mountains, he heard the thick mouth of the perpetual thunder. He slept. And dreamed.

II

Susan Delgado, his beloved, was dying before his eyes.

He watched, his arms held by two villagers on each side, his neck dog-caught in a huge, rusty iron collar. This wasn't the way it had happened—he hadn't even been there—but dreams had their own logic, didn't they?

She was dying. He could smell her burning hair, could hear their cries of Charyou tree. *And he could see the color of his own madness. Susan, lovely girl at the window, horseman's daughter. How she had flown across the Drop, her shadow that of horse and girl merged, a fabulous creature out of an old story, something wild and free! How they had flown together in the corn! Now they were flinging cornhusks at her and the husks caught fire even before they caught in her hair.* Charyou tree, charyou tree, *they cried, these enemies of light and love, and somewhere the witch was cackling. Rhea, the witch's name had been, and Susan was turning black in the flames, her skin cracking open, and—*

And what was she calling?

"The boy!" she was screaming. "Roland, the boy!"

He whirled, pulling his captors with him. The collar ripped at his neck and he heard the hitching, strangled sounds that were coming from his own throat. There was a sickish-sweet smell of barbecuing meat on the air.

The boy was looking down at him from a window high above the funeral pyre, the same window where Susan, who had taught him to be a man, had once sat and sung the old songs: "Hey Jude" and "Ease on Down the Road" and "Careless Love." He looked out from the window like the statue of an alabaster saint in a cathedral. His eyes were marble. A spike had been driven through Jake's forehead.

The gunslinger felt the strangling, ripping scream that signaled the beginning of his lunacy pull up from the bottom of his belly.

"Nnnnnnnnnn—"

III

Roland grunted a cry as he felt the fire singe him. He sat bolt upright in the dark, still feeling the dream of Mejis around him, strangling him like the collar he'd worn. In his twistings and turnings he had thrown one hand against the dying coals of the fire. He put the hand to his face, feeling the dream flee, leaving only the stark picture of Jake, plaster-white, a saint for demons.

"Nnnnnnnnnn—"

He glared around at the mystic darkness of the willow grove, both guns out and ready. His eyes were red loopholes in the last glow from the fire.

"Nnnnnnnnnn—"
Jake.

The gunslinger was up and on the run. A bitter circle of moon had risen and he could follow the boy's track in the dew. He ducked under the first of the willows, splashed through the spring, and legged up the far bank, skidding in the dampness (even now his body could relish it). Willow withes slapped at his face. The trees were thicker here, and the moon was blotted out. Tree-trunks rose in lurching shadows. The grass, now knee-high, caressed him, as if pleading with him to slow down, to enjoy the cool. To enjoy the life. Half-rotted dead branches reached for his shins, his *cojones.* He paused for a moment, lifting his head and scenting at the air. A ghost of a breeze helped him. The boy did not smell good, of course; neither of them did. The gunslinger's nostrils flared like those of an ape. The younger, lighter odor of the boy's sweat was faint, oily, unmistakable. He crashed over a deadfall of grass and bramble and downed branches, sprinted through a tunnel of overhanging willow and sumac. Moss struck his shoulders like flabby corpse-hands. Some clung in sighing gray tendrils.

He clawed through a last barricade of willows and came to a clearing that looked up at the stars and the highest peak of the range, gleaming skull-white at an impossible altitude.

There was a ring of black standing stones which looked like some sort of surreal animal-trap in the moonlight. In the center was a table of stone . . . an altar. Very old, rising out of the ground on a thick arm of basalt.

The boy stood before it, trembling back and forth. His hands shook at his sides as if infused with static electricity. The gunslinger called his name sharply, and Jake responded with that inarticulate sound of negation. The faint smear of face, almost hidden by the boy's left shoulder, looked both terrified and exalted. And there was something else.

The gunslinger stepped inside the ring and Jake screamed, recoiling and throwing up his arms. Now his face could be seen clearly. The gunslinger read fear and terror at war with some excruciating pleasure.

The gunslinger felt it touch him—the spirit of the oracle, the succubus. His loins were suddenly filled with light, a light that was soft yet hard. He felt his head twisting, his tongue thickening and becoming sensitive to even the spittle that coated it.

He didn't think about what he was doing when he pulled the half-rotted jawbone from the pocket where he had carried it since he found it in the lair of the speaking-demon at the way station. He didn't think, but it had never frightened him to operate on pure instinct. That had ever been the best and truest place for him. He held the jawbone's frozen, prehistoric grin up before his eyes, holding his other arm out stiffly, first and last fingers poked out in the ancient forked sign, the ward against the evil eye.

The current of sensuality was whipped away from him like a drape.

Jake screamed again.

The gunslinger walked to him and held the jawbone in front of Jake's warring eyes.

"See this, Jake—see it very well."

What came in response was a wet sound of agony. The boy tried to pull his gaze away, could not. For a moment it seemed that he might be pulled apart—mentally if not physically. Then, suddenly, both eyes rolled up to the whites. Jake collapsed. His body struck the earth limply, one hand almost touching the squat basalt arm that supported the altar. The gunslinger dropped to one knee and picked him up. He was amazingly light, as dehydrated as a November leaf from their long walk through the desert.

Around him Roland could feel the presence that dwelt in the circle of stones whirring with a jealous anger—its prize was being taken from it. Once the gunslinger passed out of the circle, the sense of frustrated jealousy faded quickly. He carried Jake back to their camp. By the time they got there, the boy's twitching unconsciousness had become deep sleep.

The gunslinger paused for a moment above the gray ruin of the fire. The moonlight on Jake's face reminded him again of a church saint, alabaster purity all unknown. He hugged the kid and put a dry kiss on his cheek, knowing that he loved him. Well, maybe that wasn't quite right. Maybe the truth was that he'd loved the kid from the first moment he'd seen him (as he had Susan Delgado), and was only now allowing himself to recognize the fact. For it *was* a fact.

And it seemed that he could almost feel the laughter from the man in black, someplace far above them.

IV

Jake, calling him: that was how the gunslinger awoke. He'd tied Jake firmly to one of the tough bushes that grew nearby, and the boy was hungry and upset. By the sun, it was almost nine-thirty.

"Why'd you tie me up?" Jake asked indignantly as the gunslinger loosened the thick knots in the blanket. "I wasn't going to run away!"

"You *did* run away," the gunslinger said, and the expression on Jake's face made him smile. "I had to go out and get you. You were sleepwalking."

"I was?" Jake looked at him suspiciously. "I never did anything like that be—"

The gunslinger suddenly produced the jawbone and held it in front of Jake's face. Jake flinched away from it, grimacing and raising his arm.

"See?"

Jake nodded, bewildered. "What happened?"

"We don't have time to palaver now. I have to go off for a while. I may be gone the whole day. So listen to me, boy. It's important. If sunset comes and I'm not back—"

Fear flashed on Jake's face. "You're leaving me!"

The gunslinger only looked at him.

"No," Jake said after a moment. "I guess if you were going to leave me, you already would have."

"That's using your head. Now listen, and hear me very well. I want you to stay here while I'm gone. Right here in camp. Don't stray, even if it seems like the best idea in the world. And if you feel strange—funny in any way—you pick up this bone and hold it in your hands."

Hate and disgust crossed Jake's face, mixed with bewilderment. "I couldn't. I . . . I just couldn't."

"You can. You may have to. Especially after midday. It's important. You may feel pukey or headachey when you first lay hold of it, but that'll pass. Do you understand?"

"Yes."

"And will you do what I say?"

"Yes, but why do you have to go away?" Jake burst out.

"I just do."

The gunslinger caught another fascinating glimpse of the steel that lay under the boy's surface, as enigmatic as the story he had told about coming from a city where the buildings were so tall they actually scraped the sky. It wasn't Cuthbert the boy reminded him of so much as his other close friend, Alain. Alain had been quiet, in no way prone to Bert's grandstanding quackery, and he'd been dependable and afraid of nothing.

"All right," Jake said.

The gunslinger laid the jawbone carefully on the ground next to the ruins of the fire, where it grinned up through the grass like some eroded fossil that has seen the light of day after a night of five thousand years. Jake wouldn't look at it. His face was pale and miserable. The gunslinger wondered if it would profit them for him to put the boy to sleep and question him, then decided there would be little gain. He knew well enough that the spirit of the stone circle was surely a demon, and very likely an oracle as well. A demon with no shape, only a kind of unformed sexual glare with the eye of prophecy. He wondered briefly if it might not be the soul of Sylvia Pittston, the giant woman whose religious huckstering had led to the final showdown in Tull . . .

but no. Not her. The stones in the circle were ancient. Sylvia Pittston was a jilly-come-lately compared to the thing that made its den here. It was old . . . and sly. But the gunslinger knew the forms of speaking quite well and did not think the boy would have to use the jaw-bone mojo. The voice and mind of the oracle would be more than occupied with him. The gunslinger needed to know things, in spite of the risk . . . and the risk was high. Yet for both Jake and himself, he needed desperately to know.

The gunslinger opened his tobacco poke and pawed through it, pushing the dry strands of leaf aside until he came to a minuscule object wrapped in a fragment of white paper. He rolled it between fingers that would all too soon be gone and looked absently up at the sky. Then he unwrapped it and held the contents—a tiny white pill with edges that had been much worn with traveling—in his hand.

Jake looked at it curiously. "What's that?"

The gunslinger uttered a short laugh. "The story Cort used to tell us was that the Old Gods pissed over the desert and made mescaline."

Jake only looked puzzled.

"This is a drug," the gunslinger said. "But not one that puts you to sleep. One that wakes you up all the way for a little while."

"Like LSD," the boy agreed instantly and then looked puzzled.

"What's that?"

"I don't know," Jake said. "It just popped out. I think it came from . . . you know, before."

The gunslinger nodded, but he was doubtful. He had

never heard of mescaline referred to as LSD, not even in Marten's old books.

"Will it hurt you?" Jake asked.

"It never has," the gunslinger said, conscious of the evasion.

"I don't like it."

"Never mind."

The gunslinger squatted in front of the waterskin, took a mouthful, and swallowed the pill. As always, he felt an immediate reaction in his mouth: it seemed overloaded with saliva. He sat down before the dead fire.

"When does something happen to you?" Jake asked.

"Not for a little while. Be quiet."

So Jake was quiet, watching with open suspicion as the gunslinger went calmly about the ritual of cleaning his guns.

He reholstered them and said, "Your shirt, Jake. Take it off and give it to me."

Jake pulled his faded shirt reluctantly over his head, revealing the skinny stack of his ribs, and gave it to Roland.

The gunslinger produced a needle that had been threaded into the side-seam of his jeans, and thread from an empty cartridge-loop in his gunbelt. He began to sew up a long rip in one of the sleeves of the boy's shirt. As he finished and handed the shirt back, he felt the mesc beginning to take hold—there was a tightening in his stomach and a feeling that all the muscles in his body were being cranked up a notch.

"I have to go," he said, getting up. "It's time."

The boy half rose, his face a shadow of concern, and then he settled back. "Be careful," he said. "Please."

"Remember the jawbone," the gunslinger said. He

put his hand on Jake's head as he went by and tousled the corn-colored hair. The gesture startled him into a short laugh. Jake watched after him with a troubled smile until he was gone into the willow jungle.

V

The gunslinger walked deliberately toward the circle of stones, pausing long enough to get a cool drink from the spring. He could see his own reflection in a tiny pool edged with moss and lilypads, and he looked at himself for a moment, as fascinated as Narcissus. The mind-reaction was beginning to settle in, slowing down his chain of thought by seeming to increase the connotations of every idea and every bit of sensory input. Things began to take on weight and thickness that had been heretofore invisible. He paused, getting to his feet again, and looked through the tangled snarl of willows. Sunlight slanted through in a golden, dusty bar, and he watched the interplay of motes and tiny flying things for a bit before going on.

The drug had often disturbed him: his ego was too strong (or perhaps just too simple) to enjoy being eclipsed and peeled back, made a target for more sensitive emotions—they tickled at him (and sometimes maddened him) like the touch of a cat's whiskers. But this time he felt fairly calm. That was good.

He stepped into the clearing and walked straight into the circle. He stood, letting his mind run free. Yes, it was coming harder now, faster. The grass screamed green at him; it seemed that if he bent over and rubbed his hands in it he would stand up with green paint all over his fingers and palms. He resisted a puckish urge to try the experiment.

But there was no voice from the oracle. No stirring, sexual or otherwise.

He went to the altar, stood beside it for a moment. Coherent thought was now almost impossible. His teeth felt strange in his head, tiny tombstones set in pink moist earth. The world held too much light. He climbed up on the altar and lay back. His mind was becoming a jungle full of strange thought-plants that he had never seen or suspected before, a willow-jungle that had grown up around a mescaline spring. The sky was water and he hung suspended over it. The thought gave him a vertigo that seemed faraway and unimportant.

A line of old poetry occurred to him, not a nursery voice now, no; his mother had feared the drugs and the necessity of them (as she had feared Cort and the need for this beater of boys); this verse came from the Mannifolk to the north of the desert, a clan of them still living among machines that usually didn't work . . . and which sometimes ate the men when they did. The lines played again and again, reminding him (in an unconnected way that was typical of the mescaline rush) of snow falling in a globe he had owned as a child, mystic and half fantastical:

Beyond the reach of human range
A drop of hell, a touch of strange . . .

The trees which overhung the altar contained faces. He watched them with abstracted fascination: Here was a dragon, green and twitching, here a wood-nymph with beckoning branch arms, here a living skull over-grown with slime. Faces. Faces.

The grasses of the clearing suddenly whipped and bent.

I come.

I come.

Vague stirrings in his flesh. How far I have come, he thought. From lying with Susan in sweet grass on the Drop to this.

She pressed over him, a body made of the wind, a breast of fragrant jasmine, rose, and honeysuckle.

"Make your prophecy," he said. "Tell me what I need to know." His mouth felt full of metal.

A sigh. A faint sound of weeping. The gunslinger's genitals felt drawn and hard. Over him and beyond the faces in the leaves, he could see the mountains—hard and brutal and full of teeth.

The body moved against him, struggled with him. He felt his hands curl into fists. She had sent him a vision of Susan. It was Susan above him, lovely Susan Delgado, waiting for him in an abandoned drover's hut on the Drop with her hair spilled down her back and over her shoulders. He tossed his head, but her face followed.

Jasmine, rose, honeysuckle, old hay . . . the smell of love. Love me.

"Speak prophecy," he said. "Speak truth."

Please, the oracle wept. *Don't be cold. It's always so cold here—*

Hands slipping over his flesh, manipulating, lighting him on fire. Pulling him. Drawing. A perfumed black crevice. Wet and warm—

No. Dry. Cold. Sterile.

Have a touch of mercy, gunslinger. Ah, please, I cry your favor! Mercy!

Would you have mercy on the boy?

What boy? I know no boy. It's not boys I need. O please.

Jasmine, rose, honeysuckle. Dry hay with its ghost of summer clover. Oil decanted from ancient urns. A riot for flesh.

"After," he said. "If what you tell me is useful."

Now. Please. Now.

He let his mind coil out at her, the antithesis of emotion. The body that hung over him froze and seemed to scream. There was a brief, vicious tug-of-war between his temples—his mind was the rope, gray and fibrous. For long moments there was no sound but the quiet hush of his breathing and the faint breeze which made the green faces in the trees shift, wink, and grimace. No bird sang.

Her hold loosened. Again there was the sound of sobbing. It would have to be quick, or she would leave him. To stay now meant attenuation; perhaps her own kind of death. Already he felt her chilling, drawing away to leave the circle of stones. Wind rippled the grass in tortured patterns.

"Prophecy," he said, and then an even bleaker noun. "Truth."

A weeping, tired sigh. He could almost have granted the mercy she begged, but—there was Jake. He would have found Jake dead or insane if he had been any later last night.

Sleep then.

"No."

Then half-sleep.

What she asked was dangerous, but also probably necessary. The gunslinger turned his eyes up to the faces in the leaves. A play was being enacted there for his amusement. Worlds rose and fell before him. Empires were built across shining sands where forever machines toiled in abstract electronic frenzies. Empires declined, fell, rose again. Wheels that had spun like silent liquid moved more slowly, began to squeak, began to scream, stopped. Sand choked the stainless steel gutters of concentric streets below dark skies full of stars like beds of cold jewels. And through it all, a dying wind of change blew, bringing with it the cinnamon smell of late October. The gunslinger watched as the world moved on.

And half-slept.

Three. This is the number of your fate.

Three?

Yes, three is mystic. Three stands at the heart of your quest. Another number comes later. Now the number is three.

Which three?

"We see in part, and thus is the mirror of prophecy darkened."

Tell me what you can.

The first is young, dark-haired. He stands on the brink of robbery and murder. A demon has infested him. The name of the demon is HEROIN.

Which demon is that? I know it not, even from my tutor's lessons.

"We see in part, and thus is the mirror of prophecy darkened." There are other worlds, gunslinger, and other demons. These waters are deep. Watch for the doorways. Watch for the roses and the unfound doorways.

The second?

She comes on wheels. I see no more.

The third?

Death . . . but not for you.

The man in black? Where is he?

Near. You will speak with him soon.

Of what will we speak?

The Tower.

The boy? Jake?

. . .

Tell me of the boy!

The boy is your gate to the man in black. The man in black is your gate to the three. The three are your way to the Dark Tower.

How? How can that be? Why must it be?

"We see in part, and thus is the mirror—"

God damn you.

No God damned me.

Don't patronize me, Thing.

. . .

What shall I call you, then? Star-slut? Whore of the Winds?

Some live on love that comes to the ancient places . . . even in these sad and evil times. Some, gunslinger, live on blood. Even, I understand, on the blood of young boys.

May he not be spared?

Yes.

How?

Cease, gunslinger. Strike your camp and turn back north-west. In the northwest there is still a need for men who live by the bullet.

I am sworn by my father's guns and by the treachery of Marten.

Marten is no more. The man in black has eaten his soul. This you know.

I am sworn.
Then you are damned.
Have your way with me, bitch.

VI

Eagerness.

The shadow swung over him, enfolded him. There was sudden ecstasy broken only by a galaxy of pain, as faint and bright as ancient stars gone red with collapse. Faces came to him unbidden at the climax of their coupling: Sylvia Pittston; Alice, the woman from Tull; Susan; a dozen others.

And finally, after an eternity, he pushed her away from him, once again in his right mind, bone-weary and disgusted.

No! It isn't enough! It—

"Let me be," the gunslinger said. He sat up and almost fell off the altar before regaining his feet. She touched him tentatively

(honeysuckle, jasmine, sweet attar)

and he pushed her violently, falling to his knees.

He made his drunken way to the perimeter of the circle. He staggered through, feeling a huge weight fall from his shoulders. He drew a shuddering, weeping breath. Had he learned enough to justify this feeling of defilement? He didn't know. In time he supposed he would. As he started away, he could feel her standing at the bars of her prison, watching him go from her. He wondered how long it might be before someone else crossed the desert and found her, hungry and alone.

For a moment he felt dwarfed by the possibilities of time.

VII

"You're sick!"

Jake stood up fast when the gunslinger shambled back through the last trees and came into camp. He'd been huddled by the ruins of the tiny fire, the jawbone across his knees, gnawing disconsolately on the bones of the rabbit. Now he ran toward the gunslinger with a look of distress that made Roland feel the full, ugly weight of a coming betrayal.

"No," he said. "Not sick. Just tired. Whipped." He gestured absently at the jawbone. "You can let go of that, Jake."

The boy threw it down quickly and violently, rubbing his hands across his shirt after doing it. His upper lip rose and fell in a snarl that was, the gunslinger believed, perfectly unconscious.

The gunslinger sat down—almost fell down—feeling the aching joints and the pummeled, thick mind that was the unlovely afterglow of mescaline. His crotch also pulsed with a dull ache. He rolled a cigarette with careful, unthinking slowness. Jake watched. The gunslinger had a sudden impulse to speak to the boy dan-dinh after telling him all he had learned, then thrust the idea away with horror. He wondered if a part of him—mind or soul— might not be disintegrating. To open one's mind and heart to the command of a child? The idea was insane.

"We sleep here tonight. Tomorrow we start climbing.

I'll go out a little later and see if I can't shoot something for supper. We need to make strength. I've got to sleep now. Okay?"

"Sure. Knock yourself out."

"I don't understand you."

"Do what you want."

"Ah." The gunslinger nodded and lay back. *Knock myself out,* he thought. *Knock. Myself out.*

When he woke up the shadows were long across the small grass clearing. "Build up the fire," he told Jake and tossed him his flint and steel. "Can you use that?"

"Yes, I think so."

The gunslinger walked toward the willow grove and then stopped at the sound of the boy's voice. Stopped dead.

"Spark-a-dark, where's my sire?" the boy murmured, and Roland heard the sharp *chik!chik!chik!* of the flint. It sounded like the cry of a small mechanical bird. "Will I lay me? Will I stay me? Bless this camp with fire."

Picked it up from me, the gunslinger thought, not in the least surprised to discover he was all over goosebumps and on the verge of shivering like a wet dog. *Picked it up from me, words I don't even remember saying, and will I betray such? Ah, Roland, will thee betray such true thread as this in a sad unthreaded world? Could anything justify it?*

'Tis just words.

Aye, but old ones. Good ones.

"Roland?" the boy called. "Are you all right?"

"Yar," he said gruffly, and the tang of smoke stung faintly in his nose. "Thee's made fire."

"Yes," the boy said simply, and Roland did not need to turn to know the boy was smiling.

The gunslinger got moving and bore left, this time skirting the willow grove. At a place where the ground opened out and upward in heavy open grass, he stepped back into the shadows and stood silently. Faintly, clearly, he could hear the crackle of the campfire Jake had rekindled. The sound made him smile.

He stood without moving for ten minutes, fifteen, twenty. Three rabbits came, and once they were at silflay the gunslinger pulled leather. He took them down, skinned them, gutted them, and brought them back to the camp. Jake had water already steaming over the low flames.

The gunslinger nodded to him. "That's a good piece of work."

Jake flushed with pleasure and silently handed back the flint and steel.

While the stew cooked, the gunslinger used the last of the light to go back into the willow grove. Near the first pool he began to hack at the tough vines that grew near the water's marshy verge. Later, as the fire burned down to coals and Jake slept, he would plait them into ropes that might be of some limited use later. But his intuition was that the climb would not be a particularly difficult one. He felt ka at work on the surface of things and no longer even considered it odd.

The vines bled green sap over his hands as he carried them back to where Jake waited.

They were up with the sun and packed in half an hour. The gunslinger hoped to shoot another rabbit in the meadow as they fed, but time was short and no rabbit showed itself. The bundle of their remaining food

was now so small and light that Jake carried it easily. He
had toughened up, this boy; you could see it.

The gunslinger carried their water, freshly drawn
from one of the springs. He looped his three vine
ropes around his belly. They gave the circle of stones
a wide berth (the gunslinger was afraid the boy might
feel a recurrence of fear, but when they passed above
it on a stony rise, Jake only offered it a passing glance
and then looked at a bird that hovered upwind). Soon
enough, the trees began to lose their height and lush-
ness. Trunks were twisted and roots seemed to struggle
with the earth in a tortured hunt for moisture.

"It's all so old," Jake said glumly when they paused
for a rest. "Isn't there anything young in this world?"

The gunslinger smiled and gave Jake an elbow. "You
are," he said.

Jake responded with a wan smile. "Will it be hard to
climb?"

The gunslinger looked at him, curious. "The mountains are high. Don't you think it will be a hard climb?"

Jake looked back at him, his eyes clouded, puzzled.

"No."

They went on.

VIII

The sun climbed to its zenith, seemed to hang there
more briefly than it ever had during the desert crossing, and then passed on, returning them their shadows.
Shelves of rock protruded from the rising land like the

arms of giant easy-chairs buried in the earth. The scrub grass turned yellow and sere. Finally they were faced with a deep, chimney-like crevasse in their path and they scaled a short, peeling rise of rock to get around and above it. The ancient granite had faulted on lines that were step-like, and as they had both intuited, the beginning of their climb, at least, was easy. They paused on the four-foot-wide scarp at the top and looked back over the land to the desert, which curled around the upland like a huge yellow paw. Further off it gleamed at them in a white shield that dazzled the eye, receding into dim waves of rising heat. The gunslinger felt faintly amazed at the realization that this desert had nearly murdered him. From where they stood, in a new coolness, the desert certainly appeared momentous, but not deadly.

They turned back to the business of the climb, scrambling over jackstraw falls of rock and crouch-walking up inclined planes of stone shot with glitters of quartz and mica. The rock was pleasantly warm to the touch, but the air was definitely cooler. In the late afternoon the gunslinger heard the faint sound of thunder. The rising line of the mountains obscured the sight of the rain on the other side, however.

When the shadows began to turn purple, they camped in the overhang of a jutting brow of rock. The gunslinger anchored their blanket above and below, fashioning a kind of shanty lean-to. They sat at the mouth of it, watching the sky spread a cloak over the world. Jake dangled his feet over the drop. The gunslinger rolled his evening smoke and eyed Jake half humorously. "Don't roll over in your sleep," he said, "or you may wake up in hell."

"I won't," Jake replied seriously. "My mother says—"
He broke it off.

"She says what?"

"That I sleep like a dead man," Jake finished. He looked at the gunslinger, who saw that the boy's mouth was trembling as he strove to keep back tears—*only a boy,* he thought, and pain smote him, the icepick that too much cold water can sometimes plant in the forehead. *Only a boy. Why?* Silly question. When a boy, wounded in body or spirit, called that question out to Cort, that ancient, scarred battle-engine whose job it was to teach the sons of gunslingers the beginning of what they had to know, Cort would answer: *Why is a crooked letter and can't be made straight . . . never mind why, just get up, pus head! Get up! The day's young!*

"Why am I here?" Jake asked. "Why did I forget everything from before?"

"Because the man in black has drawn you here," the gunslinger said. "And because of the Tower. The Tower stands at a kind of . . . power-nexus. In time."

"I don't understand that!"

"Nor do I," the gunslinger said. "But something has been happening. Just in my own time. 'The world has moved on,' we say . . . we've always said. But it's moving on faster now. Something has happened to time. It's softening."

They sat in silence. A breeze, faint but with an edge, picked at their legs. Somewhere it made a hollow *whooooo* in a rock fissure.

"Where do you come from?" Jake asked.

"From a place that no longer exists. Do you know the Bible?"

"Jesus and Moses. Sure."

The gunslinger smiled. "That's right. My land had a Biblical name—New Canaan, it was called. The land of milk and honey. In the Bible's Canaan, there were supposed to be grapes so big that men had to carry them on sledges. We didn't grow them that big, but it was sweet land."

"I know about Ulysses," Jake said hesitantly. "Was he in the Bible?"

"Maybe," the gunslinger said. "I was never a scholar of it, and can't say for sure."

"But the others . . . your friends—"

"No others," the gunslinger said. "I'm the last."

A tiny wasted moon began to rise, casting its slitted gaze down into the tumble of rocks where they sat.

"Was it pretty? Your country . . . your land?"

"It was beautiful," the gunslinger said. "There were fields and forests and rivers and mists in the morning. But that's only pretty. My mother used to say that the only real beauty is order and love and light."

Jake made a noncommittal noise.

The gunslinger smoked and thought of how it had been—the nights in the huge central hall, hundreds of richly clad figures moving through the slow, steady waltz steps or the faster, light ripples of the *pol-kam,* Aileen Ritter on his arm, the one his parents had chosen for him, he supposed, her eyes brighter than the most precious gems, the light of the crystal-enclosed spark-lights shining in the newly done hair of the courtesans and their half-cynical amours. The hall had been huge, an island of light whose age was beyond telling, as was the whole Central Place, which was made up of nearly a hundred

stone castles. It had been unknown years since he had
seen it, and leaving for the last time, Roland had ached
as he turned his face away from it and began his first
cast for the trail of the man in black. Even then the walls
had fallen, weeds grew in the courtyards, bats roosted
amongst the great beams of the central hall, and the gal-
leries echoed with the soft swoop and whisper of swallows. The fields where Cort had taught them archery
and gunnery and falconry were gone to hay and timothy and wild vines. In the huge kitchen where Hax had
once held his fuming and aromatic court, a grotesque
colony of Slow Mutants nested, peering at him from the
merciful darkness of pantries and shadowed pillars. The
warm steam that had been filled with the pungent odors
of roasting beef and pork had changed to the clammy
damp of moss. Giant white toadstools grew in corners
where not even the Slow Muties dared to encamp. The
huge oak subcellar bulkhead stood open, and the most
poignant smell of all had issued from that, an odor that
seemed to express with a flat finality all the hard facts of
dissolution and decay: the high sharp odor of wine gone
to vinegar. It had been no struggle to turn his face to the
south and leave it behind—but it had hurt his heart.

"Was there a war?" Jake asked.

"Even better," the gunslinger said and pitched the
last smoldering ember of his cigarette away. "There was
a revolution. We won every battle, and lost the war. No
one won the war, unless maybe it was the scavengers.
There must have been rich pickings for years after."

"I wish I'd lived there," Jake said wistfully.

"Do you say so?"

"I do."

"Time to turn in, Jake."

The boy, now only a dim shadow, turned on his side and curled up with the blanket tossed loosely over him. The gunslinger sat sentinel over him for perhaps an hour after, thinking his long, sober thoughts. Such meditation was a novel thing for him, sweet in a melancholy sort of way, but still utterly without practical value: there was no solution to the problem of Jake other than the one the Oracle had offered—and turning away was simply not possible. There might have been tragedy in the situation, but the gunslinger did not see that; he saw only the predestination that had always been there. And finally, his more natural character reasserted itself and he slept deeply, with no dreams.

IX

The climb became grimmer on the following day as they continued to angle toward the narrow V of the pass through the mountains. The gunslinger pushed slowly, still with no sense of hurry. The dead stone beneath their feet left no trace of the man in black, but the gunslinger knew he had been this way before them—and not only from the path of his climb as he and Jake had observed him, tiny and bug-like, from the foothills. His aroma was printed on every cold down-draft of air. It was an oily, sardonic odor, as bitter to the nose as the stench of the devil-grass.

Jake's hair had grown much longer, and it curled slightly at the base of his sunburned neck. He climbed tough, moving with sure-footedness and no apparent acrophobia as they crossed gaps or scaled their way up ledged facings. Twice already he'd gone up in places the gunslinger could not have managed, and anchored one of the ropes so the gunslinger could climb up hand over hand.

The following morning they climbed through a coldly damp snatch of cloud that blotted out the tumbled slopes below them. Patches of hard, granulated snow began to appear nestled in some of the deeper pockets of stone. It glittered like quartz and its texture was as dry as sand. That afternoon they found a single footprint in one of these snowpatches. Jake stared at it for a moment with awful fascination, then looked up frightfully, as if expecting to see the man in black materialize into his own footprint. The gunslinger tapped him on the shoulder then and pointed ahead. "Go. The day's getting old."

Later, they made camp in the last of the daylight on a wide, flat ledge to the east and north of the cut that slanted into the heart of the mountains. The air was frigid; they could see the puffs of their breath, and the humid sound of thunder in the red-and-purple afterglow of the day was surreal, slightly lunatic.

The gunslinger thought the boy might begin to question him, but there were no questions from Jake. The boy fell almost immediately into sleep. The gunslinger followed his example. He dreamed again of Jake as an alabaster saint with a nail through his forehead. He awoke with a gasp, tasting the cold thinness of altitude in his lungs. Jake was asleep beside him, but his sleep was not easy; he twisted and mumbled to himself, chasing his own phantoms. The gunslinger lay over uneasily, and slept again.

X

A week after Jake saw the footstep, they faced the man in black for a brief moment in time. In that moment, the gunslinger felt he could almost understand the implication of the Tower itself, for that moment seemed to stretch out forever.

They continued southeast, reaching a point perhaps halfway through the cyclopean mountain range, and just as the going seemed about to become really difficult for the first time (above them, seeming to lean out, the icy ledges and screaming buttes made the gunslinger feel an unpleasant reverse vertigo), they began to descend again along the side of the narrow pass. An angular zigzagging path led them toward a canyon floor where an ice-edged stream boiled with slatey, headlong power from higher country still.

On that afternoon the boy paused and looked back at the gunslinger, who had paused to wash his face in the stream.

"I smell him," Jake said.

"So do I."

Ahead of them the mountain threw up its final defense—a huge slab of insurmountable granite facing that climbed into cloudy infinity. At any moment the gunslinger expected a twist in the stream to bring them upon a high waterfall and the insurmountable smoothness of rock—dead end. But the air here had that odd magnifying quality that is common to high places, and it was another day before they reached that great granite face.

The gunslinger began to feel the tug of anticipation again, the feeling that it was all finally in his grasp. He'd been through this before—many times—and still he had to fight himself to keep from breaking into an eager trot.

"Wait!" The boy had stopped suddenly. They faced a sharp elbow-bend in the stream; it boiled and frothed around the eroded hang of a giant sandstone boulder. All that morning they had been in the shadow of the mountains as the canyon narrowed.

Jake was trembling violently and his face had gone pale.

"What's the matter?"

"Let's go back," Jake whispered. "Let's go back quick."

The gunslinger's face was wooden.

"Please?" The boy's face was drawn, and his jaw-line shook with suppressed agony. Through the heavy blanket of stone they still heard thunder, as steady as machines in the earth. The slice of sky they could see had itself assumed a turbulent, gothic gray above them as warm and cold currents met and warred.

"Please, *please!*" The boy raised a fist, as if to strike the gunslinger's chest.

"No."

The boy's face took on wonder. "You're going to kill me. He killed me the first time and you're going to kill me this time. *And I think you know it.*"

The gunslinger felt the lie on his lips, then spoke it: "You'll be all right." And a greater lie yet. "I'll take care."

Jake's face went gray, and he said no more. He put an unwilling hand out, and he and the gunslinger went around the elbow-bend that way, hand in hand. On the other side they came face-to-face with that final rising wall and the man in black.

He stood no more than twenty feet above them, just to the right of the waterfall that crashed and spilled from a huge ragged hole in the rock. Unseen wind rippled and tugged at his hooded robe. He held a staff in one hand. The other hand he held out to them in a mocking gesture of welcome. He seemed a prophet, and below that rushing sky, mounted on a ledge of rock, a prophet of doom, his voice the voice of Jeremiah.

"Gunslinger! How well you fulfill the prophecies of old! Good day and good day and good day!" He laughed and bowed, the sound echoing over the bellow of the falling water.

Without a thought the gunslinger had drawn his pistols. The boy cowered to his right and behind, a small shadow.

Roland fired three times before he could gain control of his traitor hands—the echoes bounced their bronze tones against the rock valley that rose around them, over the sound of the wind and water.

A spray of granite puffed over the head of the man in black; a second to the left of his hood; a third to the right. He had missed cleanly all three times.

The man in black laughed—a full, hearty laugh that seemed to challenge the receding echo of gunshots. "Would you kill all your answers so easily, gunslinger?"

"Come down," the gunslinger said. "Do that I beg ya, and we'll have answers all around."

Again that huge, derisive laugh. "It's not your bullets I fear, Roland. It's your idea of answers that scares me."

"Come down."

"We'll speak on the other side, I think," the man in black said. "On the other side we will hold much council and long palaver."

His eyes flicked to Jake and he added:

"Just the two of us."

Jake flinched away from him with a small, whining cry, and the man in black turned, his robe swirling in the gray air like a batwing. He disappeared into the cleft in the rock from which the water spewed at full force. The gunslinger exercised grim will and did not send a bullet after him—*would you kill all your answers so easily, gunslinger?*

There was only the sound of wind and water, a sound that had been in this place of desolation for a thousand years. Yet the man in black had stood there. Twelve years after his last glimpse, Roland had seen him close-up again, had spoken to him. And the man in black had laughed.

On the other side we will hold much council and long palaver.

The boy looked up at him, his body trembling. For a moment the gunslinger saw the face of Allie, the girl from Tull, superimposed over Jake's, the scar standing out on her forehead like a mute accusation, and felt brute loathing for them both (it wouldn't occur to him until much later that both the scar on Alice's forehead and the nail he saw spiked through Jake's forehead in his dreams were in the same place). Jake perhaps caught a whiff of his thought; a moan slipped from his throat. Then he twisted his lips and cut the sound off. He held the makings of a fine man, perhaps a gunslinger in his own right if given time.

Just the two of us.

The gunslinger felt a great and unholy thirst in some deep unknown pit of his body, one no draft of water or wine could touch. Worlds trembled, almost within reach of his fingers, and in some instinctual way he strove not to be corrupted, knowing in his colder mind that such strife was vain and always would be. In the end there was only ka.

It was noon. He looked up, letting the cloudy, unsettled daylight shine for the last time on the all-too-vulnerable sun of his own righteousness. *No one ever really pays for betrayal in silver,* he thought. *The price of any betrayal always comes due in flesh.*

"Come with me or stay," the gunslinger said.

The boy responded to this with a hard and humorless grin—his father's grin, had he but known it. "And I'll be fine if I stay," he said. "Fine all by myself, here in the mountains. Someone will come and save me. They'll have cake and sandwiches. Coffee in a Thermos, too. Do you say so?"

"Come with me or stay," the gunslinger repeated, and felt something happen in his mind. An uncoupling. That was the moment at which the small figure before him ceased to be Jake and became only the boy, an impersonality to be moved and used.

Something screamed in the windy stillness; he and the boy both heard.

The gunslinger began to climb, and after a moment Jake came after. Together they mounted the tumbled rock beside the steely-cold falls, and stood where the man in black had stood before them. And together they entered in where he had disappeared. The darkness swallowed them.

THE SLOW MUTANTS

CHAPTER 4

The Slow Mutants

I

The gunslinger spoke slowly to Jake in the rising and falling inflections of one who speaks in his sleep:

"There were three of us that night: Cuthbert, Alain, and me. We weren't supposed to be there, because none of us had passed from the time of children. We were still in our clouts, as the saying went. If we'd been caught, Cort would have striped us bloody. But we weren't. I don't think any of the ones that went before us were caught, either. Boys must put on their fathers' pants in private, strut them in front of the mirror, and then sneak them back on their hangers; it was like that. The father pretends he doesn't notice the new way the pants are hung up, or the traces of boot-polish mustaches still under their noses. Do you see?"

The boy said nothing. He'd said nothing since they had passed from the daylight. The gunslinger, on the other hand, had talked hectically, feverishly, to fill the silence. He had not looked back at the light as they passed into the land beneath the mountains, but the boy had. The gunslinger had read the failing of day in the soft mirror of Jake's cheek: now faint rose, now milk-glass, now pallid silver, now the last dusk-glow touch of evening, now nothing. The gunslinger had struck a false light and they had gone on.

Finally they camped. No echo from the man in black returned to them. Perhaps he had stopped to rest, too. Or perhaps he floated onward and without running lights, through nighted chambers.

"The Sowing Night Cotillion—the Commala, some of the older folk called it, after the word for rice—was held once a year in the Great Hall," the gunslinger went on. "The proper name was The Hall of Grandfathers, but to us it was only the Great Hall."

The sound of dripping water came to their ears.

"A courting rite, as any spring dance surely is." The gunslinger laughed deprecatingly; the insensate walls turned the sound into a loon-like wheeze. "In the old days, the books say, it was the welcoming of spring, what was sometimes called New Earth or Fresh Commala. But civilization, you know . . ."

He trailed off, unable to describe the change inherent in that featureless noun, the death of romance and the lingering of its sterile, carnal revenant, a world living on the forced respiration of glitter and ceremony; the geometric steps of make-believe courtship during the Sowing Night Cotil' that had replaced the truer, madder, scribble-scrabble of love which he could only intuit dimly; hollow grandeur in place of true passions which might once have built kingdoms and sustained them. He found the truth with Susan Delgado in Mejis, only to lose it again. *Once there was a king,* he might have told the boy; *the Eld whose blood, attenuated though it may be, still flows in my veins. But kings are done, lad. In the world of light, anyway.*

"They made something decadent out of it," the gun-slinger said at last. "A play. A game." In his voice was all the unconscious distaste of the ascetic and the eremite. His face, had there been stronger light to illumine it, would have shown harshness and sorrow, the purest kind of condemnation. His essential force had not been cut or diluted by the passage of years. The lack of imag-ination that still remained in that face was remarkable.

"But the Ball," the gunslinger said. "The Sowing Night Cotil' . . ."

The boy did not speak, did not ask.

"There were crystal chandeliers, heavy glass with elec-tric spark-lights. It was all light, it was an island of light.

"We sneaked into one of the old balconies, the ones that were supposed to be unsafe and roped off. But we were boys, and boys will be boys, so they will. To us everything was dangerous, but what of that? Had we not been made to live forever? We thought so, even when we spoke to each other of our glorious deaths.

"We were above everyone and could look down on everything. I don't remember that any of us said any-thing. We only drank it up with our eyes.

"There was a great stone table where the gunsling-ers and their women sat at meat, watching the dancers. A few of the gunslingers also danced, but only a few. And they were the young ones. The one who sprang the trap on Hax was one of the dancers, I seem to recall. The elders only sat, and it seemed to me they were half embarrassed in all that light, all that civilized light. They were revered ones, the feared ones, the guardians, but they seemed like hostlers in that crowd of cavaliers with their soft women . . .

"There were four circular tables loaded with food, and they turned all the time. The cooks' boys never stopped coming and going from seven until three o' the clock the next morning. The tables were *like* clocks, and we could smell roast pork, beef, lobster, chickens, baked apples. The odors changed as the tables turned. There were ices and candies. There were great flaming skewers of meat.

"Marten sat next to my mother and father—I knew them even from so high above—and once she and Marten danced, slowly and revolvingly, and the others cleared the floor for them and clapped when it was over. The gunslingers did not clap, but my father stood slowly and held his hands out to her. And she went to him, smiling, holding out her own.

"It was a moment of enormous gravity, even we felt it in our high hiding place. My father had by then taken control of his ka-tet, you must ken—the Tet of the Gun—and was on the verge of becoming Dinh of Gilead, if not all In-World. The rest knew it. Marten knew it better than any . . . except, perhaps, for Gabrielle Verriss that was."

The boy spoke at last, and with seeming reluctance. "She was your mother?"

"Aye. Gabrielle-of-the-Waters, daughter of Alan, wife of Steven, mother of Roland." The gunslinger spread his hands apart in a mocking little gesture that seemed to say *Here I am, and what of it?* Then he dropped them into his lap again.

"My father was the last lord of light."

The gunslinger looked down at his hands. The boy said nothing more.

"I remember how they danced," the gunslinger said. "My mother and Marten, the gunslingers' counselor. I remember how they danced, revolving slowly together and apart, in the old steps of courtship."

He looked at the boy, smiling. "But it meant nothing, you know. Because power had been passed in some way that none of them knew but all understood, and my mother was grown root and branch to the holder and wielder of that power. Was it not so? She went to him when the dance was over, didn't she? And clasped his hands. Did they applaud? Did the hall ring with it as those pretty boys and their soft ladies applauded and lauded him? Did it? Did it?"

Bitter water dripped distantly in the darkness. The boy said nothing.

"I remember how they danced," the gunslinger said softly. "I remember how they danced." He looked up at the unseeable stone roof and it seemed for a moment that he might scream at it, rail at it, challenge it blindly— those blind and tongueless tonnages of granite that now bore their tiny lives like microbes in its stone intestine.

"What hand could have held the knife that did my father to his death?"

"I'm tired," the boy said, and then again said no more.

The gunslinger lapsed into silence, and the boy laid over and put one hand between his cheek and the stone. The little flame in front of them guttered. The gunslinger rolled a smoke. It seemed he could see the crystal light still, in the eye of his memory; hear the shout of accolade, empty in a husked land that stood even then hopeless against a gray ocean of time. Remembering that island of light hurt him bitterly, and he wished

he had never held witness to it, or to his father's cuck-
oldry.

He passed smoke between his mouth and nostrils,
looking down at the boy. *How we make large circles in earth
for ourselves,* he thought. *Around we go, back to the start
and the start is there again: resumption, which was ever the
curse of daylight.*

How long before we see daylight again?

He slept.

After the sound of his breathing had become long
and steady and regular, the boy opened his eyes and
looked at the gunslinger with an expression of sickness
and love. The last light of the fire caught in one pupil
for a moment and was drowned there. He went to sleep.

II

The gunslinger had lost most of his time sense in the
desert, which was changeless; he lost the rest of it here
in the passage under the mountains, which was lightless.
Neither of them had any means of telling the clock, and
the concept of hours became meaningless, abnegate.
In a sense, they stood outside of time. A day might have
been a week, or a week a day. They walked, they slept,
they ate thin meals that did not satisfy their bellies.
Their only companion was a steady thundering rush
of the water, drilling its auger path through the stone.
They followed it and drank from its flat, mineral-salted
depth, hoping there was nothing in it that would make
them sick or kill them. At times the gunslinger thought
he saw fugitive drifting lights like corpse-lamps beneath

its surface, but supposed they were only projections of his brain, which had not forgotten the light. Still, he cautioned the boy not to put his feet in the water.

The range-finder in his head took them on steadily.

The path beside the river (for it *was* a path—smooth, sunken to a slight concavity) led always upward, toward the river's head. At regular intervals they came to curved stone pylons with sunken ringbolts; perhaps once oxen or stagehorses had been tethered there. At each was a steel flagon holding an electric torch, but these were all barren of life and light.

During the third period of rest-before-sleep, the boy wandered away a little. The gunslinger could hear small conversations of rattled pebbles as Jake moved cautiously.

"Careful," he said. "You can't see where you are."

"I'm crawling. It's . . . say!"

"What is it?" The gunslinger half crouched, touching the haft of one gun.

There was a slight pause. The gunslinger strained his eyes uselessly.

"I think it's a railroad," the boy said dubiously.

The gunslinger got up and walked toward the sound of Jake's voice, leading with one foot lightly to test for pitfalls.

"Here." A hand reached out and cat's-pawed the gunslinger's face. The boy was very good in the dark, better than Roland himself. His eyes seemed to dilate until there was no color left in them: the gunslinger saw this as he struck a meager light. There was no fuel in this rock womb, and what they had brought with them was going rapidly to ash. At times the urge to strike a light was well-nigh insatiable. They had discovered one could grow as hungry for light as for food.

The boy was standing beside a curved rock wall that was lined with parallel metal staves running off into the darkness. Each carried black nodes that might once have been conductors of electricity. And beside and below, set only inches off the stone floor, were tracks of bright metal. What might have run on those tracks at one time? The gunslinger could only imagine sleek electric bullets, firing their courses through this forever night with affrighted searchlight eyes going before. He had never heard of such things, but there were many remnants of the gone world, just as there were demons. The gunslinger had once come upon a hermit who'd gained a quasi-religious power over a miserable flock of kine-keepers by possession of an ancient gasoline pump. The hermit crouched beside it, one arm wrapped possessively around it, and preached wild, guttering sermons. He occasionally placed the still-bright steel nozzle, which was attached to a rotted rubber hose, between his legs. On the pump, in perfectly legible (although rust-clotted) letters, was a legend of unknown meaning: *AMOCO. Lead Free.* Amoco had become the totem of a thundergod, and they had worshipped Him with the slaughter of sheep and the sound of engines: *Rumm! Rummm! Rum-rum-rummmmm!*

Hulks, the gunslinger thought. Only meaningless hulks poking from sands that once were seas.

And now a railroad.

"We'll follow it," he said.

The boy said nothing.

The gunslinger extinguished the light and they slept.

When Roland awoke, the boy was up before him, sitting on one of the rails and watching him sightlessly in the dark.

They followed the rails like blindmen, Roland leading, Jake following. They slipped their feet along one rail always, also like blindmen. The steady rush of the river off to the right was their companion. They did not speak, and this went on for three periods of waking. The gunslinger felt no urge to think coherently, or to plan. His sleep was dreamless.

During the fourth period of waking and walking, they literally stumbled on a handcar.

The gunslinger ran into it chest-high, and the boy, walking on the other side, struck his forehead and went down with a cry.

The gunslinger made a light immediately. "Are you all right?" The words sounded sharp, angry, and he winced at them.

"Yes." The boy was holding his head gingerly. He shook it once to make sure he had told the truth. They turned to look at what they had run into.

It was a flat square plate of metal that sat mutely on the tracks. There was a seesaw handle in the center of the square. It descended into a connection of cogs. The gunslinger had no immediate sense of the thing's purpose, but the boy grasped it at once.

"It's a handcar."

"What?"

"Handcar," the boy said impatiently, "like in the old cartoons. Look."

He pulled himself up and went to the handle. He managed to push it down, but it took all his weight

STEPHEN KING   178

hung over the handle to turn the trick. The handcar moved a foot, with silent timelessness, on the rails.

"Good!" said a faint mechanical voice. It made them both jump. "Good, push ag . . ." The mechanical voice died out.

"It works a little hard," the boy said, as if apologizing for the thing.

The gunslinger pulled himself up beside Jake and shoved the handle down. The handcar moved forward obediently, then stopped. "Good, push again!" the mechanical voice encouraged.

He had felt a driveshaft turn beneath his feet. The operation pleased him, and so did the mechanical voice (although he intended to listen to *that* no longer than necessary). Other than the pump at the way station, this was the first machine he'd seen in years that still worked well. But the thing disquieted him, too. It would take them to their destination that much the quicker. He had no doubt whatever that the man in black had meant for them to find this, too.

"Neat, huh?" the boy said, and his voice was full of loathing. The silence was deep. Roland could hear his organs at work inside his body, and the drip of water, and nothing else.

"You stand on one side, I stand on the other," Jake said. "You'll have to push by yourself until it gets rolling good. Then I can help. First you push, then I push. We'll go right along. Get it?"

"I get it," the gunslinger said. His hands were in helpless, despairing fists.

"But you'll have to push by yourself until it gets rolling good," the boy repeated, looking at him.

The gunslinger had a sudden vivid picture of the Great Hall a year or so after the Sowing Night Cotillion. By then it had been nothing but shattered shards in the wake of revolt, civil strife, and invasion. This image was followed by one of Allie, the scarred woman from Tull, pushed and pulled by bullets that were killing her for no reason at all . . . unless reflex was a reason. Next came Cuthbert Allgood's face, laughing as he went downhill to his death, still blowing that gods-damned horn . . . and then he saw Susan's face, twisted, made ugly with weeping. *All my old friends*, the gunslinger thought, and smiled hideously.

"I'll push," the gunslinger said.

He began to push, and when the voice began to speak ("Good, push again! Good, push again!") he sent his hand fumbling along the post upon which the see-saw handle had been balanced. At last he found what he was surely looking for: a button. He pushed it.

"Goodbye, pal!" the mechanical voice said cheerily, and was then blessedly silent for some hours.

III

They rolled on through the dark, faster now, no longer having to feel their way. The mechanical voice spoke up once, suggesting they eat Crisp-A-La, and again to say that nothing satisfied at the end of a hard day like Larchies. Following this second piece of advice, it spoke no more.

Once the awkwardness of a buried age had been run off the handcar, it went smoothly. The boy tried to do his share, and the gunslinger allowed him small shifts, but mostly he pumped by himself, in large and chest-stretching risings and fallings. The underground river was their companion, sometimes closer on their right, sometimes further away. Once it took on huge and thunderous hollowness, as if passing through some great cathedral narthex. Once the sound of it disappeared almost altogether.

The speed and the made wind against their faces seemed to take the place of sight and to drop them once again into a frame of time. The gunslinger estimated they were making anywhere from ten to fifteen miles an hour, always on a shallow, almost imperceptible uphill grade that wore him out deceptively. When they stopped he slept like the stone itself. Their food was almost gone again. Neither of them worried about it.

For the gunslinger, the tenseness of a coming climax was as imperceivable but as real (and accretive) as the fatigue of propelling the handcar. They were close to the end of the beginning . . . or at least *he* was. He felt like a performer placed on center stage minutes before the rise of the curtain; settled in position with his first line held securely in his mind, he heard the unseen audience rattling programs and settling in their seats. He lived with a tight, tidy ball of unholy anticipation in his belly and welcomed the exercise that let him sleep. And when he *did* sleep, it was like the dead.

The boy spoke less and less, but at their stopping place one sleep-period not long before they were attacked by the Slow Mutants, he asked the gunslinger almost shyly about his coming of age.

"For I would hear more of that," he said.

The gunslinger had been leaning with his back against the handle, a cigarette from his dwindling supply of tobacco clamped in his lips. He'd been on the verge of his usual unthinking sleep when the boy asked his question.

"Why would thee sill to know that?" he asked, amused.

The boy's voice was curiously stubborn, as if hiding embarrassment. "I just would." And after a pause, he added: "I always wondered about growing up. I bet it's mostly lies."

"What you'd hear of wasn't my growing-up," the gunslinger said. "I suppose I did the first of that not long *after* what thee'd hear of—"

"When you fought your teacher," Jake said remotely. "That's what I want to hear."

Roland nodded. Yes, of course, the day he had tried the line; that was a story any boy might want to hear, all right. "My real growing-up didn't start until after my Da' sent me away. I finished doing it at one place and another along the way." He paused. "I saw a not-man hung once."

"A not-man? I don't understand."

"You could feel him but couldn't see him."

Jake nodded, seeming to understand. "He was invisible."

Roland raised his eyebrows. He had never heard the word before. "Do you say so?"

"Yes."

"Then let it be so. In any case, there were folk who didn't want me to do it—felt they'd be cursed if I did it, but the fellow had gotten a taste for rape. Do you know what that is?"

"Yes," Jake said. "And I bet an invisible guy would be good at it, too. How did you catch him?"

"That's a tale for another day." Knowing there would be no other days. Both of them knowing there would be no others. "Two years after that, I left a girl in a place called King's Town, although I didn't want to—"

"Sure you did," the boy said, and the contempt in his voice was no less for the softness of his tone. "Got to catch up with that Tower, am I right? Got to keep a-ridin', just like the cowboys on my Dad's Network."

Roland felt his face flush with heat in the dark, but when he spoke his voice was even. "That was the last part, I guess. Of my growing-up, I mean. I never knew any of the parts when they happened. Only later did I know that."

He realized with some unease that he was avoiding what the boy wanted to hear.

"I suppose the coming of age *was* part of it, at that," he said, almost grudgingly. "It was formal. Almost stylized; like a dance." He laughed unpleasantly.

The boy said nothing.

"It was necessary to prove one's self in battle," the gunslinger began.

IV

Summer, and hot.

Full Earth had come to the land like a vampire lover that year, killing the land and the crops of the tenant farmers, turning the fields of the castle-city of Gilead white and sterile. In the west, some miles distant and near the

borders that were the end of the civilized world, fighting
had alrcady begun. All reports were bad, and all of them
paled to insignificance before the heat that rested over
this place of the center. Cattle lolled empty-eyed in the
pens of the stockyards. Pigs grunted lustlessly, unmindful of sows and sex and knives whetted for the coming
fall. People whined about taxes and conscription, as they
always did; but there was an apathy beneath the empty
passion-play of politics. The center had frayed like a rag
rug that had been washed and walked on and shaken
and hung and dried. The thread that held the last jewel
at the breast of the world was unraveling. Things were
not holding together. The earth drew in its breath in the
summer of the coming eclipse.

The boy idled along the upper corridor of this stone
place which was home, sensing these things, not understanding. He was also dangerous and empty, waiting to
be filled.

It was three years since the hanging of the cook who
had always been able to find snacks for hungry boys;
Roland had lengthened and filled out both at shoulder
and hip. Now, dressed only in faded denim pants, fourteen years old, he had come to look like the man he
would become: lean and lank and quick on his feet. He
was still unbedded, but two of the younger slatterns of a
West-Town merchant had cast eyes on him. He had felt
a rcsponse and felt it more strongly now. Even in the
coolness of the passage, he felt sweat on his body.

Ahead were his mother's apartments and he
approached them incuriously, meaning only to pass
them and go upward to the roof, where a thin breeze
and the pleasure of his hand awaited.

He had passed the door when a voice called him: "You. Boy."

It was Marten, the counselor. He was dressed with a suspicious, upsetting casualness—black whipcord trousers almost as tight as leotards, and a white shirt open halfway down his hairless chest. His hair was tousled.

The boy looked at him silently.

"Come in, come in! Don't stand in the hall! Your mother wants to speak to you." He was smiling with his mouth, but the lines of his face held a deeper, more sardonic humor. Beneath that—and in his eyes—there was only coldness.

In truth, his mother did not seem to want to see him. She sat in the low-backed chair by the large window in the central parlor of her apartments, the one which overlooked the hot blank stone of the central courtyard. She was dressed in a loose, informal gown that kept slipping from one white shoulder and looked at the boy only once—a quick, glinting rueful smile, like autumn sun on a rill of water. During the interview which followed, she studied her hands rather than her son.

He saw her seldom now, and the phantom of cradle songs

(chussit, chissit, chassit)

had almost faded from his brain. But she was a beloved stranger. He felt an amorphous fear, and an inchoate hatred for Marten, his father's closest advisor, was born.

"Are you well, Ro'?" she asked him softly. Marten stood beside her, a heavy, disturbing hand near the juncture of her white shoulder and white neck, smiling on them both. His brown eyes were dark to the point of blackness with smiling.

"Yes," he said.

"Your studies go well? Vannay is pleased? And Cort?" Her mouth quirked at this second name, as if she had tasted something bitter.

"I'm trying," he said. They both knew he was not flashingly intelligent like Cuthbert, or even quick like Jamie. He was a plodder and a bludgeoner. Even Alain was better at studies.

"And David?" She knew his affection for the hawk.

The boy looked up at Marten, still smiling paternally down on all this. "Past his prime."

His mother seemed to wince; for a moment Marten's face seemed to darken, his grip on her shoulder to tighten. Then she looked out into the hot whiteness of the day, and all was as it had been.

It's a charade, he thought. *A game. Who is playing with whom?*

"You have a cut on your forehead," Marten said, still smiling, and pointed a negligent finger at the mark of Cort's latest

(thank you for this instructive day)

bashing. "Are you going to be a fighter like your father or are you just slow?"

This time she did wince.

"Both," the boy said. He looked steadily at Marten and smiled painfully. Even in here, it was very hot.

Marten stopped smiling abruptly. "You can go to the roof now, boy. I believe you have business there."

"My mother has not yet dismissed me, bondsman!"

Marten's face twisted as if the boy had lashed him with a quirt. The boy heard his mother's dreadful, woeful gasp. She spoke his name.

But the painful smile remained intact on the boy's face and he stepped forward. "Will you give me a sign of fealty, bondsman? In the name of my father whom you serve?"

Marten stared at him, rankly unbelieving.

"Go," Marten said gently. "Go and find your hand."

Smiling rather horribly, the boy went.

As he closed the door and went back the way he came, he heard his mother wail. It was a banshee sound. And then, unbelievably, the sound of his father's man striking her and telling her to shut her quack.

To shut her quack!

And then he heard Marten's laugh.

The boy continued to smile as he went to his test.

V

Jamie had come from the shops, and when he saw the boy crossing the exercise yard, he ran to tell Roland the latest gossip of bloodshed and revolt to the west. But he fell aside, the words all unspoken. They had known each other since the time of infancy, and as boys they had dared each other, cuffed each other, and made a thousand explorations of the walls within which they had both been birthed.

The boy strode past him, staring without seeing, grinning his painful grin. He was walking toward Cort's cottage, where the shades were drawn to ward off the savage afternoon heat. Cort napped in the afternoon so that he could enjoy to the fullest extent his evening tomcat forays into the mazed and filthy brothels of the lower town.

Jamie knew in a flash of intuition, knew what was to
come, and in his fear and ecstasy he was torn between
following Roland and going after the others.

Then his hypnotism was broken and he ran toward the
main buildings, screaming, "Cuthbert! Alain! Thomas!"
His screams sounded puny and thin in the heat. They
had known, all of them, in that intuitive way boys have,
that Roland would be the first of them to try the line.
But this was too soon.

The hideous grin on Roland's face galvanized him
as no news of wars, revolts, and witchcrafts could have
done.

This was more than words from a toothless mouth
given over fly-specked heads of lettuce.

Roland walked to the cottage of his teacher and
kicked the door open. It slammed backward, hit the
plain rough plaster of the wall, and rebounded.

He had never been inside before. The entrance
opened on an austere kitchen that was cool and brown.
A table. Two straight chairs. Two cabinets. A faded lino-
leum floor, tracked in black paths from the cooler set
in the floor to the counter where knives hung, and to
the table.

Here was a public man's privacy. The faded refuge
of a violent midnight carouser who had loved the boys
of three generations roughly, and made some of them
into gunslingers.

"Cort!"

He kicked the table, sending it across the room and
into the counter. Knives from the wall rack fell in twinkling jackstraws.

There was a thick stirring in the other room, a half-

STEPHEN KING   188

sleep clearing of the throat. The boy did not enter,
knowing it was sham, knowing that Cort had awakened
immediately in the cottage's other room and stood with
one glittering eye beside the door, waiting to break the
intruder's unwary neck.

"Cort, I want you, bondsman!"

Now he spoke the High Speech, and Cort swung the
door open. He was dressed in thin underwear shorts, a
squat man with bow legs, runneled with scars from top
to toe, thick with twists of muscle. There was a round,
bulging belly. The boy knew from experience that it was
spring steel. The one good eye glared at him from the
bashed and dented hairless head.

The boy saluted formally. "Teach me no more, bondsman. Today I teach you."

"You are early, puler," Cort said casually, but he also
spoke the High Speech. "Two years early at the very best,
I should judge. I will ask only once. Will you cry off?"

The boy only smiled his hideous, painful smile. For
Cort, who had seen the smile on a score of bloodied,
scarlet-skied fields of honor and dishonor, it was answer
enough—perhaps the only answer he would have
believed.

"It's too bad," the teacher said absently. "You have
been a most promising pupil—the best in two dozen
years, I should say. It will be sad to see you broken and
set upon a blind path. But the world has moved on. Bad
times are on horseback."

The boy still did not speak (and would have been
incapable of any coherent explanation, had it been
required), but for the first time the awful smile soft-
ened a little.

"Still, there is the line of blood," Cort said, "revolt and witchcraft to the west or no. I am your bondsman, boy. I recognize your command and bow to it now—if never again—with all my heart."

And Cort, who had cuffed him, kicked him, bled him, cursed him, made mock of him, and called him the very eye of syphilis, bent to one knee and bowed his head.

The boy touched the leathery, vulnerable flesh of his neck with wonder. "Rise, bondsman. In love."

Cort stood slowly, and there might have been pain behind the impassive mask of his reamed features. "This is waste. Cry off, you foolish boy. I break my own oath. Cry off and wait."

The boy said nothing.

"Very well; if you say so, let it be so." Cort's voice became dry and business-like. "One hour. And the weapon of your choice."

"You will bring your stick?"

"I always have."

"How many sticks have been taken from you, Cort?" Which was tantamount to asking: How many boys have entered the square yard beyond the Great Hall and returned as gunslinger apprentices?

"No stick will be taken from me today," Cort said slowly. "I regret it. There is only the once, boy. The penalty for overeagerness is the same as the penalty for unworthiness. Can you not wait?"

The boy recalled Marten standing over him. The smile. And the sound of the blow from behind the closed door. "No."

"Very well. What weapon do you choose?"

The boy said nothing.

Cort's smile showed a jagged ring of teeth. "Wise enough to begin. In an hour. You realize you will in all probability never see your father, your mother, or your ka-babbies again?"

"I know what exile means," Roland said softly.

"Go now, and meditate on your father's face. Much good will it do ya."

The boy went, without looking back.

VI

The cellar of the barn was spuriously cool, dank, smelling of cobwebs and earthwater. The sun lit it in dusty rays from narrow windows, but here was none of the day's heat. The boy kept the hawk here and the bird seemed comfortable enough.

David no longer hunted the sky. His feathers had lost the radiant animal brightness of three years ago, but the eyes were still as piercing and motionless as ever. You cannot friend a hawk, they said, unless you are half a hawk yourself, alone and only a sojourner in the land, without friends or the need of them. The hawk pays no coinage to love or morals.

David was an old hawk now. The boy hoped that he himself was a young one.

"Hai," he said softly and extended his arm to the tethered perch.

The hawk stepped onto the boy's arm and stood motionless, unhooded. With his other hand the boy reached into his pocket and fished out a bit of dried jerky. The hawk snapped it deftly from between his fingers and made it disappear.

The boy began to stroke David very carefully. Cort most probably would not have believed it if he had seen it, but Cort did not believe the boy's time had come, either.

"I think you die today," he said, continuing to stroke. "I think you will be made a sacrifice, like all those little birds we trained you on. Do you remember? No? It doesn't matter. After today I am the hawk and each year on this day I'll shoot the sky in your memory."

David stood on his arm, silent and unblinking, indifferent to his life or death.

"You are old," the boy said reflectively. "And perhaps not my friend. Even a year ago you would have had my eyes instead of that little string of meat, isn't it so? Cort would laugh. But if we get close enough . . . close enough to that chary man . . . if he don't suspect . . . which will it be, David? Age or friendship?"

David did not say.

The boy hooded him and found the jesses, which were looped at the end of David's perch. They left the barn.

VII

The yard behind the Great Hall was not really a yard at all, but only a green corridor whose walls were formed by tangled, thick-grown hedges. It had been used for the rite of coming of age since time out of mind, long before Cort and his predecessor, Mark, who had died of a stab-wound from an overzealous hand in this place. Many boys had left the corridor from the east end, where the teacher always entered, as men. The east end faced the Great Hall and all the civilization and intrigue of the lighted world. Many more had slunk away, beaten and bloody, from the west end, where the boys always entered, as boys forever. The west end faced the farms and the hut-dwellers beyond the farms; beyond that, the tangled barbarian forests; beyond that, Garlan; and beyond Garlan, the Mohaine Desert. The boy who became a man progressed from darkness and unlearning to light and responsibility. The boy who was beaten could only retreat, forever and forever. The hallway was as smooth and green as a gaming field. It was exactly fifty yards long. In the middle was a swatch of shaven earth. This was the line.

Each end was usually clogged with tense spectators and relatives, for the ritual was usually forecast with great accuracy—eighteen was the most common age (those who had not made their test by the age of twenty-five usually slipped into obscurity as freeholders, unable to face the brutal all-or-nothing fact of the field and the test). But on this day there were none but Jamie DeCurry, Cuthbert Allgood, Alain Johns, and Thomas Whitman. They clustered at the boy's end, gape-mouthed and frankly terrified.

"Your weapon, stupid!" Cuthbert hissed, in agony. "You forgot your weapon!"

"I have it," the boy said. Dimly he wondered if the news of this lunacy had reached yet to the central buildings, to his mother—and to Marten. His father was on a hunt, not due back for days. In this he felt a sense of shame, for he felt that in his father he would have found understanding, if not approval. "Has Cort come?"

"Cort is here." The voice came from the far end of the corridor, and Cort stepped into view, dressed in a short singlet. A heavy leather band encircled his forehead to keep sweat from his eyes. He wore a dirty girdle to hold his back straight. He held an ironwood stick in one hand, sharp on one end, heavily blunted and spatulate on the other. He began the litany which all of them, chosen by the blind blood of their fathers all the way back to the Eld, had known since early childhood, learned against the day when they would, perchance, become men.

"Have you come here for a serious purpose, boy?"

"I have come for a serious purpose."

"Have you come as an outcast from your father's house?"

"I have so come." And would remain outcast until he had bested Cort. If Cort bested him, he would remain outcast forever.

"Have you come with your chosen weapon?"

"I have."

"What is your weapon?" This was the teacher's advantage, his chance to adjust his plan of battle to the sling or spear or bah or bow.

"My weapon is David."

Cort halted only briefly. He was surprised, and very likely confused. That was good.

Might be good.

"So then have you at me, boy?"

"I do."

"In whose name?"

"In the name of my father."

"Say his name."

"Steven Deschain, of the line of Eld."

"Be swift, then."

And Cort advanced into the corridor, switching his stick from one hand to the other. The boys sighed flutteringly, like birds, as their dan-dinh stepped to meet him.

My weapon is David, teacher.

Did Cort understand? And if so, did he understand fully? If he did, very likely all was lost. It turned on surprise—and on whatever stuff the hawk had left in him. Would he only sit, disinterested and stupid, on the boy's arm, while Cort struck him brainless with the ironwood? Or seek escape in the high, hot sky?

As they drew close together, each for the nonce still on his side of the line, the boy loosened the hawk's hood with nerveless fingers. It dropped to the green grass, and Cort halted in his tracks. He saw the old warrior's eyes drop to the bird and widen with surprise and slow-dawning comprehension. *Now* he understood.

"Oh, you little fool," Cort nearly groaned, and Roland was suddenly furious that he should be spoken to so.

"At him!" he cried, raising his arm.

And David flew like a silent brown bullet, stubby wings pumping once, twice, three times, before crashing into Cort's face, talons searching, beak digging. Red drops flew up into the hot air.

"Hai! Roland!" Cuthbert screamed deliriously. "First blood! First blood to my bosom!" He struck his chest hard enough to leave a bruise there that would not fade for a week.

Cort staggered backwards, off balance. The ironwood

staff rose and beat futilely at the air about his head. The hawk was an undulating, blurred bundle of feathers.

The boy, meanwhile, arrowed forward, his hand held out in a straight wedge, his elbow locked. This was his chance, and very likely the only one he'd have.

Still, Cort was almost too quick for him. The bird had covered ninety percent of his vision, but the ironwood came up again, spatulate end forward, and Cort cold-bloodly performed the only action that could turn events at that point. He beat his own face three times, biceps flexing mercilessly.

David fell away, broken and twisted. One wing flapped frantically at the ground. His cold, predator's eyes stared fiercely into the teacher's bloody, streaming face. Cort's bad eye now bulged blindly from its socket.

The boy delivered a kick to Cort's temple, connecting solidly. It should have ended it, but it did not. For a moment Cort's face went slack; and then he lunged, grabbing for the boy's foot.

The boy skipped back and tripped over his own feet. He went down asprawl. He heard, from far away, the sound of Jamie screaming in dismay.

Cort was ready to fall on him and finish it. Roland had lost his advantage and both of them knew it. For a moment they looked at each other, the teacher standing over the pupil with gouts of blood pouring from the left side of his face, the bad eye now closed except for a thin slit of white. There would be no brothels for Cort this night.

Something ripped jaggedly at the boy's hand. It was David, tearing blindly at whatever he could reach. Both wings were broken. It was incredible that he still lived.

The boy grabbed him like a stone, unmindful of the jabbing, diving beak that was taking the flesh from his wrist in ribbons. As Cort flew at him, all spread-eagled, the boy threw the hawk upward.

"Hai! David! Kill!"

Then Cort blotted out the sun and came down atop of him.

VIII

The bird was smashed between them, and the boy felt a callused thumb probe for the socket of his eye. He turned it, at the same time bringing up the slab of his thigh to block Cort's crotch-seeking knee. His own hand flailed against the tree of Cort's neck in three hard chops. It was like hitting ribbed stone.

Then Cort made a thick grunting. His body shuddered. Faintly, the boy saw one hand flailing for the dropped stick, and with a jackknifing lunge, he kicked it out of reach. David had hooked one talon into Cort's right ear. The other battered mercilessly at the teacher's cheek, making it a ruin. Warm blood splattered the boy's face, smelling of sheared copper.

Cort's fist struck the bird once, breaking its back. Again, and the neck snapped away at a crooked angle. And still the talon clutched. There was no ear now; only a red hole tunneled into the side of Cort's skull. The third blow sent the bird flying, at last clearing Cort's face.

The moment it was clear, the boy brought the edge of his hand across the bridge of his teacher's nose, using every bit of his strength and breaking the thin bone. Blood sprayed.

Cort's grasping, unseeing hand ripped at the boy's buttocks, trying to pull his trousers down, trying to hobble him. Roland rolled away, found Cort's stick, and rose to his knees.

Cort came to his own knees, grinning. Incredibly, they faced each other that way from either side of the line, although they had switched positions and Cort was now on the side where Roland had begun the contest. The old warrior's face was curtained with gore. The one seeing eye rolled furiously in its socket. The nose was smashed over to a haunted, leaning angle. Both cheeks hung in flaps.

The boy held the man's stick like a Gran' Points player waiting for the pitch of the rawhide bird.

Cort double-feinted, then came directly at him.

Roland was ready, not fooled in the slightest by this last trick, which both knew was a poor one. The ironwood swung in a flat arc, striking Cort's skull with a dull thudding noise. Cort fell on his side, looking at the boy with a lazy unseeing expression. A tiny trickle of spit came from his mouth.

"Yield or die," the boy said. His mouth was filled with wet cotton.

And Cort smiled. Nearly all consciousness was gone, and he would remain tended in his cottage for a week afterward, wrapped in the blackness of a coma, but now he held on with all the strength of his pitiless, shadowless life. He saw the need to palaver in the boy's eyes, and even with a curtain of blood between the two of them, understood that the need was desperate.

"I yield, gunslinger. I yield smiling. You have this day remembered the face of your father and all those who came before him. What a wonder you have done!"

Cort's clear eye closed.

The gunslinger shook him gently, but with persistence. The others were around him now, their hands trembling to thump his back and hoist him to their shoulders; but they held back, afraid, sensing a new gulf. Yet this was not as strange as it could have been, because there had always been a gulf between this one and the rest.

Cort's eye rolled open again.

"The key," the gunslinger said. "My birthright, teacher. I need it."

His birthright was the guns, not the heavy ones of his father—weighted with sandalwood—but guns, all the same. Forbidden to all but a few. In the heavy vault under the barracks where he by ancient law was now required to abide, away from his mother's breast, hung his apprentice weapons, heavy cumbersome barrel-shooters of steel and nickel. Yet they had seen his father through his apprenticeship, and his father now ruled—at least in name.

"Is your need so fearsome, then?" Cort muttered, as if in his sleep. "So pressing? Aye, I feared so. So much need should have made you stupid. And yet you won."

"The key."

"The hawk was a fine ploy. A fine weapon. How long did it take you to train the bastard?"

"I never trained David. I friended him. The key."

"Under my belt, gunslinger." The eye closed again.

The gunslinger reached under Cort's belt, feeling

the heavy press of the man's belly, the huge muscles there now slack and asleep. The key was on a brass ring. He clutched it in his hand, restraining the mad urge to thrust it up to the sky in a salutation of victory.

He got to his feet and was finally turning to the others when Cort's hand fumbled for his foot. For a moment the gunslinger feared some last attack and tensed, but Cort only looked up at him and beckoned with one crusted finger.

"I'm going to sleep now," Cort whispered calmly. "I'm going to walk the path. Perhaps all the way to the clearing at the end of it, I don't know. I teach you no more, gunslinger. You have surpassed me, and two years younger than your father, who was the youngest. But let me counsel."

"What?" Impatiently.

"Wipe that look off your face, maggot."

In his surprise, Roland did as he was bid (although, being crouched hidden behind his face as we all are, could not know it).

Cort nodded, then whispered a single word. "Wait."

"What?"

The effort it took the man to speak lent his words great emphasis. "Let the word and the legend go before you. There are those who will carry both." His eyes flicked over the gunslinger's shoulder. "Fools, perchance. Let your shadow grow hair on its face. Let it become dark." He smiled grotesquely. "Given time, words may even enchant an enchanter. Do you take my meaning, gunslinger?"

"Yes. I think I do."

"Will you take my last counsel as your teacher?"

The gunslinger rocked back on his heels, a hunkered, thinking posture that foreshadowed the man. He looked at the sky. It was deepening, purpling. The heat of the day was failing and thunderheads in the west foretold rain. Lightning tines jabbed the placid flank of the rising foothills miles distant. Beyond that, the mountains. Beyond that, the rising fountains of blood and unreason. He was tired, tired into his bones and beyond.

He looked back at Cort. "I will bury my hawk tonight, teacher. And later go into lower town to inform those in the brothels that will wonder about you. Perhaps I will comfort one or two a little."

Cort's lips parted in a pained smile. And then he slept.

The gunslinger got to his feet and turned to the others. "Make a litter and take him to his house. Then bring a nurse. No, two nurses. Okay?"

They still watched him, caught in a bated moment that none of them could immediately break. They still looked for a corona of fire, or a magical change of features.

"Two nurses," the gunslinger repeated, and then smiled. They smiled in return. Nervously.

"You goddamned horse drover!" Cuthbert suddenly yelled, grinning. "You haven't left enough meat for the rest of us to pick off the bone!"

"The world won't move on tomorrow," the gunslinger said, quoting the old adage with a smile. "Alain, you butter-butt! Move your freight."

Alain set about the business of making the litter; Thomas and Jamie went together to the main hall and the infirmary.

The gunslinger and Cuthbert looked at each other. They had always been the closest—or as close as they could be under the particular shades of their characters. There was a speculative, open light in Bert's eyes, and the gunslinger controlled only with great difficulty the need to tell him not to call for the test for a year or even eighteen months, lest he go west. But they had been through a great ordeal together, and the gunslinger did not feel he could risk saying such a thing without a look on his face that might be taken for arrogance. *I've begun to scheme,* he thought, and was a little dismayed. Then he thought of Marten, of his mother, and he smiled a deceiver's smile at his friend.

I am to be the first, he thought, knowing it for the first time, although he had thought of it idly many times before. *I* am *the first.*

"Let's go," he said.

"With pleasure, gunslinger."

They left by the east end of the hedge-bordered corridor; Thomas and Jamie were returning with the nurses already. They looked like ghosts in their white and gauzy summer robes, crossed at the breast with red.

"Shall I help you with the hawk?" Cuthbert asked.

"Yes," the gunslinger said. "That would be lovely, Bert."

And later, when darkness had come and the rushing thundershowers with it; while huge, phantom caissons rolled across the sky and lightning washed the crooked streets of the lower town in blue fire; while horses stood at hitching rails with their heads down and their tails drooping, the gunslinger took a woman and lay with her.

It was quick and good. When it was over and they lay side by side without speaking, it began to hail with a brief, rattling ferocity. Downstairs and far away, someone was playing "Hey Jude" ragtime. The gunslinger's mind turned reflectively inward. It was in that hail-splattered silence, just before sleep overtook him, that he first thought that he might also be the last.

IX

The gunslinger didn't tell the boy all of this, but perhaps most of it came through anyway. He had already realized that this was an extremely perceptive boy, not so different from Alain, who was strong in that half-empathy, half-telepathy they called the touch.

"You asleep?" the gunslinger asked.

"No."

"Did you understand what I told you?"

"Understand it?" the boy asked with surprising scorn. "Understand it? Are you kidding?"

"No." But the gunslinger felt defensive. He had never told anyone about his coming of age before, because he felt ambivalent about it. Of course, the hawk had been a perfectly acceptable weapon, yet it had been a trick, too. And a betrayal. The first of many. *And tell me—am I really preparing to throw this boy at the man in black?*

"I understood it, all right," the boy said. "It was a game, wasn't it? Do grown men always have to play games? Does everything have to be an excuse for another kind of game? Do any men grow up or do they only come of age?"

"You don't know everything," the gunslinger said, trying to hold his slow anger. "You're just a boy."

"Sure. But I know what I am to you."

"And what is that?" the gunslinger asked, tightly.

"A poker chip."

The gunslinger felt an urge to find a rock and brain
the boy. Instead, he spoke calmly.

"Go to sleep. Boys need their sleep."

And in his mind he heard Marten's echo: *Go and find
your hand.*

He sat stiffly in the darkness, stunned with horror
and terrified (for the first time in his existence) of the
self-loathing that might come afterward.

X

During the next period of waking, the railway angled
closer to the underground river, and they came upon
the Slow Mutants.

Jake saw the first one and screamed aloud.

The gunslinger's head, which had been fixed straight
forward as he pumped the handcar, jerked to the right.
There was a rotten jack-o'-lantern greenness below
them, pulsating faintly. For the first time he became
aware of odor—faint, unpleasant, wet.

The greenness was a face—what might be called a
face by one of charitable bent. Above the flattened nose
was an insectile node of eyes, peering at them expres-
sionlessly. The gunslinger felt an atavistic crawl in his
intestines and privates. He stepped up the rhythm of
arms and handcar handle slightly.

The glowing face faded.

"What the hell was *that?*" the boy asked, crawling to him. "What—" The words stopped dumb in his throat as they came upon and then passed a group of three faintly glowing forms, standing between the rails and the invisible river, watching them, motionless.

"They're Slow Mutants," the gunslinger said. "I don't think they'll bother us. They're probably just as frightened of us as we are of—"

One of the forms broke free and shambled toward them. The face was that of a starving idiot. The faint naked body had been transformed into a knotted mess of tentacular limbs and suckers.

The boy screamed again and crowded against the gunslinger's leg like a frightened dog.

One of the thing's tentacle arms pawed across the flat platform of the handcar. It reeked of the wet and the dark. The gunslinger let loose of the handle and drew. He put a bullet through the forehead of the starving idiot face. It fell away, its faint swamp-fire glow fading, an eclipsed moon. The gunflash lay bright and branded on their dark retinas, fading only reluctantly. The smell of expended powder was hot and savage and alien in this buried place.

There were others, more of them. None moved against them overtly, but they were closing in on the tracks, a silent, hideous party of rubberneckers.

"You may have to pump for me," the gunslinger said. "Can you?"

"Yes."

"Then be ready."

The boy stood close to him, his body poised. His eyes

took in the Slow Mutants only as they passed, not tra-
versing, not seeing more than they had to. The boy
assumed a psychic bulge of terror, as if his very id had
somehow sprung out through his pores to form a shield.
If he had the touch, the gunslinger reasoned, that was
not impossible.

The gunslinger pumped steadily but did not increase
his speed. The Slow Mutants could smell their terror,
he knew that, but he doubted if terror alone would be
enough to motivate them. He and the boy were, after
all, creatures of the light, and whole. *How they must hate
us,* he thought, and wondered if they had hated the
man in black in the same way. He thought not, or perhaps he had passed among them only like the shadow
of a dark wing in this greater darkness.

The boy made a noise in his throat and the gunslinger turned his head almost casually. Four of them
were charging the handcar in a stumbling way—one of
them in the process of finding a handgrip.

The gunslinger let go of the handle and drew again,
with the same sleepy casual motion. He shot the lead
mutant in the head. The mutant made a sighing, sobbing noise and began to grin. Its hands were limp and
fish-like, dead; the fingers clove to one another like the
fingers of a glove long immersed in drying mud. One
of these corpse-hands found the boy's foot and began
to pull.

The boy shrieked aloud in the granite womb.

The gunslinger shot the mutant in the chest. It began
to slobber through the grin. Jake was going off the side.
The gunslinger caught one of his arms and was almost
pulled off balance himself. The thing was surprisingly

strong. The gunslinger put another bullet in the mutant's head. One eye went out like a candle. Still it pulled. They engaged in a silent tug of war for Jake's jerking, wriggling body. The Slow Mutants yanked on him like a wishbone. The wish would undoubtedly be to dine.

The handcar was slowing down. The others began to close in—the lame, the halt, the blind. Perhaps they only looked for a Jesus to heal them, to raise them Lazarus-like from the darkness.

It's the end for the boy, the gunslinger thought with perfect coldness. *This is the end he meant. Let go and pump or hold on and be buried. The end for the boy.*

He gave a tremendous yank on the boy's arm and shot the mutant in the belly. For one frozen moment its grip grew even tighter and Jake began to slide off the edge again. Then the dead mud-mitts loosened, and the Slow Mutie fell on its face behind the slowing handcar, still grinning.

"I thought you'd leave me," the boy was sobbing. "I thought . . . I thought . . ."

"Hold on to my belt," the gunslinger said. "Hold on just as tight as you can."

The hand worked into his belt and clutched there; the boy was breathing in great convulsive, silent gasps.

The gunslinger began to pump steadily again, and the handcar picked up speed. The Slow Mutants fell back a step and watched them go with faces hardly human (or pathetically so), faces that generated the weak phosphorescence common to those weird deep-sea fishes that live under incredible black pressure, faces that held no anger or hate but only what seemed to be a semiconscious, idiot regret.

"They're thinning," the gunslinger said. The drawn-up muscles of his lower belly and privates relaxed the smallest bit. "They're—"

The Slow Mutants had put rocks across the track. The way was blocked. It had been a quick, poor job, perhaps the work of only a minute to clear, but they were stopped. And someone would have to get down and move them. The boy moaned and shuddered closer to the gunslinger. The gunslinger let go of the handle and the handcar coasted noiselessly to the rocks, where it thumped to rest.

The Slow Mutants began to close in again, almost casually, almost as if they had been passing by, lost in a dream of darkness, and had found someone of whom to ask directions. A street-corner congregation of the damned beneath the ancient rock.

"Arc they going to get us?" the boy asked calmly.

"Never in life. Be quiet a second."

He looked at the rocks. The mutants were weak, of course, and had not been able to drag any of the boulders to block their way. Only small rocks. Only enough to stop them, to make someone—

"Get down," the gunslinger said. "You'll have to move them. I'll cover you."

"No," the boy whispered. "Please."

"I can't give you a gun and I can't move the rocks and shoot, too. You have to get down."

Jake's eyes rolled terribly; for a moment his body shuddered in tune with the turnings of his mind, and then he wriggled over the side and began to throw rocks to the right and the left, working with mad speed, not looking up.

The gunslinger drew and waited.

Two of them, lurching rather than walking, went for the boy with arms like dough. The guns did their work, stitching the darkness with red-white lances of light that pushed needles of pain into the gunslinger's eyes. The boy screamed and continued to throw away rocks to either side. Witch-glow leaped and danced. Hard to see now, that was the worst. Everything had gone to shadows and afterimages.

One of them, glowing hardly at all, suddenly reached for the boy with rubber boogeyman arms. Eyes that ate up half the mutie's head rolled wetly.

Jake screamed again and turned to struggle.

The gunslinger fired without allowing himself to think before his spotty vision could betray his hands into a terrible quiver; the two heads were only inches apart. It was the mutie who fell.

Jake threw rocks wildly. The mutants milled just outside the invisible line of trespass, closing a little at a time, now very close. Others had caught up, swelling their number.

"All right," the gunslinger said. "Get on. Quick."

When the boy moved, the mutants came at them. Jake was over the side and scrambling to his feet; the gunslinger was already pumping again, all out. Both guns were holstered now. They must run. It was their only chance.

Strange hands slapped the metal plane of the car's surface. The boy was holding his belt with both hands now, his face pressed tightly into the small of the gunslinger's back.

A group of them ran onto the tracks, their faces full

of that mindless, casual anticipation. The gunslinger was full of adrenaline; the car was flying along the tracks into the darkness. They struck the four or five pitiful hulks full force. They flew like rotten bananas struck from the stem.

On and on, into the soundless, flying, banshee darkness.

After an age, the boy raised his face into the made wind, dreading and yet needing to know. The ghost of gunflashes still lingered on his retinas. There was nothing to see but the darkness and nothing to hear but the rumble of the river.

"They're gone," the boy said, suddenly fearing an end to the tracks in the darkness, and the wounding crash as they jumped the rails and plunged to twisted ruin. He had ridden in cars; once his humorless father had driven at ninety on the New Jersey Turnpike and had been stopped by a cop who ignored the twenty Elmer Chambers offered with his license and gave him a ticket anyway. But he had never ridden like this, with the wind and the blindness and the terrors behind and ahead, with the sound of the river like a chuckling voice—the voice of the man in black. The gunslinger's arms were pistons in a lunatic human factory.

"They're gone," the boy said timidly, the words ripped from his mouth by the wind. "You can slow down now. We left them behind."

But the gunslinger did not hear. They careened onward into the strange dark.

XI

They went on for three "days" without incident.

XII

During the fourth period of waking (halfway through? three-quarters? they didn't know—knew only that they weren't tired enough yet to stop) there was a sharp thump beneath them; the handcar swayed, and their bodies immediately leaned to the right against gravity as the rails took a gradual turn to the left.

There was a light ahead—a glow so faint and alien that it seemed at first to be a totally new element, not earth, air, fire, nor water. It had no color and could only be discerned by the fact that they had regained their hands and faces in a dimension beyond that of touch. Their eyes had become so light-sensitive that they noticed the glow more than five miles before they approached its source.

"The end," the boy said tightly. "It's the end."

"No." The gunslinger spoke with odd assurance. "It isn't."

And it was not. They reached light but not day.

As they approached the source of the glow, they saw for the first time that the rock wall to the left had fallen away and their tracks had been joined by others which crossed in a complex spiderweb. The light laid them in burnished vectors. On some of them there were dark boxcars, passenger coaches, a stage that had

been adapted to rails. They made the gunslinger nervous, like ghost galleons trapped in an underground Sargasso.

The light grew stronger, hurting their eyes a little, but growing slowly enough to allow them to adapt. They came from dark to light like divers coming up from deep fathoms in slow stages.

Ahead, drawing nearer, was a huge hangar stretching up into the dark. Cut into it, showing yellow squares of light, were a series of perhaps twenty-four entranceways, growing from the size of toy windows to a height of twenty feet as they drew closer. They passed inside through one of the middle ways. Written above were a series of characters, in various languages, the gunslinger presumed. He was astounded to find that he could read the last one; it was an ancient root of the High Speech itself and said:

TRACK 10 TO SURFACE AND POINTS WEST

The light inside was brighter; the tracks met and merged through a series of switchings. Here some of the traffic lanterns still worked, flashing eternal reds and greens and ambers.

They rolled between the rising stone piers caked black with the passage of thousands of vehicles, and then they were in some kind of central terminal. The gunslinger let the handcar coast slowly to a stop, and they peered around.

"It's like a subway," the boy said.

"Subway?"

"Never mind. You wouldn't know what I was talking about. *I* don't even know what I'm talking about, not anymore."

The boy climbed up onto the cracked cement. They looked at silent, deserted booths where newspapers and books had once been traded or sold; a bootery; a weapon shop (the gunslinger, suddenly feverish with excitement, saw revolvers and rifles; closer inspection showed that their barrels had been filled with lead; he did, however, pick out a bow, which he slung over his back, and a quiver of almost useless, badly weighted arrows); a women's apparel shop. Somewhere a converter was turning the air over and over, as it had for thousands of years—but perhaps would not for much longer. It had a grating noise somewhere in its cycle which served to remind that perpetual motion, even under strictly controlled conditions, was still a fool's dream. The air had a mechanized taste. The boy's shoes and the gunslinger's boots made flat echoes.

The boy cried out: "Hey! Hey . . ."

The gunslinger turned around and went to him. The boy was standing, transfixed, at the book stall. Inside, sprawled in the far corner, was a mummy. It was wearing a blue uniform with gold piping—a trainman's uniform, by the look. There was an ancient, perfectly preserved newspaper on the dead thing's lap, and it crumbled to dust when the gunslinger touched it. The mummy's face was like an old, shriveled apple. Cautiously, the gunslinger touched the cheek. There was a small puff of dust. When it cleared, they were able to look through the flesh and into the mummy's mouth. A gold tooth twinkled there.

"Gas," the gunslinger murmured. "The old people made a gas that would do this. Or so Vannay told us."

"The one who taught from books."

"Yes. He."

"I bet these old people fought wars with it," the boy said darkly. "Killed *other* old people with it."

"I'm sure you're right."

There were perhaps a dozen other mummies. All but two or three were wearing the blue and gold ornamental uniforms. The gunslinger supposed that the gas had been used when the place was empty of most incoming and outgoing traffic. Perhaps once in the dim ago, the station had been a military objective of some long-gone army and cause.

The thought depressed him.

"We better go on," he said, and started toward Track 10 and the handcar again. But the boy stood rebelliously behind him.

"Not going."

The gunslinger turned back, surprised.

The boy's face was twisted and trembling. "You won't get what you want until I'm dead. I'll take my chances by myself."

The gunslinger nodded noncommittally, hating himself for what he was going to do. "Okay, Jake," he said mildly. "Long days, pleasant nights." He turned around, walked across to the stone piers, leaped easily down onto the handcar.

"You made a deal with someone!" the boy screamed after him. "I know you did!"

The gunslinger, not replying, carefully put the bow in front of the T-post rising out of the handcar's floor, out of harm's way.

The boy's fists were clenched, his features drawn in agony.

How easily you bluff this young boy, the gunslinger told himself. *Again and again his wonderful intuition—his touch—has led him to this point, and again and again you have led him on past it. And how difficult could it be—after all, he has no friends but you.*

In a sudden, simple thought (almost a vision) it came to him that all he had to do was give it over, turn around, take the boy with him, and make him the center of a new force. The Tower did not have to be obtained in this humiliating, nose-rubbing way, did it? Let his quest resume after the boy had a growth of years, when the two of them could cast the man in black aside like a cheap wind-up toy.

Surely, he thought cynically. *Surely.*

He knew with sudden coldness that turning backward would mean death for both of them—death or worse: entombment with the Slow Muties behind them. Decay of all the faculties. With, perhaps, the guns of his father living long after both of them, kept in rotten splendor as totems not unlike the unforgotten gas pump.

Show some guts, he told himself falsely.

He reached for the handle and began to pump it. The handcar moved away from the stone piers.

The boy screamed: *"Wait!"* And began running on the diagonal, toward where the handcar would emerge nearer the darkness ahead. The gunslinger had an impulse to speed up, to leave the boy alone yet at least with an uncertainty.

Instead, he caught him as he leaped. The heart beneath the thin shirt thrummed and fluttered as Jake clung to him.

The end was very close now.

XIII

The sound of the river had become very loud, filling even their dreams with its thunder. The gunslinger, more as a whim than anything else, let the boy pump them ahead while he shot a number of the bad arrows, tethered by fine white lengths of thread, into the dark.

The bow was also very bad, incredibly preserved but with a terrible pull and aim despite that, and the gunslinger knew nothing would improve it. Even re-stringing would not help the tired wood. The arrows would not fly far into the dark, but the last one he sent out came back wet and slick. The gunslinger only shrugged when the boy asked him how far to the water, but privately he didn't think the arrow could have traveled more than sixty yards from the rotted bow—and lucky to get that far.

And still the river's thunder grew louder, closer.

During the third waking period after the station, a spectral radiance began to grow again. They had entered a long tunnel of some weird phosphorescent rock, and the wet walls glittered and twinkled with thousands of minute starbursts. The boy called them *fol-suls.* They saw things in a kind of eerie, horror-house surreality.

The brute sound of the river was channeled to them by the confining rock, magnified in its own natural amplifier. Yet the sound remained oddly constant, even as they approached the crossing point the gunslinger was sure lay ahead, because the walls were widening, drawing back. The angle of their ascent became more pronounced.

The tracks arrowed through the new light. To the

gunslinger the clumps of *fot-suls* looked like the captive tubes of swamp gas sometimes sold for a pretty at the Feast of Reaptide fair; to the boy they looked like endless streamers of neon tubing. But in its glow they could both see that the rock that had enclosed them so long ended up ahead in ragged twin peninsulas that pointed toward a gulf of darkness—the chasm over the river.

The tracks continued out and over that unknowable drop, supported by a trestle aeons old. And beyond, what seemed an incredible distance, was a tiny pinprick of light, not phosphorescence or fluorescence, but the hard, true light of day. It was as tiny as a needle-prick in a dark cloth, yet weighted with frightful meaning.

"Stop," the boy said. "Stop for a minute. Please."

Unquestioning, the gunslinger let the handcar coast to a stop. The sound of the river was a steady, booming roar, coming from beneath and ahead. The artificial glow from the wet rock was suddenly hateful. For the first time he felt a claustrophobic hand touch him, and the urge to get out, to get free of this living burial, was strong and nearly undeniable.

"We'll go on," the boy said. "Is that what he wants? For us to drive the handcar out over . . . *that* . . . and fall down?"

The gunslinger knew it was not but said: "I don't know what he wants."

They got down and approached the lip of the drop carefully. The stone beneath their feet continued to rise until, with a sudden, angling drop, the floor fell away from the tracks and the tracks continued alone, across blackness.

The gunslinger dropped to his knees and peered

down. He could dimly make out a complex, nearly incredible webwork of steel girders and struts, disappearing down toward the roar of the river, all in support of the graceful arch of the tracks across the void.

In his mind's eye he could imagine the work of time and water on the steel, in deadly tandem. How much support was left? Little? Hardly any? None? He suddenly saw the face of the mummy again, and the way the flesh, seemingly solid, had crumbled to powder at the effortless touch of his finger.

"We'll walk now," the gunslinger said.

He half expected the boy to balk again, but he preceded the gunslinger out onto the rails, crossing on the welded steel slats calmly, with sure feet. The gunslinger followed him out over the chasm, ready to catch him if Jake should put a foot wrong.

The gunslinger felt a fine slick of sweat cover his skin. The trestle was rotten, very rotten. It thrummed beneath his feet with the heady motion of the river far beneath, swaying a little on unseen guy wires. *We're acrobats,* he thought. *Look, Mother, no net. I'm flying.*

He knelt once and examined the crossties they were walking on. They were caked and pitted with rust (he could feel the reason on his face—fresh air, the friend of corruption; they must be very close to the surface now), and a strong blow of the fist made the metal quiver sickly. Once he heard a warning groan beneath his feet and felt the steel settle preparatory to giving way, but he had already moved on.

The boy, of course, was over a hundred pounds lighter and safe enough, unless the going became progressively worse.

Behind them, the handcar had melted into the general gloom. The stone pier on the left extended out perhaps twenty yards. It jutted further than the one on the right, but this was also left behind and then they were alone over the gulf.

At first it seemed that the tiny prick of daylight remained mockingly constant (perhaps even drawing away from them at the exact pace they approached it—that would be a fine bit of magic indeed), but gradually the gunslinger realized that it was widening, becoming more defined. They were still below it, but the tracks were rising to meet it.

The boy gave a surprised grunt and suddenly lurched to the side, arms pinwheeling in slow, wide revolutions. It seemed that he tottered on the brink for a very long time indeed before stepping forward again.

"It almost went on me," he said softly, without emotion. "There's a hole. Step over if you don't want to take a quick trip to the bottom. Simon says take one giant step."

That was a game the gunslinger knew as Mother Says, remembered well from childhood games with Cuthbert, Jamie, and Alain, but he said nothing, only stepped over.

"Go back," Jake said, unsmiling. "You forgot to say 'May I?'"

"Cry your pardon, but I think not."

The crosstie the boy had stepped on had given way almost entirely and flopped downward lazily, swinging on a rotten rivet.

Upward, still upward. It was a nightmare walk and so seemed to go on much longer than it did; the air itself seemed to thicken and become like taffy, and the gunslinger felt as if he might be swimming rather than

walking. Again and again his mind tried to turn itself
to thoughtful, lunatic consideration of the awful space
between this trestle and the river below. His brain viewed
it in spectacular detail, and how it would be: the scream
of twisting, giving metal, the lurch as his body slid off to
the side, the grabbing for nonexistent handholds with
the fingers, the swift rattle of bootheels on treacherous,
rotted steel—and then down, turning over and over, the
warm spray in his crotch as his bladder let go, the rush
of wind against his face, rippling his hair up in a caricature of fright, pulling his eyelids back, the dark water
rushing to meet him, faster, outstripping even his own
scream—

Metal screamed beneath him and he stepped past it
unhurriedly, shifting his weight, at that crucial moment
not thinking of the drop, or of how far they had come,
or of how far might be left. Not thinking that the boy
was expendable and that the sale of his honor was now,
at last, nearly negotiated. What a relief it would be when
the deal was done!

"Three ties out," the boy said coolly. "I'm gonna
jump. Here! Right here! *Geronimo!*"

The gunslinger saw him silhouetted for a moment
against the daylight, an awkward, hunched spread-eagle,
arms out as if, should all else fail, there was the possibility of flight. He landed and the whole edifice swayed
drunkenly under his weight. Metal beneath them pro-
tested and something far below fell, first with a crash,
then with a splash.

"Are you over?" the gunslinger asked.

"Yar," the boy said, "but it's very rotten. Like the ideas
of certain people, maybe. I don't think it will hold you

any further than where you are now. Me, but not you. Go back. Go back now and leave me alone."

His voice was cold, but there was hysteria underneath, beating as his heart had beat when he jumped back onto the handcar and Roland had caught him.

The gunslinger stepped over the break. One large step did it. One giant step. *Mother, may I? Yes-you-may.* The boy was shuddering helplessly. "Go back. I don't want you to kill me."

"For love of the Man Jesus, *walk*," the gunslinger said roughly. "It's going to fall down for sure if we stand here palavering."

The boy walked drunkenly now, his hands held out shudderingly before him, fingers splayed.

They went up.

Yes, it was much more rotten now. There were frequent breaks of one, two, even three ties, and the gunslinger expected again and again that they would find the long empty space between rails that would either force them back or make them walk on the rails themselves, balanced giddily over the chasm.

He kept his eyes fixed on the daylight.

The glow had taken on a color—blue—and as it came closer it became softer, paling the radiance of the *fot-suls*. Fifty yards or a hundred still to cover? He could not say.

They walked, and now he looked at his feet, crossing from tie to tie. When he looked up again, the glow ahead had grown to a hole, and it was not just light but a way out. They were almost there.

Thirty yards now. No more than that. Ninety short feet. It could be done. Perhaps they would have the man in black yet. Perhaps, in the bright sunlight the evil flowers in his mind would shrivel and anything would be possible.

The sunlight was blocked out.

He looked up, startled, peering like a mole from its hole, and saw a silhouette filling the light, eating it up, allowing only chinks of mocking blue around the outline of shoulders and the fork of crotch.

"Hello, boys!"

The man in black's voice echoed to them, amplified in this natural throat of stone, the sarcasm of his good cheer taking on mighty overtones. Blindly, the gunslinger sought the jawbone, but it was gone, lost somewhere, used up.

He laughed above them and the sound crashed around them, reverberating like surf in a filling cave. The boy screamed and tottered, a windmill again, arms gyrating through the scant air.

Metal ripped and sloughed beneath them; the rails canted through a slow and dreamy twisting. The boy plunged, and one hand flew up like a gull in the darkness, up, up, and then he hung over the pit; he dangled there, his dark eyes staring up at the gunslinger in final blind lost knowledge.

"Help me."

Booming, racketing: "No more games. Come now, gunslinger. Or catch me never."

All the chips on the table. Every card up but one. The boy dangled, a living Tarot card, the Hanged Man, the Phoenician sailor, innocent lost and barely above the wave of a stygian sea.

Wait then, wait awhile.

"Do I go?"

His voice is so loud, he makes it hard to think.

"Help me. Help me, Roland."

The trestle had begun to twist further, screaming, pulling loose from itself, giving—

"Then I shall leave you."

"No! You shall NOT!"

The gunslinger's legs carried him in a sudden leap, breaking the paralysis that held him; he took a true giant's step above the dangling boy and landed in a skidding, plunging rush toward the light that offered the Tower frozen on his mind's eye in a black still life . . .

Into sudden silence.

The silhouette was gone, even the beat of his heart was gone as the trestle settled further, beginning its final slow dance to the depths, tearing loose, his hand finding the rocky, lighted lip of damnation; and behind him, in the dreadful silence, the boy spoke from too far beneath him.

"Go then. There are other worlds than these."

Then the trestle tore away, the whole weight of it; and as the gunslinger pulled himself up and through to the light and the breeze and the reality of a new ka, he twisted his head back, for a moment in his agony striving to be Janus—but there was nothing, only plummeting silence, for the boy made no cry as he fell.

Then Roland was up, pulling himself onto the rocky escarpment that looked toward a grassy plain, toward where the man in black stood spread-legged, with arms crossed.

The gunslinger stood drunkenly, pallid as a ghost, eyes huge and swimming beneath his forehead, shirt smeared with the white dust of his final, lunging crawl.

It came to him that there would be further degradations
of the spirit ahead that might make this one seem infinitesimal, and yet he would still flee it, down corridors and
through cities, from bed to bed; he would flee the boy's
face and try to bury it in cunts and killing, only to enter
one final room and find it looking at him over a candle
flame. He had become the boy; the boy had become
him. He was become a werewolf of his own making. In
deep dreams he would become the boy and speak the
boy's strange city tongue.

This is death. Is it? Is it?

He walked slowly, drunkenly down the rocky hill
toward where the man in black waited. Here the tracks
had been worn away, under the sun of reason, and it
was as if they had never been.

The man in black pushed his hood away with the
backs of both hands, laughing.

"So!" he cried. "Not an end, but the end of the beginning, eh? You progress, gunslinger! You progress! Oh,
how I admire you!"

The gunslinger drew with blinding speed and fired
twelve times. The gunflashes dimmed the sun itself, and
the pounding of the explosions slammed back from the
rock-faced escarpments behind them.

"Now-now," the man in black said, laughing. "Oh,
now-now-*now*. We make great magic together, you and
I. You kill me no more than you kill yourself."

He withdrew, walking backwards, facing the gunslinger, grinning and beckoning. "Come. Come. Come.
Mother, may I? Yes-you-may."

The gunslinger followed him in broken boots to the
place of counseling.

THE GUNSLINGER
AND THE MAN
IN BLACK

CHAPTER 5

The Gunslinger and
the Man in Black

I

The man in black led him to an ancient killing ground to make palaver. The gunslinger knew it immediately: a golgotha, place-of-the-skull. And bleached skulls stared blandly up at them—cattle, coyotes, deer, rabbits, bumbler. Here the alabaster xylophone of a hen pheasant killed as she fed; there the tiny, delicate bones of a mole, perhaps killed for pleasure by a wild dog.

The golgotha was a bowl indented into the descending slope of the mountain, and below, in easier altitudes, the gunslinger could see Joshua trees and scrub firs. The sky overhead was a softer blue than he had seen for a twelve-month, and there was an indefinable something that spoke of the sea in the not-too-great distance.

I am in the West, Cuthbert, he thought wonderingly. *If this is not Mid-World, it's close by.*

The man in black sat on an ancient ironwood log. His boots were powdered white with dust and the uneasy bone-meal of this place. He had put his hood up again, but the gunslinger could see the square shape of his chin clearly, and the shading of his jaw.

The shadowed lips twitched in a smile. "Gather wood, gunslinger. This side of the mountains is gentle, but at this altitude, the cold still may put a knife in one's belly. And this is a place of death, eh?"

"I'll kill you," the gunslinger said.

"No you won't. You can't. But you can gather wood to remember your Isaac."

The gunslinger had no understanding of the reference. He went wordlessly and gathered wood like a common cook's boy. The pickings were slim. There was no devil-grass on this side and the ironwood would not burn. It had become stone. He returned finally with a large armload of likely sticks, powdered and dusted with disintegrated bone, as if dipped in flour. The sun had sunk beyond the highest Joshua trees and had taken on a reddish glow. It peered at them with baleful indifference.

"Excellent," the man in black said. "How exceptional you are! How methodical! How resourceful! I salute you!" He giggled, and the gunslinger dropped the wood at his feet with a crash that ballooned up bone dust.

The man in black did not start or jump; he merely began laying the fire. The gunslinger watched, fascinated, as the ideogram (fresh, this time) took shape. When it was finished, it resembled a small and complex double chimney about two feet high. The man in black lifted his hand skyward, shaking back the voluminous sleeve from a tapered, handsome hand, and brought it down rapidly, index and pinky fingers forked out in the traditional sign of the evil eye. There was a blue flash of flame, and their fire was lighted.

"I have matches," the man in black said jovially, "but I thought you might enjoy the magic. For a pretty, gunslinger. Now cook our dinner."

The folds of his robe shivered, and the plucked and gutted carcass of a plump rabbit fell on the dirt.

The gunslinger spitted the rabbit wordlessly and roasted it. A savory smell drifted up as the sun went down. Purple shadows drifted hungrily over the bowl where the man in black had chosen to finally face him. The gunslinger felt hunger begin to rumble endlessly in his belly as the rabbit browned; but when the meat was cooked and its juices sealed in, he handed the entire skewer wordlessly to the man in black, rummaged in his own nearly flat knapsack, and withdrew the last of his jerky. It was salty, painful to his mouth, and tasted like tears.

"That's a worthless gesture," the man in black said, managing to sound angry and amused at the same time.

"Nevertheless," the gunslinger said. There were tiny sores in his mouth, the result of vitamin deprivation, and the salt taste made him grin bitterly.

"Are you afraid of enchanted meat?"

"Yes indeed."

The man in black slipped his hood back.

The gunslinger looked at him silently. In a way, the face that the hood had hidden was an uneasy disappointment. It was handsome and regular, with none of the marks and twists which indicate a man who has been through awesome times and has been privy to great secrets. His hair was black and of a ragged, matted length. His forehead was high, his eyes dark and brilliant. His nose was nondescript. The lips were full and sensual. His complexion was pallid, as was the gun-slinger's own.

The gunslinger said finally, "I expected an older man."

"Why? I am nearly immortal, as are you, Roland—for now, at least. I could have taken a face with which you would have been more familiar, but I elected to show you the one I was—ah—born with. See, gunslinger, the sunset."

The sun had departed already, and the western sky was filled with sullen furnace light.

"You won't see another sunrise for what may seem a very long time," the man in black said.

The gunslinger remembered the pit under the mountains and then looked at the sky, where the con-stellations sprawled in clockspring profusion.

"It doesn't matter," he said softly, "now."

II

The man in black shuffled the cards with flying hands. The deck was huge, the designs on the back convoluted. "These are Tarot cards, gunslinger—of a sort. A mixture of the standard deck to which have been added a selec-tion of my own development. Now watch carefully."

"What will I watch?"

"I'm going to tell your future. Seven cards must be turned, one at a time, and placed in conjunction with the others. I've not done this since the days when Gil-ead stood and the ladies played at Points on the west lawn. And I suspect I've *never* read a tale such as yours." Mockery was creeping into his voice again. "You are the world's last adventurer. The last crusader. How that must please you, Roland! Yet you have no idea how close you stand to the Tower now, as you resume your quest. Worlds turn about your head."

"What do you mean, resume? I never left off."

At this the man in black laughed heartily, but would not say what he found so funny. "Read my fortune then," Roland said harshly.

The first card was turned.

"The Hanged Man," the man in black said. The darkness had given him back his hood. "Yet here, in conjunction with nothing else, it signifies strength, not death. You, gunslinger, are the Hanged Man, plodding ever onward toward your goal over the pits of Na'ar. You've already dropped one co-traveler into that pit, have you not?"

The gunslinger said nothing, and the second card was turned.

"The Sailor! Note the clear brow, the hairless cheeks, the wounded eyes. He drowns, gunslinger, and no one throws out the line. The boy Jake."

The gunslinger winced, said nothing.

The third card was turned. A baboon stood grinningly astride a young man's shoulder. The young man's face was turned up, a grimace of stylized dread and horror on his features. Looking more closely, the gunslinger saw the baboon held a whip.

"The Prisoner," the man in black said. The fire cast uneasy, flickering shadows over the face of the ridden man, making it seem to move and writhe in wordless terror. The gunslinger flicked his eyes away.

"A trifle upsetting, isn't he?" the man in black said, and seemed on the verge of sniggering.

He turned the fourth card. A woman with a shawl over her head sat spinning at a wheel. To the gunslinger's dazed eyes, she appeared to be smiling craftily and sobbing at the same time.

"The Lady of the Shadows," the man in black remarked. "Does she look two-faced to you, gunslinger? She is. Two faces at least. She broke the blue plate!"

"What do you mean?"

"I don't know." And—in this case, at least—the gunslinger thought his adversary was telling the truth.

"Why are you showing me these?"

"Don't ask!" the man in black said sharply, yet he smiled. "Don't ask. Merely watch. Consider this only pointless ritual if it eases you and cools you to do so. Like church."

He tittered and turned the fifth card.

A grinning reaper clutched a scythe with bony fingers. "Death," the man in black said simply. "Yet not for you."

The sixth card.

The gunslinger looked at it and felt a strange, crawling anticipation in his guts. The feeling was mixed with horror and joy, and the whole of the emotion was unnameable. It made him feel like throwing up and dancing at the same time.

"The Tower," the man in black said softly. "Here is the Tower."

The gunslinger's card occupied the center of the pattern; each of the following four stood at one corner, like satellites circling a star.

"Where does that one go?" the gunslinger asked.

The man in black placed the Tower over the Hanged Man, covering it completely.

"What does that mean?" the gunslinger asked.

The man in black did not answer.

"What does that mean?" he asked raggedly.

The man in black did not answer.

"Goddamn you!"

No answer.

"Then be damned to you. What's the seventh card?"

The man in black turned the seventh. A sun rose in a luminously blue sky. Cupids and sprites sported around it. Below the sun was a great red field upon which it shone. Roses or blood? The gunslinger could not tell. *Perhaps*, he thought, *it's both.*

"The seventh card is Life," the man in black said softly. "But not for you."

"Where does it fit the pattern?"

"That is not for you to know now," the man in black said. "Or for me to know. I'm not the great one you seek, Roland. I am merely his emissary." He flipped the card carelessly into the dying fire. It charred, curled, and flashed to flame. The gunslinger felt his heart quail and turn icy in his chest.

"Sleep now," the man in black said carelessly. "Perchance to dream and that sort of thing."

"What my bullets won't do, mayhap my hands will," the gunslinger said. His legs coiled with savage, splendid suddenness, and he flew across the fire at the other, arms outstretched. The man in black, smiling, swelled in his vision and then retreated down a long and echoing corridor. The world filled with the sound of sardonic laughter, he was falling, dying, sleeping.

He dreamed.

III

The universe was void. Nothing moved. Nothing was.

The gunslinger drifted, bemused.

"Let's have a little light," the voice of the man in black said nonchalantly, and there was light. The gunslinger thought in a detached way that light was pretty good.

"Now darkness overhead with stars in it. Water down below."

It happened. He drifted over endless seas. Above, the stars twinkled endlessly, yet he saw none of the constellations which had guided him across his long life.

"Land," the man in black invited, and there was; it heaved itself out of the water in endless, galvanic convulsions. It was red, arid, cracked and glazed with sterility. Volcanoes blurted endless magma like giant pimples on some ugly adolescent's baseball head.

"Okay," the man in black was saying. "That's a start. Let's have some plants. Trees. Grass and fields."

There was. Dinosaurs rambled here and there, growling and whoofing and eating each other and getting stuck in bubbling, odiferous tarpits. Huge tropical rain-forests sprawled everywhere. Giant ferns waved at the sky with serrated leaves. Beetles with two heads crawled on some of them. All this the gunslinger saw. And yet he felt big.

"Now bring man," the man in black said softly, but the gunslinger was falling . . . falling up. The horizon of this vast and fecund earth began to curve. Yes, they had all said it curved, his teacher Vannay had claimed it had been proved long before the world had moved on. But this—

Further and further, higher and higher. Continents took shape before his amazed eyes, and were obscured with clocksprings of clouds. The world's atmosphere held it in a placental sac. And the sun, rising beyond the earth's shoulder—

He cried out and threw an arm before his eyes.

"Let there be light!"

The voice no longer belonged to the man in black. It was gigantic, echoing. It filled space, and the spaces between space.

"Light!"

Falling, falling.

The sun shrank. A red planet stamped with canals whirled past him, two moons circling it furiously. Beyond this was a whirling belt of stones and a gigantic planet that seethed with gases, too huge to support itself, oblate in consequence. Further out was a ringed world that glittered like a precious gem within its engirdlement of icy spicules.

"Light! Let there be—"

Other worlds, one, two, three. Far beyond the last, one lonely ball of ice and rock twirled in dead darkness about a sun that glittered no brighter than a tarnished penny.

Beyond this, darkness.

"No," the gunslinger said, and his word on it was flat and echoless in the black. It was darker than dark, blacker than black. Beside this, the darkest night of a man's soul was as noonday, the darkness under the mountains a mere smudge on the face of Light. "No more. Please, no more now. No more—"

"LIGHT!"

"No more. No more, please—"

The stars themselves began to shrink. Whole nebulae drew together and became glowing smudges. The whole universe seemed to be drawing around him.

"Please no more no more no more—"

The voice of the man in black whispered silkily in his ear: "Then renege. Cast away all thoughts of the Tower. Go your way, gunslinger, and begin the long job of saving your soul."

He gathered himself. Shaken and alone, enwrapt in the darkness, terrified of an ultimate meaning rushing at him, he gathered himself and uttered the final answer on that subject:

"NEVER!"

"THEN LET THERE BE LIGHT!"

And there *was* light, crashing in on him like a hammer, a great and primordial light. Consciousness had no chance of survival in that great glare, but before it perished, the gunslinger saw something clearly, something he believed to be of cosmic importance. He clutched it with agonized effort and then went deep, seeking refuge in himself before that light should blind his eyes and blast his sanity.

He fled the light and the knowledge the light implied, and so came back to himself. Even so do the rest of us; even so the best of us.

IV

It was still night—whether the same or another, he had no immediate way of knowing. He pushed himself up from where his demon spring at the man in black had carried him and looked at the ironwood where Walter o' Dim (as some along Roland's way had named him) had been sitting. He was gone.

A great sense of despair flooded him—God, all that to do over again—and then the man in black said from behind him: "Over here, gunslinger. I don't like you so close. You talk in your sleep." He tittered.

The gunslinger got groggily to his knees and turned around. The fire had burned down to red embers and gray ashes, leaving the familiar decayed pattern of exhausted fuel. The man in black was seated next to it, smacking his lips with unlovely enthusiasm over the greasy remains of the rabbit.

"You did fairly well," the man in black said. "I never could have sent that vision to your father. He would have come back drooling."

"What was it?" the gunslinger asked. His words were blurred and shaky. He felt that if he tried to rise, his legs would buckle.

"The universe," the man in black said carelessly. He burped and threw the bones into the fire where they first glistened and then blackened. The wind above the cup of the golgotha keened and moaned.

"Universe?" the gunslinger said blankly. It was a word with which he was unfamiliar. His first thought was that the other was speaking poetry.

"You want the Tower," the man in black said. It seemed to be a question.

"Yes."

"Well, you shan't have it," the man in black said, and smiled with bright cruelty. "No one cares in the counsels of the great if you pawn your soul or sell it outright, Roland. I have an idea of how close to the edge that last pushed you. The Tower will kill you half a world away."

"You know nothing of me," the gunslinger said quietly, and the smile faded from the other's lips.

"I made your father and I broke him," the man in black said grimly. "I came to your mother as Marten— there's a truth you always suspected, is it not?—and took her. She bent beneath me like a willow . . . although (this may comfort you) she never broke. In any case it was written, and it was. I am the furthest minion of he who now rules the Dark Tower, and Earth has been given into that king's red hand."

"Red? Why do you say red?"

"Never mind. We'll not speak of him, although you'll learn more than you cared to if you press on. What hurt you once will hurt you twice. This is not the beginning but the beginning's end. You'd do well to remember that . . . but you never do."

"I don't understand."

"No. You don't. You never did. You never will. You have no imagination. You're blind that way."

"What did I see?" the gunslinger asked. "What did I see at the end? What was it?"

"What did it seem to be?"

The gunslinger was silent, thoughtful. He felt for his tobacco, but there was none. The man in black did not offer to refill his poke by either black magic or white. Later he might find more in his grow-bag, but later seemed very far away now.

"There was light," the gunslinger said finally. "Great white light. And then—" He broke off and stared at the man in black. He was leaning forward, and an alien emotion was stamped on his face, writ too large for lies or denial. It was awe or wonder. Perhaps they were the same.

"You don't know," he said, and began to smile. "O great sorcerer who brings the dead to life. You don't know. You're a fake!"

"I know," the man in black said. "But I don't know . . . what."

"White light," the gunslinger repeated. "And then—a blade of grass. One single blade of grass that filled everything. And I was tiny. Infinitesimal."

"Grass." The man in black closed his eyes. His face looked drawn and haggard. "A blade of grass. Are you sure?"

"Yes." The gunslinger frowned. "But it was purple."

"Hear me now, Roland, son of Steven. Would you hear me?"

"Yes."

And so the man in black began to speak.

V

The universe (he said) is the Great All, and offers a paradox too great for the finite mind to grasp. As the living brain cannot conceive of a nonliving brain—although it may think it can—the finite mind cannot grasp the infinite.

The prosaic fact of the universe's existence alone defeats both the pragmatist and the romantic. There was a time, yet a hundred generations before the world moved on, when mankind had achieved enough technical and scientific prowess to chip a few splinters from the great stone pillar of reality. Even so, the false light of science (knowledge, if you like) shone in only a few developed countries. One company (or cabal) led the way in this regard; North Central Positronics, it called itself. Yet, despite a tremendous increase in available facts, there were remarkably few insights.

"Gunslinger, our many-times-great grandfathers conquered the-disease-which-rots, which they called cancer, almost conquered aging, walked on the moon—"

"I don't believe that," the gunslinger said flatly.

To this the man in black merely smiled and answered, "You needn't. Yet it was so. They made or discovered a hundred other marvelous baubles. But this wealth of information produced little or no insight. There were no great odes written to the wonders of artificial insemination—having babies from frozen mansperm—or to the cars that ran on power from the sun. Few if any seemed to have grasped the truest principle of reality: new knowledge leads always to yet more awesome mysteries. Greater physiological knowledge of the brain makes the existence of the soul less possible yet more probable by the nature of the search. Do you see? Of course you don't. You've reached the limits of your ability to comprehend. But never mind—that's beside the point."

"What *is* the point, then?"

"The greatest mystery the universe offers is not life but size. Size encompasses life, and the Tower encompasses size. The child, who is most at home with wonder, says: Daddy, what is above the sky? And the father says: The darkness of space. The child: What is beyond space? The father: The galaxy. The child: Beyond the galaxy? The father: Another galaxy. The child: Beyond the other galaxies? The father: No one knows.

"You see? Size defeats us. For the fish, the lake in which he lives is the universe. What does the fish think when he is jerked up by the mouth through the silver limits of existence and into a new universe where the air drowns him and the light is blue madness? Where huge bipeds with no gills stuff it into a suffocating box and cover it with wet weeds to die?

"Or one might take the tip of a pencil and magnify it. One reaches the point where a stunning realization strikes home: The pencil-tip is not solid; it is composed of atoms which whirl and revolve like a trillion demon planets. What seems solid to us is actually only a loose net held together by gravity. Viewed at their actual size, the distances between these atoms might become leagues, gulfs, aeons. The atoms themselves are composed of nuclei and revolving protons and electrons. One may step down further to subatomic particles. And then to what? Tachyons? Nothing? Of course not. Everything in the universe denies nothing; to suggest an ending is the one absurdity.

"If you fell outward to the limit of the universe, would you find a board fence and signs reading DEAD END? No. You might find something hard and rounded, as the chick must see the egg from the inside. And if you should peck through that shell (or find a door), what great and torrential light might shine through your opening at the end of space? Might you look through and discover our entire universe is but part of one atom on a blade of grass? Might you be forced to think that

by burning a twig you incinerate an eternity of eterni-
ties? That existence rises not to one infinite but to an
infinity of them?

"Perhaps you saw what place our universe plays in the
scheme of things—as no more than an atom in a blade
of grass. Could it be that everything we can perceive,
from the microscopic virus to the distant Horsehead
Nebula, is contained in one blade of grass that may
have existed for only a single season in an alien time-
flow? What if that blade should be cut off by a scythe?
When it begins to die, would the rot seep into our own
universe and our own lives, turning everything yellow
and brown and desiccated? Perhaps it's already begun
to happen. We say the world has moved on; maybe we
really mean that it has begun to dry up.

"Think how small such a concept of things makes us,
gunslinger! If a God watches over it all, does He actually mete out justice for a race of gnats among an infini-
tude of races of gnats? Does His eye see the sparrow fall
when the sparrow is less than a speck of hydrogen floating disconnected in the depth of space? And if He does
see . . . what must the nature of such a God be? Where
does He live? How is it possible to live beyond infinity?

"Imagine the sand of the Mohaine Desert, which you
crossed to find me, and imagine a trillion universes—
not worlds but *universes*—encapsulated in each grain
of that desert; and within each universe an infinity of
others. We tower over these universes from our pitiful
grass vantage point; with one swing of your boot you
may knock a billion billion worlds flying off into darkness, in a chain never to be completed.

"Size, gunslinger . . . *size* . . .

"Yet suppose further. Suppose that all worlds, all universes, met in a single nexus, a single pylon, a Tower. And within it, a stairway, perhaps rising to the Godhead itself. Would you dare climb to the top, gunslinger? Could it be that somewhere above all of endless reality, there exists a Room? . . .

"You dare not."

And in the gunslinger's mind, those words echoed: *You dare not.*

VI

"Someone has dared," the gunslinger said.

"Who would that be?"

"God," the gunslinger said softly. His eyes gleamed. "God has dared . . . or the king you spoke of . . . or . . . is the room empty, seer?"

"I don't know." Fear passed over the man in black's bland face, as soft and dark as a buzzard's wing. "And, furthermore, I don't ask. It might be unwise."

"Afraid of being struck dead?"

"Perhaps afraid of . . . an accounting."

The man in black was silent for a while. The night was very long. The Milky Way sprawled above them in great splendor, yet terrifying in the emptiness between its burning lamps. The gunslinger wondered what he would feel if that inky sky should split open and let in a torrent of light.

"The fire," he said. "I'm cold."

"Build it up yourself," said the man in black. "It's the butler's night off."

VII

The gunslinger drowsed awhile and awoke to see the man in black regarding him avidly, unhealthily.

"What are you staring at?" An old saying of Cort's occurred to him. "Do you see your sister's bum?"

"I'm staring at you, of course."

"Well, don't." He poked up the fire, ruining the precision of the ideogram. "I don't like it." He looked to the east to see if there was the beginning of light, but this night went on and on.

"You seek the light so soon."

"I was made for light."

"Ah, so you were! And so impolite of me to forget the fact! Yet we have much to discuss yet, you and I. For so has it been told to me by my king and master."

"Who is this king?"

The man in black smiled. "Shall we tell the truth then, you and I? No more lies?"

"I thought we had been."

But the man in black persisted as if Roland hadn't spoken. "Shall there be truth between us, as two men? Not as friends, but as equals? There is an offer you will get rarely, Roland. Only equals speak the truth, that's my thought on't. Friends and lovers lie endlessly, caught in the web of regard. How tiresome!"

"Well, I wouldn't want to tire you, so let us speak the

truth." He had never spoken less on this night. "Start by telling me what exactly you mean by glammer."

"Why, enchantment, gunslinger! My king's enchantment has prolonged this night and will prolong it until our palaver is done."

"How long will that be?"

"Long. I can tell you no better. I do not know myself." The man in black stood over the fire, and the glowing embers made patterns on his face. "Ask. I will tell you what I know. You have caught me. It is fair; I did not think you would. Yet your quest has only begun. Ask. It will lead us to business soon enough."

"Who is your king?"

"I have never seen him, but you must. But before you meet him, you must first meet the Ageless Stranger." The man in black smiled spitelessly. "You must slay him, gunslinger. Yet I think it is not what you wished to ask."

"If you've never seen your king and master, how do you know him?"

"He comes to me in dreams. As a stripling he came to me, when I lived, poor and unknown, in a far land. A sheaf of centuries ago he imbued me with my duty and promised me my reward, although there were many errands in my youth and the days of my manhood, before my apotheosis. You are that apotheosis, gunslinger. You are my climax." He tittered. "You see, someone has taken you seriously."

"And this Stranger, does he have a name?"

"O, he is named."

"And what is his name?"

"Legion," the man in black said softly, and somewhere

in the easterly darkness where the mountains lay, a rock-slide punctuated his words and a puma screamed like a woman. The gunslinger shivered and the man in black flinched. "Yet I do not think that is what you wished to ask, either. It is not your nature to think so far ahead."

The gunslinger knew the question; it had gnawed him all this night, and he thought, for years before. It trembled on his lips but he didn't ask it . . . not yet.

"This Stranger is a minion of the Tower? Like yourself?"

"Yar. He *darkles*. He *tincts*. He is in all times. Yet there is one greater than he."

"Who?"

"Ask me no more!" the man in black cried. His voice aspired to sternness and crumbled into beseechment. "I know not! I do not wish to know. To speak of the things in End-World is to speak of the ruination of one's own soul."

"And beyond the Ageless Stranger is the Tower and whatever the Tower contains?"

"Yes," whispered the man in black. "But none of these things are what you wish to ask."

True.

"All right," the gunslinger said, and then asked the world's oldest question. "Will I succeed? Will I win through?"

"If I answered that question, gunslinger, you'd kill me."

"I *ought* to kill you. You need killing." His hands had dropped to the worn butts of his guns.

"Those do not open doors, gunslinger; those only close them forever."

"Where must I go?"

"Start west. Go to the sea. Where the world ends is where you must begin. There was a man who gave you advice . . . the man you bested so long ago—"

"Yes, Cort," the gunslinger interrupted impatiently.

"The advice was to wait. It was bad advice. For even then my plans against your father had proceeded. He sent you away and when you returned—"

"I'd not hear you speak of that," the gunslinger said, and in his mind he heard his mother singing: *Baby-bunting, baby dear, baby bring your basket here.*

"Then hear this: when you returned, Marten had gone west, to join the rebels. So all said, anyway, and so you believed. Yet he and a certain witch left you a trap and you fell into it. Good boy! And although Marten was long gone by then, there was a man who sometimes made you think of him, was there not? A man who affected the dress of a monk and the shaven head of a penitent—"

"Walter," the gunslinger whispered. And although he had come so far in his musings, the bald truth still amazed him. "*You.* Marten never left at all."

The man in black tittered. "At your service."

"I ought to kill you now."

"That would hardly be fair. Besides, all of that was long ago. Now comes the time of sharing."

"You never left," the gunslinger repeated, stunned. "You only changed."

"Sit," the man in black invited. "I'll tell you stories, as many as you would hear. Your own stories, I think, will be much longer."

"I don't talk of myself," the gunslinger muttered.

"Yet tonight you must. So that we may understand."

"Understand what? My purpose? You know that. To find the Tower is my purpose. I'm sworn."

"Not your purpose, gunslinger. Your mind. Your slow, prodding, tenacious mind. There has never been one quite like it, in all the history of the world. Perhaps in the history of creation."

"This is the time of speaking. This is the time of histories."

"Then speak."

The man in black shook the voluminous arm of his robe. A foil-wrapped package fell out and caught the dying embers in many reflective folds.

"Tobacco, gunslinger. Would you smoke?"

He had been able to resist the rabbit, but he could not resist this. He opened the foil with eager fingers. There was fine crumbled tobacco inside, and green leaves to wrap it in, amazingly moist. He had not seen such tobacco for ten years.

He rolled two cigarettes and bit the ends of each to release the flavor. He offered one to the man in black, who took it. Each of them took a burning twig from the fire.

The gunslinger lit his cigarette and drew the aromatic smoke deep into his lungs, closing his eyes to concentrate the senses. He blew out with long, slow satisfaction.

"Is it good?" the man in black inquired.

"Yes. Very good."

"Enjoy it. It may be the last smoke for you in a very long time."

The gunslinger took this impassively.

"Very well," the man in black said. "To begin then:

"You must understand the Tower has always been, and there have always been boys who know of it and lust for it, more than power or riches or women . . . boys who look for the doors that lead to it . . ."

VIII

There was talk then, a night's worth of talk and God alone knew how much more (or how much was true), but the gunslinger remembered little of it later . . . and to his oddly practical mind, little of it seemed to matter. The man in black told him again that he must go to the sea, which lay no more than twenty easy miles to the west, and there he would be invested with the power of *drawing*.

"But that's not exactly right, either," the man in black said, pitching his cigarette into the remains of the campfire. "No one wants to invest you with a power of any kind, gunslinger; it is simply *in* you, and I am compelled to tell you, partly because of the sacrifice of the boy, and partly because it is the law; the natural law of things. Water must run downhill, and you must be told. You will draw three, I understand . . . but I don't really care, and I don't really want to know."

"The three," the gunslinger murmured, thinking of the Oracle.

"And then the fun begins! But, by then, I'll be long gone. Goodbye, gunslinger. My part is done now. The chain is still in your hands. 'Ware it doesn't wrap itself around your neck."

Compelled by something outside him, Roland said, "You have one more thing to say, don't you?"

"Yes," the man in black said, and he smiled at the gunslinger with his depthless eyes and stretched one of his hands out toward him. "Let there be light."

And there was light, and this time the light was good.

IX

Roland awoke by the ruins of the campfire to find himself ten years older. His black hair had thinned at the temples and there had gone the gray of cobwebs at the end of autumn. The lines in his face were deeper, his skin rougher.

The remains of the wood he had carried had turned to something like stone, and the man in black was a laughing skeleton in a rotting black robe, more bones in this place of bones, one more skull in this golgotha.

Or is it really you? he thought. *I have my doubts, Walter o' Dim . . . I have my doubts, Marten-that-was.*

He stood up and looked around. Then, with a sudden quick gesture, he reached toward the remains of his companion of the night before (if it was indeed the remains of Walter), a night that had somehow lasted ten years. He broke off the grinning jawbone and jammed it carelessly into the left hip pocket of his jeans—a fitting enough replacement for the one lost under the mountains.

"How many lies did you tell me?" he asked. Many, he was sure, but what made them good lies was that they had been mixed with the truth.

The Tower. Somewhere ahead, it waited for him—the nexus of Time, the nexus of Size.

He began west again, his back set against the sunrise, heading toward the ocean, realizing that a great passage of his life had come and gone. "I loved you, Jake," he said aloud.

The stiffness wore out of his body and he began to walk more rapidly. By that evening he had come to the end of the land. He sat on a beach which stretched left and right forever, deserted. The waves beat endlessly against the shore, pounding and pounding. The setting sun painted the water in a wide strip of fool's gold.

There the gunslinger sat, his face turned up into the fading light. He dreamed his dreams and watched as the stars came out; his purpose did not flag, nor did his heart falter; his hair, finer now and gray at the temples, blew around his head, and the sandalwood-inlaid guns of his father lay smooth and deadly against his hips, and he was lonely but did not find loneliness in any way a bad or ignoble thing. The dark came down and the world moved on. The gunslinger waited for the time of the *drawing* and dreamed his long dreams of the Dark Tower, to which he would someday come at dusk and approach, winding his horn, to do some unimaginable final battle.

ACKNOWLEDGMENTS

Grateful acknowledgment is made for permission to reprint an excerpt from *Look Homeward, Angel* by Thomas Wolfe. Copyright Charles Scribner's Sons, 1929; copyright renewed © Edward C. Ashwell, Administrator, C.T.A., and/or Fred W. Wolfe, 1957. Reprinted with permission of Scribner, an imprint of Simon & Schuster Adult Publishing Group.

"The Gunslinger" copyright © Mercury Press, Inc., 1978, for *The Magazine of Fantasy and Science Fiction*, October 1978.

"The Way Station" copyright © Mercury Press, Inc., 1980, for *The Magazine of Fantasy and Science Fiction*, April 1980.

"The Oracle and the Mountain" copyright © Mercury Press, Inc., 1981, for *The Magazine of Fantasy and Science Fiction*, February 1981.

"The Slow Mutants" copyright © Mercury Press, Inc., 1981, for *The Magazine of Fantasy and Science Fiction*, July 1981.

"The Gunslinger and the Dark Man" copyright © Mercury Press, Inc., 1981, for *The Magazine of Fantasy and Science Fiction*, November 1981.

ABOUT THE AUTHOR

Stephen King is the author of more than fifty books, all of them worldwide bestsellers. His recent work includes the short story collection *The Bazaar of Bad Dreams*, *End of Watch*, *Finders Keepers*, *Mr. Mercedes* (an Edgar Award winner for Best Novel), *Revival*, *Doctor Sleep*, and *Under the Dome*. His novel *11/22/63* was named a top ten book of 2011 by *The New York Times Book Review* and won the Los Angeles Times Book Prize for best Mystery/Thriller. He is the recipient of the 2014 National Medal of Arts and the 2003 National Book Foundation Medal for Distinguished Contribution to American Letters. He lives in Bangor, Maine, with his wife, novelist Tabitha King.